THE FALLEN GIRLS

PAUL J. TEAGUE

Storm

Ebook ISBN: 978-1-80508-485-3
Paperback ISBN: 978-1-80508-489-1

Cover design: Lisa Horton
Cover images: Trevillion, Shutterstock

Published by Storm Publishing.
For further information, visit:
www.stormpublishing.co

ALSO BY PAUL J. TEAGUE

PROLOGUE

1975 – CHURCH OF ST MARY AND THE ANGELS: MOTHER & BABY UNIT

Mandy looked down at the gravel drive. If she jumped, she'd more likely end up crippled than dead. The height wasn't enough.

The baby stirred in its blanket. Poor mite, it was cold on that balcony. Goosebumps covered Mandy's arms. The tips of her fingers were numbing, and even the baby's breaths sent out a tiny wisp of condensation. The grass beyond the driveway looked crisp and white, and the air was completely still. In the distance, she could hear traffic from the city centre. Under any other circumstances, it would have been a beautiful night.

She hadn't even given him a name. Not officially, anyway. Oliver, that was what she called him. Her beautiful baby Oliver. They'd have goaded her if she had dared admit to giving him a name.

'He's not really yours,' that bitch of a nun would sneer at her. 'Don't get too used to it. The new parents will be here in a couple of days, and he'll get some proper care. He'll have a decent mother then, one who's married and doesn't sleep with the first boy who smiles at her.'

He was eight days old already, weighing in at five pounds

and seven ounces when he was born. A little on the small side for a boy, they'd said. She could never have imagined loving him so deeply and so soon. Is this how her mother felt about her? If she did, she never showed it.

He looked so beautiful in his tiny Babygros. They hadn't even let her buy anything for him. He was dressed in second-hand clothes donated to the church by the good people of Hull. Mandy had wondered if they knew their charity was going to help fallen girls like her. She reckoned they, too, would have scorned her had they known. It was only one time. And he'd told her she was special and beautiful. She'd never known such attentiveness; it was like she was the only girl in the entire world. He was nowhere to be seen now.

'Mandy, you know this is stupid. Come down from there. You'll hurt the baby. You'll hurt little Oliver—'

The name seemed to stick in the nun's throat, like a poisonous morsel paralysing her airways. She must have looked in Mandy's diary if she knew about the name. That woman was a monster. They were all monsters. They were like bogeymen, coming to take her precious baby under the cover of night.

The other girls had tried to warn her.

'Did you sign the papers?' they had asked.

'Yes, but I didn't know what they were,' Mandy had replied. 'That social worker told me it was for the best. My dad wouldn't let me back home if I didn't. How was I to know what it said? It was a load of fancy words I didn't understand.'

'It's done then,' her friends had replied, one of them squeezing her hand. 'Not that we have any choice in the matter either.'

'Come on, Mandy, dear. It's time to pack the baby's things. It'll all be fine in the morning, you'll see.'

They'd come out in force to talk her down. That was Sister Kay. Mandy liked Sister Kay. She'd whisper kind things to her when she was settling down for the night. Or in those beautiful quiet moments when the baby would latch onto the bottle and feed contentedly, with only a dim light to illuminate the room. She could have stayed like that forever. They wouldn't allow her to breastfeed, even though she was swollen and sore.

'You're a lovely girl and good mummy to that wee boy,' she'd whisper, like she didn't want Sister Brennan to hear. 'He's lucky to have you. Just remember, you'll always be his mum. Look how well he's feeding. Only days old, and he knows you're his mummy already.'

The kindness of Sister Kay's voice was a siren call. Mandy liked her soft tone. She was Scottish, she thought. The nun's obvious concern almost charmed her off the stone balcony. Mandy hadn't thought things through. She was dressed only in her nightie, and her entire body had begun to shake with the cold. Her feet were bare, and she had slippers under the bed but hadn't thought to put them on. Her frozen toes could barely feel the icy stone beneath them. She pulled Oliver in for warmth. He nestled in like he belonged there. He did belong there. They could say whatever they liked about her, the baby was hers.

She'd rushed for the balcony when she woke to hear their hushed voices. Mandy sensed immediately that something was going on outside. There was an atmosphere of anticipation beyond her bedroom door, like a bunch of jackals were gathering to plan their next kill.

The other girls didn't know how it happened. The first they'd know about it would be when one of them wasn't at breakfast or dinner. The baby would be gone, too. They'd be whisked away from the home, without time for goodbyes. Sometimes they'd hear screams, but they were somewhere else in the building, in the back rooms, which the girls seldom saw. Occasionally, they'd see more cars parked out the front; it was often a clue that something was going on.

A bat flew just over her head and startled her. Mandy moved her right foot to steady herself, but it was so cold she couldn't feel the edge of the thick stone balustrade. For a moment, she thought she was going to stumble. If it had been high enough, she truly wished they could fall to their deaths and be together forever. As she felt herself lurching forwards, Sister Kay's arm wrapped around her waist and allowed her to catch her balance. She looked at her with red eyes.

'You poor girl,' Sister Kay whispered gently.

Mandy stepped down from the balcony's edge; she could barely move from the cold. She was immediately surrounded by bodies. Sister Kay held her, pulling her in tight to make her warm.

'You poor, dear girl,' she kept repeating. 'Thank goodness you're safe. I thought you were going to hurt yourself for a moment there. Burrow into me. You'll catch your death of cold.'

It took Mandy a few moments to come around, such was the comfort of Sister Kay's embrace. She moved her fingers and realised Oliver was no longer there. It was all happening so quickly; she could barely keep up with what was going on. Somebody threw a blanket around the two of them and she caught the tail-end of a sentence. It was a voice she'd heard before.

'—keep her occupied for a few minutes. We won't be long.'

It was that social worker. The one who'd made her sign the papers. She didn't like him; he gave her the creeps.

Her mind seemed to thaw at the same time as her body. Her thoughts began to flow freely like ice melting on a stream in the morning sunshine.

'You're taking my baby!' she screamed. 'Leave my baby!'

'Shh, it's all right, my darling,' Sister Kay whispered. 'Let them do this.'

Mandy tore herself away from the cocoon she'd created and ran back into the room. Sister Brennan was there, the baby in her arms. The social worker was hurriedly throwing all of Oliver's clean clothes into a holdall. The bag wasn't hers. She'd never seen it before. It looked like leather and seemed expensive.

'In the name of Jesus, shut that door,' Sister Brennan seethed, her tone full of contempt. 'She'll wake the rest of the girls up and we'll have a riot on our hands.'

Sister Kay pushed the door, responding to a commanding glance from Sister Brennan. The priest was there, too, skulking at the edges, looking like an undecided Judas, not yet quite committed to his betrayal.

Mandy rushed at Sister Brennan, her eyes on Oliver, who had now sensed something was going on. The baby began to cry, and Mandy tried to snatch him out of the nun's arms.

'Get away with you, girl!' Sister Brennan shouted at her, pushing her with her free arm so she fell to the ground. Mandy took the impact on her wrist; it twisted as she struck the old, worn floorboards.

'You deserve it, you silly girl! You've brought all this shame on yourself, what with your immoral behaviour—'

'Okay, we're done,' the social worker started. 'You'll feel better about it in the morning when your mother and father come to take you home again. You'll soon forget him—'

'I hate you!' Mandy screamed, tears of pain and frustration now streaming down her face. She moved to pull herself up, to make one more attempt to rescue her baby, but she stumbled back, dizzy.

The social worker left the room with the priest following close behind, the baby's carrycot and a basket of terry nappies in his hands.

Mandy looked in desperation as Sister Brennan rushed towards the door, the precious baby in her arms.

Sister Kay put out her hand to help Mandy up from the floor, her face red with anguish.

'Leave the girl be!' Sister Brennan snapped. 'And lock the door behind you. This little hussy can have the rest of the night to think about what she's done. She deserves everything that's happened to her tonight. The baby is going to live with some decent parents now. He can have a proper family.'

Mandy wept as Sister Brennan marched through the door, the last glimpse of her beautiful boy blurred by her tears. Sister Kay looked at her for a moment, hesitated, and then moved over to the door as Sister Brennan summoned her from along the landing.

'I'm sorry, Mandy,' she stuttered. 'I'm so sorry.'

The door clicked shut and Mandy listened as the key turned from the outside.

'I fucking hate you all,' she screamed. 'I hate you. I'll kill you. One day, I'll come back here and kill every last one of you.'

ONE

'Did you really have to pick the night before we were going to move to the other side of the country to announce your midlife crisis? For heaven's sake, Léon, you might have timed it better.'

The sound of the guy in the flat above banging his drums had made Hollie's head start throbbing well over an hour ago. Léon had picked the worst possible time to call, and she knew she was taking out her frustration on him. But damn, it felt good.

'I told you; it's been a slow burn kind of thing—' Léon protested from his end of the WhatsApp call. He looked uncomfortable and she was enjoying it. It was a bit soon for her to barge into the drummer's flat and smash one of his drums over his head, so Léon would have to be the fall guy for now.

'You were only away for a couple of weeks,' Hollie resumed, 'and the kids were with you, too. I mean – where did you even find the opportunity to meet this woman?'

Hollie recognised how tense things had got at home, but he didn't have to resort to the most hackneyed trick in the book. When all else fails, run from your marital difficulties and ship in a woman ten years younger instead. She never thought this would be the way her marriage imploded, yet millions of women had likely thought the same thing over the centuries.

Léon started to explain once again how it was a chance meeting when his parents had been looking after the kids. It was Hollie who'd asked for them to stay with his parents in France for a short time. It was she who had set up the situation which would destroy her family.

Hollie's hackles began to rise, and she diverted her attention as a preference to laying into Léon further. That bloody drummer. She couldn't work out what the hell he was supposed to be playing, but if someone could have written a piece of music depicting a thumping migraine, this would be it. It was thudding, persistent, monotonous and wearing all at once. No wonder drummers never got the girl, not if the girl had to put up with that racket.

This wasn't the first time he'd done it, either. She'd only been in the flat for ten days, yet she'd had to put up with his impromptu practice sessions four times already.

Hollie took a long, slow breath and tried to calm herself down. The woman on the mindfulness downloads she'd been playing on her phone seemed to have her life sorted. Not only was her stomach perfectly toned, but also every inch of her looked honed to perfection. Hollie needed a bit of that right now.

The flat depressed her. It was painted magnolia for starters, with only the white glossed doors breaking the blandness. The carpets were worn and tired, the patterns from a time long forgotten. The walls were marked by the spectral discolouring of pictures hung up over previous years, ghosts of former occupants who'd tried to assert their personality on the place. The cooker was a living testament to all the meals that had ever been prepared there, seeing as it looked like nobody had bothered to give it a proper clean within living memory. The only consolation was the window facing out into Pearson

Park and that outlook, at least, held some happy memories for her.

She recalled a picnic with a group of friends from university, cobbled together from cheap items bought in the local corner store. None of them had any money at the time, yet that didn't seem to matter. They were young and had their lives ahead of them.

She'd enjoyed a passionate kiss on one of the benches once, late at night, a box full of chips perched on their laps, giggling after too many beers in a nearby pub. She was certain that was the night that Isabella was conceived.

Hollie had been lucky to find the flat at such short notice after Léon's bombshell, she knew that, but what a pit for a professional woman in her forties. They'd had a nice, detached rental lined up while the house in Lancaster sold and they sorted out the relocation. Only, Léon thought now would be the perfect time to fall in love with a Frenchwoman in her mid-thirties and screw up everything right at the last minute. So the detached place was swiftly cancelled, a cheap flat procured using only the internet to verify that it even existed, and now Hollie had a six-month contract in which to enjoy the accommodation she'd so hastily agreed to let.

Léon's voice drifted back into her consciousness. He'd stopped blaming her now with his disgruntled spouse's Top-Three hits: long hours at work, too preoccupied with police cases and placing the family in danger in the line of duty. He was wise enough not to mention the non-existent sex life. He'd now turned to the kids, the kids they'd had together. At least Isabella was well clear of it. Hollie was beginning to think that taking a year out sounded like an attractive option.

Over the past ten days living in Hull, in between wanting to murder the drummer, feeling she was failing desperately in her new job, and wanting to live anywhere but the shitty flat on Pearson Park, she'd realised Léon did have a fair point. The marriage had become a stale checkmate in which they parented the kids as if they were good pals rather than lovers, and day-to-day life had become a matter of well-rehearsed routine. There was no way she was admitting it to him, but they probably were due for a shakeup. She'd have preferred it to involve marriage guidance rather than a new woman. But when it came to the kids, he could get stuffed.

'You know you can't look after them properly, not with the hours you keep,' Léon reminded her, his voice so calm and confident that there was very little she could send back by way of defence.

'I take it you've heard of childcare—' she began.

'But I can work at home. I can be there for them in the morning and when they come home from school. You know you can't do that, Hollie. It's been a struggle ever since Isabella left for uni. And now she's travelling, we're stuffed.'

He paused and moved closer to his webcam like he was trying to peer around the side to get a better look at her flat.

'What the hell is that noise? It sounds like your dishwasher is about to explode.'

Hollie ignored the remark. If she told him about how the drummer was making her life hell, she'd burst into tears and there was no way she was opening herself up to that possibility. Not while she was fighting for her kids.

'Listen, Léon, the children aren't negotiable. I know I work crappy hours, but it goes with the territory. I've always made the kids a priority, you know that, so don't try to paint me as some absent mother; I'm not and I won't have you suggesting that I am. This has always been our life. You can't throw it all back at me now your head's been turned by—'

She hesitated and knew as the word came out of her mouth that it was inflammatory, unhelpful, spiteful and graceless. But she went for it anyway.

'—a young bit of totty who's not even got a few stretch marks to show for life—'

Hollie was distracted momentarily by an incoming call notification vibrating her phone. She ignored it at first, not wanting to give Léon further ammunition about her lifestyle.

'I've told you already, Veronique is thirty-eight and has a seven-year-old daughter from a previous relationship. This is no casual fling. We're in love.'

'I've got to go, Léon,' she said, curt and dismissive.

'A call from work?' Léon challenged.

Whoever was chasing her had rung off and dialled again. It looked important.

'Look, this isn't going away, Hollie. Once the house sells, I want to go to France. We'll split the money and at least you can get out of that flat. Izzy can decide where she's staying when she gets back. But we have to think about Noah and Lily. I know it's raw now, but you know you can't look after them properly. Not with the hours you keep—'

To her shame, Hollie froze her movements, paused for a few seconds, then ended the call. She'd told Léon the broadband was dodgy. With any luck, he'd fall for the old blue-screen-of-death technique.

She answered her mobile phone, which was now on the third ring back. It was the office – she knew that much already – but there was no way Léon was getting the satisfaction of seeing her pick it up while on the WhatsApp call.

She noticed the time on the phone display as she picked up: 10.36 on Sunday night. She braced herself. Less than nine days on the job, the induction process was not yet completed, and here it was already: the first out-of-hours call.

'Yes,' she answered, firm and unforgiving. It wouldn't do for her new team to think they could interrupt her at any time of day or night without good reason.

'Sorry to disturb you, ma'am. It's DS Anderson.'

'Go ahead, detective.'

'We've got an incident at the Humber Bridge. I thought you'd want to be in on it.'

'What is it?'

'Someone has been thrown from a length of rope over the bridge. They were left hanging over the Clive Sullivan Way. A lorry smashed into the body before it could stop—'

'Is it suicide, DS Anderson? Why are we involved?'

'No, not suicide, ma'am. Murder. There's no doubt foul play was involved.'

'Who's the victim? Is it gang-related?'

'No, ma'am, nothing to do with gangs. It's unusual, ma'am, that's for sure. The victim is a nun, as yet unidentified. The body's one hell of a mess, but early indications are she was old. It looks like this woman was in her seventies.'

TWO

She'd replaced the incessant pounding of the drum kit up the stairs with a sea of flashing blue lights and the roar of traffic passing on the opposite carriageway. Lancaster was a sleepy town; it seemed to Hollie that Hull never slept.

She clocked DS Ben Anderson's disapproving face as she arrived at the scene. She'd let it pass for now, but there was a storm brewing with that man. She could feel it coming.

'What's the score here, then?' Hollie asked, looking around at the immediate area. It was what was known in policing terms as a fucking mess. Both lanes of the dual carriageway were closed, with police and emergency vehicles at either side of the bridge overhead doing their best to protect the crime scene. Even the Humber Rescue team was there, it being so close to the estuary and their HQ. The cold, hostile water might have been a blessing for the victim; death must have been fast and violent when it came at the end of a rope.

'Charles Ruane has come and gone in the time it took you to get here—'

There it was: the dig. She'd just been through all this with Léon, and now here was her deputy having a go at her. So, she'd messed it up and ended up getting lost in Hessle. Her satnav had sent her in circles. When Hollie had been a student in the city, she'd relied on public transport. Hull's roads and shortcuts were a mystery to her still. It would take some time before they became as familiar to her as her old patch. In the meantime, she was half an hour later than expected at one of the highest profile crime scenes the city had seen in some years.

'Charles Ruane?'

'The forensic pathologist. I think you met him briefly last week?'

'Of course,' Hollie replied. 'Doctor Ruane.'

The past week had been a sea of faces. When DS Anderson used the job title, rather than the name, she remembered who he was talking about: an older man, the type she'd call a gentleman. Old school, old manners, the calm confidence of a person who'd been doing the job for many years. She'd liked him in the short exchange they'd had. She hadn't expected to be dealing with him quite so soon.

'It was a rubber-stamping job. Dead at the scene. He's confirmed the approximate age: definitely a female in her seventies.'

'How do we know she's a nun?' Hollie asked, realising the stupidity of her question the moment it parted her lips.

'You've seen how nuns dress, I assume?' Anderson answered, intolerance plastered across his face. 'Of course, she might have been at a hen party.'

'Of course,' Hollie replied. She felt her face reddening and was thankful for the flashing lights and semi-darkness which must have hidden the worst of it.

'Anything we can identify her with?'

Hollie attempted to wrestle the conversation back in her favour.

'There's not much of her left. Dental records are a possibility,' Anderson suggested, throwing her a bone. 'But they'll take a little time to get checked, of course.'

Anderson looked upwards. Hollie took a moment to focus on what she was supposed to be looking at. She gasped when she saw it.

'For fuck's sake, every bloody smartphone and press photographer in the city is going to have that recorded.'

High above them, gathered at the side of the Humber Bridge where the body had been thrown over, was a crowd of officers retrieving what was left of the corpse. From that far away, it looked like some macabre Halloween spoof local students might have dreamt up. She didn't need to be up close to imagine what they were dealing with.

'We've called in an abseiling specialist to advise,' Anderson continued. 'Uniform are doing their best to stop the press from taking photographs, but it's so open up there, it's a fool's errand. It's not like we can put a tent over her. At least they won't publish a picture as terrifying as that on their front pages.'

'No, but it's sure as hell doing the rounds on social media. Who would want to do that to a nun? An old lady?'

'As I said, Doctor Ruane confirmed the basics and said he'd take a closer look at the body parts once they've been retrieved from the surrounding area.'

'Is that the lorry?' Hollie pointed over towards the central crash barrier several metres ahead of them. A large, Heath Robinson affair of a tarpaulin had been draped over the lorry's front cab.

'Yes, that's it. The lorry driver was lucky. He got a concussion and a broken collarbone. He's at Hull Royal Infirmary being patched up.'

Hollie spotted a mischievous look in Anderson's eyes.

'Would you like to take a look, boss? Bearing in mind Doctor Ruane said he didn't need to see any more to pronounce her dead.'

Hollie had seen her fair share of mangled bodies. While she'd grown accustomed to the violence of it, she never got used to the sight. She had no wish to see the scattered remains of this nun.

'I'll pass, but thanks for the invite,' she answered, her face blank so as not to give anything away. 'Besides, I've had better invitations at this time on a Sunday night. I'll wait until Doctor Ruane and his team have had some time to tidy her up a bit.'

For the briefest moment, she caught the whiff of a smile. There was a human in there, after all. It was fair enough he should resent her being there. She was a transfer from another force, and Anderson had clearly expected to get the promotion as an internal candidate. Well, hard luck, she'd got the job. He'd have to learn to live with it or get his arse moved to another team.

Hollie looked up again, then drew a deliberate breath before speaking.

'You'd need some length of rope to throw a person off the side of the bridge, wouldn't you?'

'It's standard mountaineering or sailing rope,' Anderson chimed in, the answer sounding pre-prepared in its confident delivery. 'The clearance from the road is thirty metres. You can buy ropes like that from Amazon at ten metres, twenty metres and thirty metres. It'll cost less than fifty quid to buy one long enough to suspend an old lady like that.'

'Okay, so we need to get straight onto that rope and where it came from,' Hollie remarked. 'How was it secured?'

'It was clipped around one of the bridge's support cables and she was thrown off the side over the railings. So that points more to climbing rope.'

'Was she dead when she was thrown over?'

'Doctor Ruane couldn't say, and he may not even know when he gets his hands on the body parts. It's going to be like a five-hundred-piece puzzle by the time we put her together—'

'Okay, that's enough, DS Anderson. Let's not forget an old lady lost her life here today.'

Hollie had spotted a junior member of the team approaching. If she was going to turn them into a coherent policing unit, it wouldn't do for the younger members to pick up on black humour from the senior officers. That was a privilege for the world-weary who'd seen and done it all. DC Gordon looked like he'd barely left school – she couldn't believe how fast they were making it to detective constable these days. He seemed timid, as if he thought he'd be interrupting something. He was clutching his phone.

'Good evening, ma'am—'

'Good evening, DC Gordon. Have you been playing rugby?'

His shoes were plastered in wet mud and his trousers were streaked green and brown.

'I took a tumble on the grass, ma'am, but it was worth it. We found something.'

DC Gordon touched the phone's screen to bring up a picture.

'What is it, Gordon?' Anderson asked. 'I hope you didn't go screwing up any evidence again?'

Hollie looked at Anderson and raised her eyebrow slightly. There was enough light for him to see. He backed down. There was history in this team she had yet to learn. Much of it didn't sound good.

'No, sir, definitely not. I saw something up the grass bank close to where the lorry hit the central reservation. It's been secured and bagged properly, sir, but I got a picture of it so you can take a look.'

Anderson relaxed his shoulders. They'd all been young once. Most of them had screwed up at a major crime scene at some point. You only tended to do it once in your career. But if it happened twice, it was generally recommended that it was time for a new job, preferably well away from policing.

'What have you got for us?' Hollie asked, making her tone as soft as she could. If the younger members of the unit were scared to venture anything, it didn't make for much of a team spirit.

'It's a sign, ma'am. It was hanging around the nun's neck. The lorry driver said he saw it, but uniform couldn't find it. I saw it blowing up the banking over there. We may even get prints off it if we're lucky.'

DC Gordon touched his screen and then spread pinched fingers to enlarge an image captured on his camera.

'Here,' he said, turning his phone so they could both see it clearly.

Sitting flat on the ground was a white sheet of plastic, the sort of object which might be used for signage or something similar. Spray-painted in red were the words *Pure Evil*.

THREE

1974: MANDY'S STORY

Mandy stared down at the page, but however hard she looked, she failed to see what the rest of the class was seeing. For all she knew, they'd given her the wrong book as a joke. The words and letters were a jumbled mess. It had always been that way. She'd accepted at primary school that she was as stupid as the other kids said. But at secondary school, things were much worse.

'Right, Mandy Tyson, let's waste a few minutes of everybody's life and see if you can help us out—'

Mandy hated Mr Adams. He had the perfect appearance for the name; he looked just like Lurch from *The Addams Family*. He was tall, for starters. So tall he had to lower his head a little when he entered the classroom. It wasn't that the door frames weren't big enough, just that he was so close to the top he must have felt like a lorry driver figuring out if he had sufficient clearance to go under a railway bridge. She'd have felt sorry for him if he wasn't so spiteful towards her. He had the same dead eyes as the creepy butler, too. The kids all called him The Henchman, but Mandy preferred Lurch. He had an uncanny habit of appearing from nowhere. She wished she could summon him with a bell, like in the TV series, rather than him appearing at her side when she was staring blankly at her schoolwork.

He was standing there now, looking down at what she'd written, judging her, deriding her, wishing she wasn't in his class. At least, that's what Mandy imagined he was thinking. He picked up her exercise book. There were no words in it, just the beginning of a sketch. After a cursory glance, he threw the book back at her. It overshot the desk and landed at the feet of the class bully.

'You'd best pick that up, Tyson,' Mr Adams said, his voice cold and without emotion. 'Then I want you to read from the text. At least that way I know it's had some opportunity to get into your brain. There's enough space in there. You wouldn't think it would be so difficult to absorb some new information.'

The class gave a collective giggle at his teasing. Mandy got out of her chair and walked slowly over to the exercise book.

'She's got blood on her seat!' one of the boys shouted.

Mandy looked back at her desk. To her horror, there was a spot of blood on the plastic chair. She'd had cramping all day since she woke up; this must be what it was about. She'd heard the other girls talking about things like this in hushed tones. She'd hoped when her time came it would happen at the weekend or during the school holidays. She was surprised she hadn't felt it, but then she was wearing her thickest tights. At fifteen, she was later than most of the other girls, too. It was like they had joined a club that she was excluded from.

'Tyson's on the rag,' shouted another pimple-faced kid.

Mandy felt her face burning like a fire had been lit inside her. She couldn't decide whether to get the exercise book or return to her chair. Even the girls were merciless. They might at least have given her some support. Instead, they were no doubt relieved somebody else had taken the bullet. They goaded her and teased her, calling her a dirty cow.

Mandy made a move back to her seat.

'What do you think you're doing?' Adams asked. 'You've already made one mess in my classroom. You're not leaving another. Pick up that exercise book and get back to your desk.'

Had Adams seen what had happened? Was he being deliberately cruel?

Mandy walked over to the exercise book and knelt to pick it up.

Willy Jarvis, the class idiot, pinched his nose and called out for the benefit of the rest of the class, 'Phwoar, you can smell her from here! Best get the nose clips out, everybody.'

Mandy fought to hold the tears back, but she couldn't do it. A single drop made its way down her left cheek, followed by a second on the right.

She returned to her desk, hesitating before she sat on the chair. There wasn't much there; her dark skirt couldn't be showing too much. But like a pack of wolves, they'd smelt her embarrassment and now they were all howling at the prospect of a feast.

'May I go to the toilet, Mr Adams?' she asked, cursing her faltering voice.

'Pardon?' Adams asked. 'Speak up, Tyson. I can't hear you.'

'May I go to the toilet?' she tried again.

Adams looked directly at her. Where normally his eyes seemed soulless and empty, now she saw bitterness and resentment. This man, who hated his job, had found his mark.

'No, Mandy Tyson, you may not go to the toilet during lesson time. You know the rules. And you've barely lifted a finger to tackle that comprehension exercise. I can't figure out if you're lazy, thick, stupid or all three. I'm beginning to think it might be all three rolled into one sullen teenager.'

Mandy sniffed and hesitated before sitting down.

'Urrgghh!' shouted Jarvis. He was so pimply she wondered if one day he might explode. One big pop and he'd be gone. If only.

'So, let's have a go at reading the text,' Mr Adams continued. 'From the top of page seven.'

Mandy opened the textbook and found the page number. She looked at the words. There was very little there she could grasp on to. She took a stab at the first word. There was laughter from the class. How long would this go on? Surely the bell was due any minute.

Mandy made a couple more tries at forging some sense from the printed words, and then the end of the lesson sounded, and the entire class was instantly less interested in her and more preoccupied with how quickly Adams would let them depart.

Within minutes, they were packed away and leaving their seats. Adams seemed as pleased as the youngsters that the ordeal was over. Mandy moved slowly, not wanting to be one of the first out. As different groups passed by her desk, they made some cruel reference to her plight.

'Don't worry, Tyson, just go with the flow!'

'Red alert! Red alert! Tyson's in town—'

'What lesson are you in next period, Tyson?'

The last comment came from a girl. While Mandy didn't have any friends at the school, she didn't expect her own gender to sell her out. That hurt most. The boys were dickheads; she was used to that.

Adams left the classroom without a word of concern. The door was left open, ready for the next class, and she was biding her time, waiting to stand and assess the damage. At least she had her coat. She could make her way to the toilets and clean herself up there. She knew enough from the whispers of her classmates that the school nurse could usually sort out a pad in an emergency.

Mandy took a tissue out of her pocket and did the best she could to clean off the chair. She then slipped her coat off the back and put it on, relieved it was as long as her skirt.

The corridors had quietened now, so she made her way up

towards the admin block, where the school nurse could usually be found. She was not in her office, so Mandy would need to ask for her in the staffroom. This was the teaching staff's inner sanctuary; all pupils feared having to knock there. She had no option. It was only a short break, and she had to sort herself out before the next lesson.

She knocked gingerly on the door. Nobody answered. She rapped louder. An impatient female teacher opened it, a cup of coffee in her hand. Mandy didn't know her; she taught art as far as she could remember.

'What is it?' the teacher asked, abrupt and dismissive.

Mandy caught sight of the teachers gathered in clusters on comfortable chairs, some of them smoking, most of them laughing. Even Adams was there, a smile on his face. It was like watching animals in their natural habitat.

'Can I speak to the nurse?' Mandy asked.

'She's on her break. Is it urgent?' the teacher asked.

'I've started my period—'

'Oh, you poor girl.'

The teacher's manner eased immediately.

'Has your mum spoken to you yet?'

Mandy shook her head.

'Not really,' she replied.

'You know it's completely normal, don't you? You're not bleeding to death or anything. You just need to sort yourself out with a pad.'

Mandy nodded. She'd pieced together various snippets of information. She knew it looked worse than it was. She'd heard it was a curse but didn't know why. She also knew it was something to do with babies, but she couldn't figure out how.

'Wait here a moment,' the teacher said. The door closed behind her, and the lively buzz of chatting teachers was muffled momentarily.

The teacher returned with her handbag. She let the

staffroom door close behind her and pulled something out of her bag.

'Do you know what to do with this?' she asked quietly.

Mandy hadn't got much of a clue what to do with it, but she gave a small nod.

'It takes a bit of getting used to, but you'll soon get the hang of it.'

'Thank you,' Mandy said quietly.

She put the pad in her coat pocket and turned to exit the admin block. The teacher hovered at the door a moment, then returned to the staffroom. The bell would be sounding at any moment, and Mandy knew she had very little time to sort herself out before the next lesson. She made for the nearest toilet, grabbed several paper towels from the dispenser, ran them under the tap, and retreated to one of the cubicles. She balanced her coat on the toilet's cistern as the coat hook on the door had long since been snapped off. She then released the button on her school skirt and twisted it around so she could attend to the patch of blood without having to remove it. It wasn't so bad, she was relieved to see, so she began to sponge it down.

Without warning, Mandy was startled by a voice. She'd thought she was alone.

'She's in here. I saw her going in—'

There were footsteps and then a violent kick to the door. The lock, loosened already by years of abuse, broke away from its mount. There were four of them, all from Mandy's class.

'Got your period, Mandy?' one of them scowled. It was Lucy. They'd been friends at primary school, but it hadn't survived the transfer to secondary education.

'Grab her!' shouted an auburn-haired girl, and before Mandy could put up a resistance, they'd got her arms and were forcing her head into the toilet bowl.

Mandy was repelled by the smell, but somebody forced her

head down and one of them flushed so that water splashed over her hair.

The school bell sounded halfway through the flush and the various hands released her from their grasp. The group of girls were gone as quickly as they arrived, a sudden storm caring little what damage was left in its wake.

Mandy sat sobbing on the floor, the bottom of her long hair dripping where it had been dangling in the water.

FOUR

'I don't think we're going to be able to solve this case, boss.'

Hollie looked at DS Anderson, to see if this was another wisecrack. It was wearing a bit thin after their seven o'clock drive over from HQ. He had a straight face, so she took a chance on him.

'Why do you say that?'

'Because when we looked for evidence, there was nun.'

It was too early in the morning to have to deal with awkward colleagues, but she knew if she let this slide, she'd have to pull much tighter on the reins at a later date.

'I'd appreciate it if you kept that sort of comment to yourself, DS Anderson. An elderly woman lost her life here last night in the most horrific of circumstances. I think we owe her a bit of respect, don't you?'

For one brief moment, she thought he was going to screw up his face, but he resisted the impulse.

'Yes, boss, of course.'

Never was an affirmation so insincerely delivered. It reminded her of Léon telling her he loved her the week before she left the family home for Hull; somehow the will just wasn't there.

She sensed things coming to a head with Anderson, but she couldn't let it get in the way of the investigation. The inappropriate remarks, the crass asides, and the snarky comments were all attempts to wear down her authority. Hollie would have to tackle it soon or she'd miss her chance.

She wanted to walk the crime scene for herself before the morning briefing, even if it did entail a ridiculously early start after an even more ridiculously late finish. She'd barely slept anyway as her mind was racing all night.

'It's quite an incline up here,' she continued, eager to change the subject. The massive concrete supports of the Humber Bridge were looming up ahead, and they'd pulled up as close as possible in the car park nearby. It wasn't fully light yet, but they could see well enough with all the streetlamps in the area.

'Well, there's no doubt he'd have had no trouble getting a vehicle into the car park, even if it does officially close at night.'

Hollie was keen to return to work matters and avoid chit-chat. She hadn't got the bandwidth for all the interpersonal issues; she was nervous enough about having to deliver her first briefing that morning. It seemed too soon: she was still familiarising herself with a new police force and a sea of unfamiliar faces. Lancaster was a small-town station; she knew everybody there. Humberside seemed vast by comparison.

'Yeah, I reckon it wouldn't have taken much to get a car or a van in here under cover of night. I'm not sure if there's CCTV in the car park, did you notice any?'

Hollie glanced around the immediate area.

'There's nothing around here, I didn't see anything obvious when we drove in. I'll get one of the team onto it when we're back at base. There has to be a camera tucked away somewhere in this area.'

They'd reached a fork on the path to the bridge. To their right were steps and, directly ahead, a sloped pathway for wheeled access.

'Do you reckon he used a wheelchair to move her?' Hollie suggested. 'It's unlikely he carried her, and I can't imagine she'd have walked voluntarily. He'd have been able to wheel her up here, though whoever did it must have some upper body strength. Have you ever pushed a wheelchair?'

Anderson paused at the steps and looked up the incline ahead of him.

'I have pushed one, once. The old-fashioned, heavy models can be an effort up a hill. I'd say it would take quite a shove to get someone up this slope, even if she was in her seventies. We know she wasn't heavy from—'

Hollie could see the cogs whirring in Anderson's head. He was about to make a crass remark and she braced for it. She almost released a sigh of relief when he diverted course and stayed on topic.

'We know from what was left of her last night that she was not a heavy woman. But I don't think you'd need extraordinary strength to push her up here. I do agree that it's unlikely that she walked or was carried.'

'I wonder if she was drugged then – or maybe sedated? That's if she wasn't already dead, of course. This is just too public a place to kill a woman who isn't compliant. One shout and it would give the game away. I know we're clutching at straws, but it makes sense if she was brought up here this way.'

'We've ruled out parking on the road side of the bridge,' Anderson continued. 'That would have alerted bridge staff. Besides, he'd have to pass through the ticket booths to do that; there are far too many witnesses for that to be a sensible option and there are definitely cameras there.'

Hollie put her foot on the first concrete step, then drew it back to the path.

'No, I want to walk up the way the killer probably came. I want to see if the route reveals anything to us. I know the scenes of crime team do an excellent job of cataloguing everything, but you can't beat walking in the same footsteps as the killer and getting a feel for it.'

Hollie wasn't entirely sure DS Anderson agreed with her on that score, but at least he'd been agreeable last night when she suggested driving up there at some ungodly hour. They'd been tired, wet and worn out by the time they left. She was glad that they could leave it to uniform to sort out the resulting traffic chaos, but she was anxious to get started on the case.

The sloped path was not steep to walk up, and she tried to imagine pushing one of the kids up in a pushchair when they were much younger. She reckoned she wouldn't have had too many problems with that, so she revised her opinion on the strength required to get a wheelchair up there.

'Okay, I reckon any normal, healthy person could do this,' she said when they reached the top.

The side path merged with the main footpath across the bridge, and the towering concrete pillars and network of cables came into clear view directly in front of her.

'Wow, this is some structure, it's stunning,' she remarked.

'It never gets old,' Anderson agreed. 'It's one hell of a feat of engineering, that's for sure.'

Hollie noticed immediately that there was good screening between pedestrians and traffic. The cars raced by to their left, but it was possible to speak without shouting, and with barriers and cabling separating them, the road felt a safe distance away.

'There's no way you could park a car there and throw a body over, even if you did risk going through the ticket barriers,' she continued. 'Whoever did it, must have entered the bridge via this pedestrian route.'

They walked further along, past a massive concrete block which appeared to anchor some of the cables. Immediately after, they reached the fencing which ran alongside the edge of the bridge.

'I expected it to be higher,' Hollie said. 'It was difficult to get an idea of scale when we were looking up from the road last night, but this is only waist height.'

'It's not without controversy,' Anderson replied. 'They get occasional jumpers. It's easy enough to climb over and leap into the road. Most jumpers go further along and throw themselves into the water though.'

'Damn, that's a horrible thing to do. How desperate must you be to hurl yourself into the water?'

The waters of the Humber seemed formidable from that height. It was a wide, deep, dark channel capable of swallowing a body and carrying it far out to sea. It made Hollie shudder to even think about it.

There were few signs of the police team that had been there the night before, though they'd now vacated the area fully having gathered all the available evidence. A torn-off strip of police tape was still attached to the fencing, and there was a notice attached to the side of the fence appealing for witnesses.

'So, this is where she went over—' Anderson began, placing his hand on the top of the barrier and looking over to the Clive Sullivan Way immediately below. The cars flew by beneath them, but it was not as noisy as Hollie had expected.

'Whoever it was who threw her over, must have been trying to make a statement,' Hollie suggested. 'I mean, if you just wanted her dead, you'd leave the body on waste ground or throw it into a river. It doesn't get more public than this. So why make such a spectacle of it?'

'Maybe they have an axe to grind?' Anderson proposed. 'I can't think that something political would result in this, but she was a nun, right? So, it's religious, I'm guessing. I'm assuming she was Roman Catholic—'

'I think we have to be careful not to rush in too fast on that theory. I'm no expert, but not all nuns are Roman Catholics and I've seen nuns on TV who aren't wearing habits. We'll need to do some digging back in the office, but I'm hoping the habit will help us to get her identified at least. If we can find out the identity of her order, that should deliver a name.'

'Yes, that's fair enough. So, what do we know about the Church that might cause an elderly woman to be murdered? I know her death might not be related to her job, but it's a good starting point, isn't it?'

Hollie looked over into the road. She couldn't contemplate ever climbing over that fencing. She'd been on various high structures in her life, and most of them had tall barriers to discourage jumpers.

'It's possible she was murdered because she was in the wrong place at the wrong time, of course—'

'Yeah, but it's not like she'd have been frequenting the usual haunts like a pub or a nightclub. Don't nuns live in convents? She'd have been pretty safe there, I'd have thought—'

'Yes, agreed, and there's also the question of why she was killed so publicly. Most killers dump the body or hide it, they don't do their best to draw attention to it.'

'Exactly. I'm guessing they wanted to make a point. Why might someone have a bone to pick with the Church?'

'Well, the cases of abuse are well known,' Hollie suggested. 'It would be unusual for a nun to be involved in that – but not impossible. Did the Church run orphanages or institutions like that? I don't know that much about it, I'm embarrassed to admit. We'll need to get this checked out back at HQ.'

'You mean you don't go to church every Sunday?' Anderson turned to her, his face completely straight.

For one moment, she thought he was deadly serious.

'Yes, good one.' She shrugged it off. 'It's easy enough to tie a rope around this railing and throw a body over the side. I can't believe how easy that would be looking at it now. But I'm convinced she must have been dead when she went over, or drugged. You'd have to hold a gun to my head to get me to climb over that barrier. It would be terrifying.'

'Baby adoptions,' Anderson said out of the blue.

'What?' Hollie asked. 'What about them?'

'I saw a film a couple of years ago. *Philomena*, with that Steve Coogan guy. It was pretty good, actually. Judi Dench was in it, too. That was the Catholic Church. She had a kid out of wedlock and the Church adopted it without her permission.'

'Oh, I remember that. It was pretty dark, if I remember.'

'Yes, you can say that again. But that was in Ireland, and this is Hull. I can't imagine things like that going on here.'

Hollie didn't agree with that assessment. Her mind had just gone into overdrive. This was precisely the sort of situation which might make someone with a grievance hurl an elderly nun over the side of a bridge. She checked herself and thought back to the multitude of cases where a murder had appeared to be one thing, only to turn out to be something completely different.

'If there's one thing I've learned over the years, it's not to rush in too fast with a theory. Let's keep an open mind for now and see what the team have to say at the briefing.'

FIVE

Hollie felt like an anxious teenager cowering in the school toilets before a PE lesson. She'd done this a thousand times before, so why the panic now? The top brass was there, that's why. And this was a shitstorm of a case to cut her teeth on in a new patch.

But it was more than that. She'd been tossing and turning in bed all night, once she'd finally dragged herself away from the crime scene. There were two crime scenes as it turned out: one overhead, at the bridge railings, and the carnage on the road below. She'd learned over the years to shut herself off from trying to empathise with a victim in their final moments, but this death seemed particularly horrific, even more so after her early visit to the bridge with DS Anderson. Experience taught her crimes like that either came from a very disturbed mind or from a place of great anger and hatred.

The kids were preying on her mind, too. She was fuming with Léon. She thought they were mates, even if the frisson of marital passion had long since been bludgeoned by the pressures of her work, the constant demands of the children and the impending stress of their relocation to Humberside. But he'd lined himself up a bit on the side. And he was right: the leverage was all in his favour when it came to his capacity to care for the children properly.

It was five to nine. An incident room had been hastily set up already – officers had been dealing with the aftermath overnight – and she was leading the morning briefing. They'd all be there, watching her performance, trying to figure out if the press attention from her pre-transfer case had been worth all the fuss. Hollie knew how this played out among her colleagues. She'd just be the next in a long line of pricks in charge until she proved otherwise.

There was a shuffle from beyond the cubicle door. She hadn't heard anybody creep in. There was a sniff; someone was crying.

Hollie flushed the toilet even though she'd only been perched there with the lid down. It was best to gift whoever it was a warning; she'd give them a minute's grace to make themselves presentable if they wanted to.

Hollie made a big deal of sliding the latch. Wiping her eyes in the mirror was DC Jenni Langdon, the newest member of her team – except for herself – and a recent transfer from uniform, if she recalled her briefing notes correctly. The look on Jenni's face reflected in the bathroom mirror might have been her own a couple of decades previously.

The moment Jenni noticed her, she ran her sleeve over her eyes and pretended to be doing something else.

'Good morning, ma'am. I've got a damn eyelash stuck in my eye. What a way to start the day. The guys will think I've been in here crying.'

The small sniff at the end of her sentence confirmed Hollie was right about her being upset.

'We haven't had a proper chance to talk yet,' Hollie began.

'I'm so sorry we haven't caught up. I've been up to my ears with induction tasks and meeting the senior team. I am sorry. How's it going?'

'Good, thanks.'

Jenni attempted to brush it off. Her eyes were red. That was either one huge eyelash or something had got to her.

'And now here we are on our first case already. Looks like the induction and grace period is over. They're letting me loose on this one. How do you feel about being on the case?'

Jenni gave a final sniff. She'd composed herself now. Hollie would save the touchy-feely bit for later. Now wasn't the time.

'It's a bit daunting. And the rest of the team have worked together for so long. Even Harry – DC Gordon, I mean. He was with them when – well, you know what happened when DI MacKenzie died. His getting killed in the line of duty like that has created a strong bond between them. I guess going through something like that would pull you together. That's why you're here, of course. I feel a bit out of the loop sometimes, like I'm a nuisance.'

'Well, you and me both.' Hollie attempted to reassure her. 'I feel like the new girl at school. And as you said, there's some history with these guys. You'll be fine, DC Langdon – just keep putting one foot in front of the other and the case will play out as it pleases. We're just the sheepdogs trying to get the sheep into the pen. Sometimes the sheep don't play ball.'

Jenni nodded and sneaked a glance in the mirror. Her eyes looked better now. It was just in the nick of time, too, as the meeting was about to kick off.

Hollie led the way and Jenni rallied herself, following behind her superior officer as if nothing had happened.

The briefing room was packed. Even the deputy chief constable was there. They'd not met properly yet, but Hollie knew it was important when the DCC showed their face that early in the morning.

'Good morning, everybody,' Hollie said, at a volume that strongly suggested it was time to shut up talking about last night's TV and get a game face on.

Everything was ready; the briefing notes were being distributed, the detailed crime scene report included, and a rapidly assembled investigation team primed for action. She just had to shut the kids out of her mind and focus on the matter at hand.

Hollie made the introductions so that everybody in the room was familiar with the senior team and key personnel, then started the briefing.

'Thanks for being here at this time of day, everybody. As you can guess, the press and social media are all over this one. We need to wrestle back the initiative and stop playing catch-up.'

She surveyed the room. DCC Warburton and DCI Osmond were both watching her intently.

'Okay, DS Anderson, bring us up to speed, please.'

Anderson had a clutch of freshly printed images which he pinned to the incident room board positioned at the front. There were gasps from some of the officers who hadn't been at the scene the previous night. However long she worked as a cop, she'd never see it all. Hollie observed how even the most hardened of faces flinched at the sight of the victim.

'One dead nun, identity unknown. Thought to be in her seventies. Nobody reported missing so far, so we haven't a clue where she's based or if she's even local. She was thrown over the side of the bridge with a length of rope wrapped around her waist. We don't know yet if she was dead when she fell. Either way, a lorry smashed into her on the carriageway below. Thanks to some sterling work by DC Gordon over there, we also retrieved this—'

Anderson held up a photograph of the plastic sign and attached it to his display of macabre pictures.

'This is what the lorry driver says was hanging around her neck when she was thrown over. As you can see, there doesn't appear to be much love lost between the victim and her killer – or killers.'

'Have you thought any more about how the killer took the victim up to the bridge, DS Anderson?'

'No, boss. A seventy-year-old lady is not very heavy and would be relatively easy for a fit man – or woman – to throw off a bridge like that. Neither can we rule out an accomplice or accomplices.'

'I should note that DS Anderson and I walked around the crime scene at the bridge first thing this morning. We feel strongly that the victim must have been transported somehow from the adjacent car park to the crime scene, there seems no other realistic way of getting her there. We think it possible that a wheelchair was used, and that the victim may have been dead already, or drugged.'

'Is there any CCTV footage available from on or around the bridge?' DS Patel asked.

Amber Patel was one of the team. She had a great reputation, and Hollie had been impressed by her file. They'd not had much time to talk so far, but she seemed sharp and professional.

'We didn't spot any in the parking area when we visited the crime scene first thing, but the cameras may well have been concealed by trees,' Hollie said. 'There must be CCTV on the bridge?'

'Yes,' DC Gordon replied, stepping forward and moving towards the front of the room. 'I've already checked that, ma'am. The bridge team were unable to lift them off the system for us last night, but we'll be over there straight away this morning. There's no guarantee they'll have been caught on camera, but we're on it.'

'Thank you, DS Gordon,' Hollie continued. 'Please make sure you check the environment around the car park and the pathway to the bridge to see if it's also covered by cameras. What about the lorry driver?'

'He's awake and conscious, but still in shock—' DC Gordon began.

'You've been busy, DC Gordon.'

'We don't hang around in this team,' Anderson interjected.

Hollie looked at him. He'd meant it just as it sounded. He might as well have announced she didn't belong here. She'd have to watch Anderson. She'd seen his sort before – bitter, resentful and still angry that she'd got the DI job rather than him. He was stuck at the detective sergeant level with a boss who knew considerably less about the local area than he did. Well, screw him, she'd seen off worse.

'Thanks for making the early calls,' Hollie continued, giving DC Gordon a smile that she hoped came over warmer than the one she'd recently received from the deputy chief constable.

'Clearly a major element in identifying the victim is going to revolve around the habit she was wearing at the time of her death. Does anybody have any background knowledge that might help with that?'

DCI Osmond started speaking.

'You'll find nuns feature in a number of religions—'

'Fuck me, he thinks he's the Pope now,' Anderson mumbled. Hollie glared at him.

'Most people might associate them with the Roman Catholic Church, but you'll also find them in the Church of England and among the Lutherans in the Protestant Church.'

This was all news to Hollie. She was beginning to wish she'd paid more attention in school assemblies.

'Thank you, sir, that's extremely useful information. DS Patel, we need to dig much deeper here and get an idea of which religious order wears a habit like the one worn by the victim.'

'Yes, ma'am,' DS Patel confirmed.

'So, has anything else come in overnight?'

Hollie surveyed the faces in front of her.

'We have yet to hear from Doctor Ruane,' she said, answering her own question, 'and the scenes of crime officers. Did we get any prints or evidence from the bridge?'

Anderson shook his head.

'You saw for yourself, boss, it was piss—' Anderson looked at the DCC. 'It was throwing it down with rain last night. There's very little chance we'll get anything useful, but we'll get a clearer steer this morning.'

'Okay then—'

The DCC stirred and Hollie deferred to her seniority. It looked like she had something she wanted to say.

'Thank you, DI Turner, and let me welcome you formally to Humberside. Your reputation precedes you and I know you'll take a strong and confident lead with the team on this.'

DCC Rose Warburton looked like brass through and through. She seemed to be a woman used to being listened to, even though she didn't appear to have anything meaningful to say. It was interesting she'd decided to attend the briefing, though. Hollie wasn't sure why she'd do that. It can't have been just to say hello to her. Her answer was quick in coming.

'Needless to say, there's going to be a lot of pressure to get a fast result on this one. A nun in her seventies was thrown from the region's most high-profile structure. It's not good. And these pictures on social media—'

She held up her phone. It was a photograph of what was left of the nun's body spread across the carriageway. It was not blurred and the person posting it had made no attempt to screen the horror of what had happened the previous night.

Hollie had learned many years ago that it didn't pay to show too much emotion in the office. Some of the older detectives pounced on it, like whippets chasing a rabbit. It just served their prehistoric dialogue that a woman wasn't up to the job. So, while her face was fixed, her mind was doing somersaults. This was a fucking disaster. With images like that all over social media, the brass would be on her back night and day until she delivered a result. The weight of responsibility felt like it might crush her. Whilst Hollie was an old hand at leading investigations of this size and scope, she felt hampered by her limited knowledge of the area and fledgling relationships with the team. They would not give her an inch, that much was clear. The media would have a feeding frenzy, too. She wondered if it was too soon to hand in her notice.

'I shall be personally keeping an eye on the progress of this case, so we'll have a chance to get to know each other, DI Turner.'

That was a veiled threat if ever Hollie had heard one.

'And we'll start this evening with a press conference at The Royal Hotel. The media team are working on a press release for this morning. We can't hold back after an incident like this. DI Turner and DS Anderson, you will both join me at half past six this evening when we'll brief the press. We'll time it for the live regional TV programmes for maximum impact. Let's make sure we have something useful to tell them by then.'

DCC Warburton delivered her instructions and left the room, with all the confidence of a person who can make unreasonable demands without any thought as to how they might be achieved.

'Well, we'd better get to it then,' Hollie announced, giving the impression that it was business as usual, and it was no big deal that the DCC would be on her arse every step of the way. Inside, she was shell-shocked by the DCC's proclamation. Her heart was pounding so hard, she half-expected it to burst out of her chest in front of her colleagues. Maybe she'd be joining Jenni Langdon in the ladies' toilets for a cry after all.

SIX

1974: MANDY'S STORY

Mandy grabbed the pile of newspapers and manoeuvred them into her bag. Mr Mouncey had sorted them into order and the house numbers and streets were written across the tops in blue pen. She sneaked a look at *The Sun*; there was usually some snippet about one of her favourite pop bands in there. She hated the broadsheets. Not only were they heavy, but they also never had anything interesting to read inside. It was all boring stuff like inflation, something about Watergate, and lots of stories referring to the IRA, whoever they were. It felt like a million miles away from her life in Hull. *The Sun* was easier to read, too; the posh papers used words she couldn't make head or tail of.

By the end of the week, she would have enough money saved to buy the latest David Essex single. It took a couple of weeks' pay to buy a new single since the prices had gone up, and she was desperate to get a copy of 'Gonna Make You a Star'. The last single she bought was by The Osmonds – 'Love Me for a Reason' – but she was close to wearing that out now and desperately wanted to add a new one to her small collection.

'Watch yourself on the roads this morning,' Mr Mouncey

warned. 'There might be some black ice. It can catch you out at this time of year.'

'Will do.' Mandy smiled. She loved it in the newsagents at that time of day. She'd sneak out of the house before her mum and dad were out of bed or, if her dad was on a late shift, before he'd got back home. The house felt like it was hers at that time of day and she dared to imagine a life away from them, in a home of her own. Whenever her father was around, she'd have an anxious feeling in the pit of her stomach. She could never be sure what his mood would be, or if it was her or her mother who'd be on the receiving end of his rage.

She would find a council flat at first, of course. But she'd work hard, earn a wage at one of the local stores in town, and try to buy a small terrace in one of the cheaper parts of the city. All she could think of was to find her own place, as far away as possible from *him*.

The world felt like it belonged to her when she stepped out of her front door at just before half past six. There was little traffic on the streets in her part of the city, it being a Saturday round, and the only noise that could be heard was the hum of the Co-op milk float as it made its way up and down the roads, bottles chinking as they were deposited on doorsteps.

Mr Mouncey was always nice to her. He'd let her take a small item of confectionery from the shelves some days. If she got lucky, it would stretch to a Curly Wurly or a Super Mousse, more often it was a couple of Fruit Salads or a Fizzy Lizzy. She would look at the row of Old Jamaica chocolate bars and speculate on how rich and sophisticated you'd need to be to eat chocolate like that.

'I got the puncture fixed on the bike,' Mr Mouncey announced as she pulled the flap down over the bag and picked it up to throw it over her shoulder. 'It should be good as new now.'

Mandy smiled and thanked him. Her mum and dad

couldn't afford a bike for her like the other kids at school. Not since her mum's nerves had been giving her problems and she'd quit her small job cleaning offices. Mandy didn't really know how nerves made somebody ill, but it seemed to affect a lot of women her mum's age. She hoped it wouldn't happen to her when she got older.

The truth was – and she knew it – Mr Mouncey didn't need to make a bike available for her. Eddie Swift, who delivered the papers on weekdays, had a Chopper bike of his own. But Mr Mouncey must have seen the look of disappointment on her face when she came in asking after the Saturday paper round job advertised in the window, on a handwritten postcard, taped alongside all the other notices.

Wanted
Paperboy
Saturdays only
25p per week

It had resulted in a big battle with her dad.

'What about your studies?' he'd shouted, thumping his fist on the table so Mandy's drink splashed onto the tablecloth. It made her flinch every time.

'You've got your CSEs coming up soon. You might even squeeze out a couple of O levels if you try really hard. A Saturday job will just distract you. Besides, you never stick to anything, so why would you be any good at this?'

'But, Dad, I want to be able to buy things, like people at school do—'

She knew she was walking on eggshells, but she wanted – she *needed* – this.

'What like? We buy your clothes and food!'

'I want to buy records and stuff. And felt pens. Mine are all worn out.'

'I'm sick to death of hearing that bloody Osmonds record of yours. They're all a bunch of drugged-up hippies. They need a good, short haircut, the lot of them.'

He was up off his chair now, storming around the room, sucking out the oxygen. Mandy pushed ahead. It made little difference if he was cursing about this or something else. At least a small job was her first step towards freedom.

'I could pay a little of it into the family allowance money to help Mum?'

That did it. It wasn't much, but an extra twenty pence a month in the family coffers would pay for a week's milk bill or buy some groceries. It was funny how her father always managed to find the money for cigarettes.

The deal was done, albeit hard-won. He'd make her work for her victory; the criticism and carping would continue throughout the day.

She had marched directly up to Mr Mouncey's shop on the street corner. He was clearly expecting a boy for the role. He didn't say anything, but she could see he was eyeing her up, trying to figure out if she was up to it. He gave her the job, but it was almost over before it began.

'What kind of bike do you have?'

'I don't have one,' she'd replied. 'We can't afford one. I'm paying part of my money over to my mum and dad to help with the food bills. I thought you'd provide one.'

She'd seen Mr Mouncey's expression relax the moment she mentioned having to share her wages with her parents. He knew her father, too. Mouncey's was where he bought his cigarettes.

'Look, lass, I've got an old delivery bike out the back. You come here at half past six on Saturday, and I'll have it ready for you.'

Mandy had run out of the shop as if he'd just given her the best job in the world. Her own money at last. She'd had to eke out her Christmas and birthday money previously, but now she could buy things for herself. Eighty pence for herself each month felt like a fortune.

Mandy didn't bother telling Mr Mouncey she couldn't ride a bike. She'd never had a bike; how would she know how to ride one? She'd seen the other kids doing it. How hard could it be?

When the first Saturday came, the solid, black bicycle was parked outside and ready for her. Mr Mouncey had shown her how to load the newspapers in delivery order and to place her bag in the rectangular basket at the front of the bike.

'Aren't you going to ride it then?' he'd asked on that first week.

'Well, the first delivery is across the road, so I'll just wheel it over.'

Mr Mouncey had nodded. She reckoned he knew, but he wasn't letting on.

She'd waited until he was safely back in the shop until she gave it a try. It was an old-fashioned, heavy bicycle and the basket made it difficult to see the front wheel. It took a lot of wobbling, a couple of near-misses and a few grazed hands before she got the hang of it. But she was determined to keep the job and be good at it. It was the first step to her freedom.

On the day she bought the David Essex single, Mr Mouncey slipped her an extra ten pence.

'I reckon you deserve it for all those grazed knees.' He smiled. 'I figure I'd better pay you some compensation or you'll be joining a union and going on strike.'

'Thanks, Mr Mouncey.' Mandy beamed. She'd be able to pay her dad and buy the David Essex record and a magazine or two. They had great posters in the *Jackie* and *Diana* magazines. She clutched her pay packet tight in her hand, eager to get home, have her breakfast and head for the city, where she could buy the record in Woolworths.

It had been a good day. By half past five that evening, she'd listened to the record nine times, and she reckoned she almost knew all the words. The single was played on a small, Dansette record player which she'd picked up at a jumble sale for a bargain price.

The tenth play was interrupted by the angry voice of her father. The front door slammed, and she felt their small house shake at the force of it. He'd been to the match and had a drink; she could always tell. She heard him shouting about a player called Wagstaff and, if it wasn't for him, the entire team would be down the plughole. She hadn't a clue what he was ranting about, but his oppressive presence brought an invisible, thick cloud into the house.

She turned up the music so she didn't have to listen. She could imagine her mother cowering there, taking whatever nonsense he threw her way and never challenging him to stop.

As his voice got louder so did the volume on the Dansette. Mandy hated this. She'd do anything to get her own place, away from her father.

He had set about her mother now. She pictured her in the kitchen, flinching at every piece of abuse he hurled at her. He never hit her, but he might as well have done. Whatever was up with her mum's nerves couldn't have been helped by his shouting.

She caught the gist of it. He was bemoaning his lot, being the sole wage earner, wishing she'd pull herself together and go back to her job. It was only cleaning, he said. How hard could it be? Mandy had seen how much it took out of her. She would never do a job like that. However tight things got, there always seemed to be enough to go around for a drink after the match and to have a packet of ciggies on the go.

There was a sudden thumping up the stairs. Mandy felt the vibration in the floorboards. She turned the music up to shut it out. Her father burst through the door. The force of it startled her.

'Will you turn that bloody racket down? I'm sick of hearing that David Essex bloke. He looks like a bird with that long bloody hair of his—'

Her father stumbled into the room, a little worse for wear, his foot striking the Dansette player, which Mandy had pulled out, as far as the lead would stretch, into the space in front of her bed. The needle shot across the record, making an abrupt scraping sound before the automated system brought the needle arm back to its cradle.

'Thank God for that,' her father shouted. 'Now keep the bloody noise down.'

He staggered out of her bedroom, along the landing and towards his own. Mandy gently shut her door and returned to her record player, turning the volume right down so it could only be heard when she lay her head against the speaker. She only got half a minute into the song before it began to repeat, the grooves on the vinyl damaged by her father's kick. Mandy stopped the record and sighed. She tried to hold back her tears. It was only a record, after all; he hadn't struck her.

SEVEN

Hollie sensed the change in the atmosphere. The DCC had just started their day by tossing a shit bomb into the middle of the briefing room. Her immediate boss – DCI Phil Osmond – hadn't yet roused himself to snap everything back into place, so Hollie took the initiative.

'Okay, everybody, you heard what DCC Warburton said. We're on the clock with this one. Somebody must have seen something, even at that time of night. It's a massive, great bridge at the gateway to a port city, which crosses a busy dual carriage-way. Let's get the victim a name and I want those CCTV logs on the bridge going through with a fine-tooth comb. DS Anderson and DC Gordon, you're on the CCTV footage—'

She watched DS Anderson's face wrinkle as she assigned him to his task for the day. Harry Gordon couldn't wait to get going; he looked like a whippet waiting to be let loose on a track.

'DS Patel, I'd like you to arrange for someone to pay our lorry driver a visit at Hull Royal if he's up to it—'

'Yes, ma'am.'

'And tell whoever does the interview to go easy on him. He's probably still in shock and may have PTSD. Oh, and take the lead on following up with uniform and the crime scene team, please. I need a list of anybody who saw anything of interest in my hands ASAP. The rest of you know your jobs. Come and see me if you have further questions, but I'll walk the room before I head off.'

The team dispersed, the buzz of chatter resuming the moment she'd dismissed them.

'Was there anything specific you wanted to assign me to?' DC Langdon asked, a look of expectation written all over her face. Any sign of tears was long gone. Whatever was bothering her had been placed on the back burner.

'You're working with me,' Hollie replied. 'It can't be that difficult to find out who's missing a nun. I'd like you to start by ringing around. Go as far as Beverley if you need to. I'm going to take a leap of faith and work on the theory that the murderer approached from the Hull side of the bridge, seeing as that's where he killed her. We can't rule out the other options, but let's start with the obvious first. Are you okay to get ringing around convents and churches while I check in on the rest of the team?'

Jenni looked like a dog with a bone.

'No problem. I'll get to it straight away.'

Hollie took a moment.

'Nicely done. You'd never know you're new to the team,' DCI Osmond began. He'd been waiting and watching all the time, and she'd forgotten about him.

He was a neatly groomed man, with tidy hair and a freshly shaved face. His trousers and shirt were crisp and neatly ironed. His voice was softer than she'd imagined it would be.

'Thank you, sir,' Hollie replied. That was a start, at least. She hadn't cocked up her first briefing.

'How are you settling in?' Osmond asked as he walked up to her.

Hollie reflected on her current domestic problems. Apart

from the crappy apartment, the separation from her husband, the impending loss of her youngest kids and that drummer in the accommodation upstairs, and the fact she felt out of her depth even though she'd been operating on cases like this for years, it was going swimmingly.

'Everything's great, sir, thank you. It's been a couple of decades since I lived in Hull. It's changed a fair bit, but I can just about find my way around still.'

'Yes, you studied here, didn't you?'

'In the late nineties. I didn't finish my course. I went back to Lancashire to be closer to my parents and to train for the police. I was here for maybe two-and-a-half years – something like that.'

'Did you like it here?'

'Yes, at the time. I just had a strong pull back home, though. I was pregnant with my first child and felt I was better off cutting short my studies and making sure I could provide for my daughter. That, and I couldn't wait to join the police. I'd seen them at work close up and I knew immediately that's what I wanted to do for a living.'

'Well, my door is always open,' DCI Osmond continued. 'It's likely to take a little while to adjust to how we do things around here. I take it you're okay with the press conference tonight?'

'Yes, I've done my fair share.' Hollie smiled. 'What are the local media like around here?'

'Most of them are happy to still be in business, I think. You've got BBC Radio Humberside and Viking FM, as far as radio is concerned. Same with TV. It's the BBC and the Calendar team. The papers are *Hull Daily Mail* and the *Yorkshire Post*. There are others, but that's who you'll see doing the rounds. We've got a good relationship with them all. You know how it works: we feed them, and they help us. They're a reliable bunch, though, I'd say. No loose cannons I'm aware of at the moment.'

'That's good to hear,' Hollie replied. She became aware of DS Anderson lurking outside the briefing room. He should have moved his arse by now and got his hands on that CCTV footage. She'd have the DCC breathing down her neck if they didn't get a move on.

'Okay, I'll leave you to get on. Keep me in the loop, won't you? I don't like surprises, so please don't give me any.'

'Will do, sir,' Hollie confirmed, and he was gone, straight back to his office, no doubt, and out of harm's way.

DS Anderson skulked into the briefing room and closed the door behind him.

'What did Crazy Horses have to say?' Anderson asked.

'I beg your pardon?'

'Osmond. "Crazy Horses". It was a pop song The Osmonds sang in the seventies. That's why we call him Crazy Horses.'

'And is he?' Hollie asked. As nicknames go, it was a good one. She hoped it wasn't too accurate, though.

'Depends how you catch him,' Anderson continued. 'He's had a nervous breakdown in the past. He was away for six months until he had to come back. Yeah, I'd say he's a little bit crazy.'

So here it was: her first challenge. This was not the modern police force they were expected to deliver. Anderson's language might have been acceptable in the past, but it wasn't now.

'DS Anderson, I don't need to remind you the force takes a supportive attitude towards mental health issues. I'd appreciate it if you checked your language, particularly within earshot of the junior team members. How they hear us speaking makes a big impact on how they feel at work.'

'Yeah, of course, boss, whatever,' was Anderson's response.

Hollie decided to leave it at that for now. The case came

first. This guy barely knew her, and team dynamics tended to get shaped by cases.

'What did you want to see me about?' Hollie changed the subject. It worked with the kids when they were pulling on her chain, and it usually worked with her colleagues, too.

'This case,' Anderson replied. 'The boss – the old boss – used to keep me close. We worked well together, like a left hand and a right one. I just wanted to say I hope you and I can do the same. Don't see me as one of the troops. I've got your back. You've got mine. We old farts need to stick together and all that. This mental health airy-fairy stuff is all well and good. But coppers like us, we've seen some dark things. And when push comes to shove, you can't just waltz off on a mental health day when there's a case like this to solve.'

Hollie let his words hang a while. She got the gist of what he was saying, but the tone in which it was delivered made her uneasy. She'd need to watch this one like a hawk.

'I hear what you say,' Hollie replied, her poker face straight and emotionless. 'Let's crack on with the case and see how we all get on.'

'Just to let you know I'm here for you when you need me.'

He gave her a small wink. It was just brief enough to be passed off as an eye flicker. But she was certain it was a wink. DC Gordon saved her by tapping at the door.

'All right to go, sir?' DC Gordon asked. 'I've got a pool car pulled up out the front. The Humber Bridge team have the footage ready.'

'Best get going,' Hollie said, relieved to have an excuse to send Anderson on his way. Harry Gordon was cut from a different cloth; he was a different generation of police officers. She questioned the wisdom of teaming them up as she watched them walk away but decided the case was more important than internal matters for now. She'd iron out those problems along the way. It made her appreciate her team in Lancaster, though.

They'd been used to each other, accustomed to each other's quirks and methods. She was starting from scratch in Hull, in more ways than one.

Her phone vibrated in her pocket, and she activated the screen to see who it was. She might have guessed. Léon.

> Don't forget to get back to me. We need to tell the kids what's happening. Let me know when you've decided.

Hollie felt her face flushing.

'Okay to interrupt, ma'am?'

It was Jenni Langdon.

'Of course, DC Langdon,' Hollie replied, placing her phone back in her pocket. Léon would have to wait for now.

'I've been ringing round the Roman Catholic churches, I thought I might as well start with the obvious. I found a match to the nun's habit using a photo matching app on Google, so that narrowed it down straight away. That, and the fact that there's only a couple of convents in our area anyway. Anyhow, we've got an early breakthrough. A nun has gone missing. It wasn't reported immediately because she'd been showing early signs of dementia, apparently. She often wandered off but usually turned up safe.'

'Have we got a name?' Hollie queried. This was just what she needed ahead of the press conference. A name and a strong lead would keep the DCC happy.

'Yes, ma'am.'

Jenni Langdon looked down at the scrawled information on the scrap of paper in her hand.

'It's a Sister Brennan, ma'am. Sister Sophia Brennan.'

EIGHT

'You've got an address, I take it?'

'Yes, ma'am. It's an old building somewhere along Holderness Road. She was based at the Convent of the Sacred Heart of Mary. When I spoke to the lady in charge, she said they're concerned about one of the nuns there. She was about to call the police anyway. She didn't seem to be aware of the incident at the bridge, so I didn't mention what happened, just in case it's not connected. She said the missing nun is in her seventies.'

'Damn, it looks like we might be delivering bad news. This is great work, well done. You come with me, DC Langdon. We'll do this one together.'

Jenni's face lit up. That was a good start. At least someone on the team wanted to work with her. Besides, Hollie had resolved to be hands-on at first; it was the only way she'd learn to navigate the new force fast and grow more familiar with her team members. As a DI, there were always papers to be shuffled and desks to be sat behind, but she preferred to be out in the field as much as possible.

She dispatched DC Langdon to book out a car and checked in on the other staff before leaving. As head of the Murder

Investigation Team, she'd work most closely with a small group of core personnel. But she knew from experience that support staff relationships could be just as important at crunch times, so she took a few moments to spread some goodwill before disappearing from the office.

It was a twenty-minute drive across the city from Police HQ to Holderness Road, so Hollie was grateful for the opportunity to chat.

'Are you okay to drive?' Hollie asked. 'I've not quite got the hang of the city. I never drove while I was a student here.'

'You were a student here?' Jenni queried.

'For a while,' Hollie replied. 'I didn't finish my course. I was at the University of Humberside, not the posh one. How about you? Are you a local girl?'

'I went to the posh university,' Jenni replied. 'I'm not sure it was a good use of money, as I'd always wanted to work for the police. I was studying architecture, would you believe it? It bored me senseless. I'd rather chase bad guys for a living.'

Hollie could understand that all right. She pulled her phone out of her pocket and gave it a glance. She thought it had vibrated but couldn't be certain with the uneven surface of the road they were driving along. It was Léon again. She couldn't put him off forever. But she didn't want the call overheard by a colleague.

'I saw you were involved in some big cases in Lancaster. You come up all over on internet searches. I'm excited to have you here. I think it will be good for the team.'

Jenni paused a moment as if considering whether to say something else.

'You looked like you were about to ask me something,' Hollie encouraged. 'So long as you're not after a pay rise, go ahead.'

'Have you moved with family?' she asked. 'I just wondered. I don't mean to be nosey or anything.'

'No, it's fine,' Hollie replied, wondering how much to reveal so early into this new working relationship.

'I'm married, with three kids. Two of them with my husband Léon—'

She'd not mention the marriage difficulties just yet. It seemed a bit soon to break down in tears in front of a junior colleague.

'That's Noah and Lily, they're ten and thirteen. Lily's struggling a bit at secondary school, Noah's heading there next year. I have an older daughter from a previous relationship. Isabella – or Izzy as she prefers to be known. She was born right here, in Hull, actually.'

Hollie immediately regretted the admission about Hull, but the driver in front took care of her having to give any further explanation. Jenni's foot slammed on the brake and the car came to a sudden stop. The driver in front had just stopped dead in the road, before taking a sudden turn into a driveway, forcing Jenni to brake harshly to avoid ploughing into the back of them.

'Fuck! Sorry, ma'am. I didn't mean to—'

'Don't worry about it,' Hollie reassured her. 'I'm sure we'll be used to hearing bad language after we've worked a few cases together. I'm tempted to get uniform around there to breathalyse that driver, but they looked like they were ancient. I'd guess at least eighty years old, possibly even ninety. At least they were sticking to the speed limit at the time.'

DC Langdon put the car back in gear and carried on driving. The driver behind them sounded their horn.

'Bet they wouldn't be so quick to make that noise if they knew who was in the car in front.' Hollie smiled. 'The things we see when we're in unmarked vehicles.'

Jenni laughed.

Hollie looked out of the window for a couple of minutes, and they drove in silence. DC Langdon seemed confident and chatty, so she decided to risk it.

'I hope you don't mind me mentioning it, but you seemed upset when I saw you in the toilets this morning. Is everything all right?'

Jenni's hands tensed on the steering wheel.

'You don't have to say anything if you don't want to,' Hollie continued. 'But I am here if you ever need to talk. And I don't bite, I promise.'

Jenni was concentrating hard on the road again.

'We've got another one ahead of us. I don't know what's up. It's like it's national bad driver day.'

Hollie made a sound in agreement.

'Is it still normal for an officer to grab you from behind?' It sounded like the part of Jenni that wanted to be truthful had just won some internal tussle.

Hollie was shocked by what she'd just said.

'Are you saying someone touched you inappropriately?' Hollie checked.

'I think so. I can't be sure. It felt like it was on purpose. His hand touched my breast, too. Does stuff like that still go on in the force?'

'If it felt like it was intentional, I'm certain it was. Don't doubt yourself. This is how they undermine you. How did it happen?'

'It was first thing this morning at the coffee machine. He made some comments about it being nice to start the day with a pretty face to look at. I couldn't believe he said it at first. He came up really close, then he leaned over to get a sugar sachet and he brushed my breast. It was slow, too. I'm certain it was deliberate.'

'Is that why you were crying earlier?'

'I was crying because I was so frustrated with myself. I'm a copper, for heaven's sake. I've dealt with several dickheads and wasters and I'm only twenty-five. Yet when one of my colleagues does something like that, I'm completely useless. I just froze while he grinned at me. I grew up in a house with my mum playing Spice Girls all the time. I'm supposed to be the girl-power generation. And all I did was freeze.'

'It's okay,' Hollie offered. 'We never expect it when it comes. Don't be harsh on yourself. That's how they get you. You can't believe they've dared to do it. They're supposed to be your mates. You rely on these guys in dangerous situations. That makes it feel like an even bigger betrayal.'

'It just made me feel so... ineffectual. What do you do in a situation like that?'

'If I'm being honest, I may well have done the same,' Hollie answered. 'But, if we're talking textbook responses here, you should challenge him – or her, of course – in a loud, firm voice and make it clear it's unacceptable. Then you should report the incident and keep a written and dated record, just in case it happens again.'

Hollie watched Jenni's hands tense on the wheel again.

'I can't report it,' she began. 'I have to work with him. I couldn't land him in trouble like that. It would be so uncomfortable.'

'Who was it?' Hollie asked. 'I can sort it for you and get it nipped in the bud.'

For a moment, Hollie really believed the name was on the tip of Jenni's tongue. She opened her mouth to speak.

'I'd rather not, DI Turner. Besides, we're here now.'

NINE

1974: MANDY'S STORY

Mandy skipped school on the day that would alter the course of her life. She'd meant to go, but her form teacher seldom asked any questions when she showed her face, so long as she waved a folded piece of paper at him and declared she'd been absent due to period problems. The young form teacher's face would redden. Mandy would wave the fake letter and tell him he could read it for himself, and then the absence would be marked in the register. And the problem went away.

Mandy knew she couldn't keep it up forever. He'd rumble her soon enough, but it was working for now. And it meant she could avoid PE and games days, which were the most excruciating for her. Another time, after the incident in the classroom, the girls in her form had snatched her bag when they were changing for PE. They'd rifled through it until they'd found the box of tampons her mum had bought for her once she'd seen the soiled skirt. There had been no chat, no talk about the birds and the bees. Just a clean school skirt in the airing cupboard the next day and a small box left on her bed when she got home from school. Her mum had given her some of her own supply to keep her going, but only left her with the scrunched-up instructions to guess what to do with them.

The girls had emptied her supplies out onto the changing room benches, opened them up, and waved them at her like tiny mice. That's when Mandy decided school wasn't for her. She'd leave as soon as she'd done her exams, got a job in town, and sorted out that council flat.

She made it as far as the school gate, walked past a cackle of girls, and then thought better of it. She'd been getting braver with her skiving, starting first with single lessons, then afternoons and now the big one: she was going for a full day. If she could get away with this twice a week, she reckoned she could last it out until the summer holidays. Her father would belt her if he ever found out, but that was a bridge she'd cross when she came to it.

Mandy made a sharp turn at the gate and walked in the opposite direction of her home. She had not dared stray anywhere near her street, or along the bus route, in case anybody spotted her and mentioned the sighting to her mum. Her mum would go spare, frantic that Mandy's father would eventually learn what she'd been up to. Then they'd both pay for it.

Mandy felt an immediate relief from the prospect of facing a day at school and a lightness came over her, a sense of freedom and of being able to do anything with her time. Her sandwiches were packed into her school bag, so she could last a day without money, as long as she was home by the usual time so as not to raise suspicion.

Finding a bench, Mandy sat, pulled off her school tie, and then removed her jumper so she could turn it inside out to hide the school emblem. Underneath her coat, nobody would see the seams; it would look like a regular jumper. She also removed her hairband and shook out her hair; she liked the way that made her look more mature. She knew she looked much older than fifteen when she was out of school uniform.

Happy she wasn't a walking target for any police officers on the lookout for truants, she rejoined Beverley Road and made her way towards the town. The road was busy enough with pedestrians and vehicles for her not to be spotted. She was confident the busyness of the city would now hide her.

She got to the city centre just before ten o'clock, after making a couple of stops along the way for a sit-down. She'd just be finishing maths if she was in school. It made as little sense as words on a page. She'd never use algebra anyway. She could add up her money okay. Why would she need all that fancy stuff?

Mandy knew where she was heading. Sydney Scarborough's: the record shop. Next to Woolies, it was the place to go for music lovers. Syd's had a much better selection, though.

It was quiet in the shop, it being a weekday and still morning. It was a treasure trove of music packed with albums and singles. She barely knew where to start. The woman at the cash desk looked up and acknowledged her.

'Good morning. Is there anything I can help you with?'

Mandy thought she was talking to somebody else at first. She wasn't used to being addressed like an adult.

'No, thanks. I'm just looking. The charts are so good at the moment, I can't make up my mind what to buy.'

The truth was her pockets were empty. But the shop was warm, and she assumed it was normal for the staff to see music enthusiasts working their way through the racks of records.

Mandy made her way to the E section first, heading directly for David Essex's *Rock On* album. She examined the track listings and hummed the tune to 'Lamplight' under her breath, remembering what a catchy tune it had. There was something about that picture on the album cover. He had such beautiful eyes, and his hair was like nothing she'd ever seen before.

She moved through the albums, one by one, checking on

The Osmonds, Slade, Suzi Quatro and all her other favourites. The woman behind the counter had put Terry Jacks on the record player and she was now humming the tune to 'Seasons in the Sun'. Mandy hadn't got a clue what it was about, but it always brought a tear to her eye.

She'd been in Syd's for almost an hour when she noticed the assistant looking at her. Maybe she'd been foolish, coming in with her bag and hanging around for so long. Besides, albums were far too expensive for her to buy with paper round money; singles were much more her thing.

'Thanks very much,' she called over to the assistant in as confident a voice as she could muster. She figured if she didn't skulk out of the shop, it would be obvious she hadn't stolen anything.

From Paragon Street and the shadow of the City Hall, Mandy made her way over to Woolworths on Whitefriargate, taking time to look in any interesting shop windows along the way.

Woolies was the place where she bought her singles; it was cheapest there. She walked past the pick 'n' mix, a wonderful array of every sweet she could imagine. She didn't know what made her do it. It was almost by impulse. Somebody had left a sweet at the side of one of the containers. It was unwrapped, so she scooped it up and popped it into her mouth.

Mandy couldn't believe what she'd just done. She stopped and looked around. Nobody was looking. Nobody had seen her. She took another, popped it straight into her mouth, and walked on towards the record counter.

The record section at Woolworths didn't offer quite the same selection as Syd's, but it gave her plenty to be getting on with. Besides, everything in the charts was there, and that was really all she cared about. She spent a little time perusing the albums but was distracted by the devil sitting on her shoulder, whispering a wild suggestion. What if she were to steal a new copy of 'Gonna Make You a Star'? The shop was so quiet at that time of day. Usually, when she came into the city centre at the weekends, the store assistants watched groups of kids like hawks. But midweek, with just a few adults walking around the store, the staff were distracted, adjusting displays and putting out new stock.

Everything in her head told her not to succumb to the temptation. But she'd worked hard to earn the money for that single and her dad had ruined it without a second thought.

She had the single in her hand now. She looked from side to side. She was completely alone. She slipped the record up her jumper and tucked one of the corners of the sleeve into the waistband of her skirt so it wouldn't fall to the floor when she walked away.

Mandy knew it was wrong; she knew it was stealing. But she didn't care. She'd paid for that record with her money. If she felt too bad about it when she got home, she'd bring back the damaged single and replace it on the shelves. It still wasn't right, but it would even things up, at least.

She pretended to thumb through some other records so as not to make it too obvious what she'd been up to. She then turned and walked away slowly, anxious not to draw attention to herself. Inside, it felt like everybody was looking at her, but she knew that was just her guilt. They couldn't possibly have known. Mandy hovered by the stationery area for a couple of minutes, then her nerves got the better of her and she rushed out of the store.

She ran a short distance along the street until she reached an empty bench. She sat, her heart pounding fast, her face flushed with heat. She'd never experienced something like this before. It was a rush of fear and panic mixed with the ecstasy of exhilaration. She'd done a terrible thing and had got away with it.

Sitting on the bench, hardly daring to remove the single

from underneath her jumper to conceal it better in her school bag, she tried her best to calm herself. She became aware of a purposeful movement to her side. It felt like somebody was heading over to her. They were. It was a man, making his way directly to the bench.

'Excuse me,' he said. 'Have you just been shopping in Woolworths?'

'Yes. No, I mean.' She was a useless thief.

'I'd like to see what you just hid underneath your jumper, please.'

TEN

'Right, brace yourself. This is likely to be difficult,' Hollie warned.

She was saying it as much for her own benefit as Jenni's. There was something about these old church buildings that gave Hollie the chills. Its dark brickwork, the ornate carvings along the gables and bargeboards, and the institutional feel of the place transported her back to a time when she was younger and afraid of authority. She thought of Isabella and how the Church might have viewed her teenage pregnancy. Somehow these places always made her feel guilty about something she hadn't done; they'd have given her short shrift as a pregnant teenager in a place like this.

Hollie focused on the job in hand.

'You're sure they haven't seen the news coverage from last night?'

'That's what the lady said,' Jenni replied, pulling on the handbrake.

The two women got out of the car. The convent was fronted by a gravel drive, so parking was straightforward. It was an imposing, double-fronted building constructed with red brick and slate on the roof. The windows were grand and ornate; Hollie guessed it was Victorian or similar. Half-net curtains hung in the lower windows, so it was difficult to get an idea of what it might be like inside.

Hollie waited on the doorstep for a moment, readying herself to enter an austere world, alien to her, and one which might have condemned her not so many years ago. She was pleased Jenni was with her – it helped to distract her from her thoughts.

'I haven't a clue what goes on in these convents,' Jenni confided. 'The whole thing is a bit of a mystery to me. I haven't been to church since – well, since I was a teenager.'

'I'm the same,' Hollie whispered. 'I reckon we're just about to fill in a gap in our education. By the way, you refer to the nuns as Sister and the Mother Superior as Reverend Mother or just Mother.'

'That's impressive knowledge,' Jenni remarked.

'Thank Google.' Hollie smiled. 'I checked it on my phone while you were driving.'

Thanks to Jenni's detective work, the nuns were already primed for their arrival. They'd have likely heard the car tyres on the gravel, too, but Hollie rang the doorbell, anyway. It was old-fashioned, the metalwork weathered and in need of a polish. It was the sort of doorbell that was so old she wasn't sure if it would even be connected. She heard a bell ring inside. It wasn't electronic; it sounded like the real thing.

'Mine plays the theme to *Star Wars*—' Jenni giggled, stopping short when the brass handle turned, and the heavy front door opened. The woman who greeted them seemed so small and fragile against the sturdiness of the door that it was a wonder she had the strength to pull it open.

Hollie took her ID from her pocket, and Jenni followed her lead.

'Good morning. I'm DI Turner and this is my colleague DC

Langdon. A member of your convent spoke to DC Langdon earlier today. I believe you're concerned about Sister Sophia Brennan?'

Hollie and Jenni let the nun study their identification for a moment. After all, Hollie wanted to encourage vulnerable old ladies to take care on their doorsteps. She, of all people, knew the world was a dangerous place.

'That was me who you spoke to earlier,' the nun began. 'I'm the Mother Superior here, Mother Maria Davies. Thank you for taking it so seriously. Come in, please.'

Hollie stepped into a vast hallway, with a ceiling higher than she'd ever seen in a residential property before. The floor still had its original tiles, and a brass chandelier hung from the ceiling which was lined with ornate plaster coving. Otherwise, the place was bare, save for a few black-and-white photos on the walls and a healthy-looking pot plant to the side of a dark-wood coat rail.

'What a wonderful building,' Jenni remarked. 'How old is it?'

'The Sisters have been here since 1941,' Mother Davies explained as she led them along the hallway. 'Please, come into the lounge and take a seat. Can I get you both a drink?'

'I'd love a coffee,' Hollie replied. 'DC Langdon?'

'Just a glass of water for me. Thank you, Mother – er, Sister. I beg your pardon.'

Kindly, Mother Davies made nothing of Jenni's minor blunder, but Hollie couldn't hold in her laughter once they were left alone, with another vast, wooden door providing the sound-proofing.

'I guess it really has been some time since you went to church.' Hollie smiled. 'Remember, it's Reverend Mother according to Google, or just Mother Davies. I know it feels weird saying it.'

'I can't believe I just said that,' Jenni replied, pulling a face. 'How old is that lady? She must be in her nineties.'

'I guess the younger generations aren't rushing to become nuns—' Hollie began. She was about to comment that she might be tempted to sign up as a new recruit, depending on how things worked out with her husband, but she checked herself. She had to keep things professional and friendly for now, despite her natural impulses.

'DS Anderson told me to always refuse drinks,' Jenni commented. 'He reckons they might have spat in them. Or worse, even.'

'I prefer to take them,' Hollie advised. 'It gives me a chance to snoop unobserved while they're making them. Besides, nuns don't strike me as the sort of people who'd spit in your drink.'

Hollie stood and studied a black-and-white picture on the wall.

'This picture looks like it was taken some years ago. She looks like a stern old boot. Shh, she's coming back.'

The door groaned open, and Mother Davies joined them, empty-handed.

'I've asked one of the sisters to attend to your drinks,' she informed them. 'They won't be long.'

Mother Davies took a chair opposite them. The frame was constructed of dark wood and the upholstery had seen better days. Jenni took out her phone and opened up the recording app in order to log the conversation. She explained to Mother Davies what she was doing.

'So, tell us about Sister Brennan,' Hollie said, taking a seat on the small sofa next to Jenni.

'She hasn't been seen since yesterday evening,' Mother Davies began. 'Poor Sister Brennan has been getting confused of late – that's not entirely unusual. But she's seemed troubled recently. We all just put it down to her condition, but this is unusual for her. I'm ashamed to say we didn't realise she hadn't come home last night. I'm deeply concerned she may have come to some harm.'

Hollie felt Jenni's eyes on her and hoped she wouldn't give the game away too soon.

'You didn't know she hadn't returned?' Hollie queried.

'It's a convent, detective, not a prison.'

That was her told.

'Does Sister Brennan have a medical diagnosis?' Hollie picked up. 'Does she have dementia, for instance?'

'She's being tested for early-stage Alzheimer's,' Mother Davies replied. 'You know, most days, she's absolutely fine. But it's the little things that give it away. She forgets the names of the other sisters or gets disoriented when she leaves the convent. Several times one of us has had to walk up the road to collect her from someplace or other when she couldn't work out where she was. It creeps up on you. But these past few weeks, she's been troubled in her mind. She's been muttering to herself about making amends, mainly. But she prays every day. God hears her. She must have made her peace with Him. I don't understand it.'

'Do you have any idea what might have been on her mind?' Hollie wondered. 'Had she fallen out with anyone? Might someone hold a grudge against her?'

Mother Davies considered that for a while, then shook her head.

'We have a peaceful life here, detective. I'm not aware of Sister Brennan having any enemies. Why would a nun make enemies?'

There was a momentary silence while Hollie thought that over, and it was Jenni who interrupted it.

'How long has Sister Brennan been living at this convent?'

Mother Davies mumbled as she worked out the dates.

'I've been here for forty-nine years now—'

Jenni gave Hollie a horrified glance. The message was

received. This woman had been living in the convent since before both Jenni and Hollie were born.

'—so, Sister Brennan came to the convent in 1979, soon after the Church started making moves to close down the mother and baby home at the Church of St Mary and the Angels. She'd been there for more than ten years, I believe—'

Hollie and Jenni both spoke at the same time.

'A mother and baby home?'

'What went on there?'

Hollie thought back to the flippant comment DS Anderson had made on the bridge that morning. This was promising.

'It was a unit where unmarried and underage girls went before and after their babies were born.'

Hollie thought that answer was on the brief side, bearing in mind what happened there.

'Might her work at the mother and baby home at the Church of St Mary and the Angels have anything to do with her disappearance?'

Mother Davies became immediately defensive.

'I don't know what you mean by that, detective.'

Jenni looked at Hollie and allowed her boss to do the talking.

'You've told us that Sister Brennan spent some time working at the home in the seventies. The mother and baby units are pretty controversial places these days. I wondered if somebody might be holding a grudge.'

'What sort of grudge?'

Mother Davies knew all right, but it seemed to Hollie that she was going to have to drag it out of her.

'The Catholic Church separated unmarried mothers from their babies. You just told us that Sister Brennan worked at one of those homes in this city. Surely she'd have people with a grudge queueing up after all these years?'

Mother Davies sighed, like this was, perhaps, well-trodden ground for her.

'I know how people view that policy in hindsight, but at the time it was thought to be the right way to deal with things. It's controversial and divisive, yes. But it was what was considered best for the girls. Sister Brennan wasn't the only person who worked there—'

'Did you?' Hollie pushed.

'No, I did not. My calling was here, in this convent. I see no reason why anybody would bear a grudge against Sister Brennan any more than they might towards somebody else who worked there. I wasn't aware of her having any enemies. She has always kept herself to herself since I've known her. She's led a quiet life of devotion here.'

Hollie let that hang a while, allowing Mother Davies to say more if she wanted to. She didn't, so Jenni broke the silence once again.

'When did you start to become concerned that she might be at risk?' Jenni asked.

'She went out to visit Father Duffy—'

'Father Duffy?' Jenni asked.

'Yes, he's one of the parish priests. He lives on the Bransholme Estate now. He still does Church work, though. He and Sister Brennan go way back. He worked with her at the mother and baby unit.'

Hollie exchanged another glance with her colleague, and Jenni took a note.

'And she never returned?' Hollie checked.

'No. And when I telephoned Father Duffy, he said she'd never arrived. Now, if Sister Brennan had got lost and confused, somebody would have given us a call. It's the advantage of the uniform, you see. Everybody knows who we are.'

'Does Sister Brennan have a mobile phone?' Jenni suggested.

It was a good question; Hollie should have thought of that herself.

'Oh, no, as you can see, we live very simple lives here, officers.'

She nodded at the television in the corner. It was of the old-fashioned variety: a wooden casing, a curved, thick glass screen, supported by four wooden legs. There was even an aerial on top. Hollie didn't think they worked since digital TV had become a thing. Tucked underneath the sturdy TV set was a video recorder which looked like it might be a collector's item. She wondered what type of films the nuns watched for their entertainment. *The Sound of Music*, perhaps?

Jenni was trying to catch Hollie's attention. Hollie looked down at her colleague's notepad. She'd written a note in block capitals.

I CHECKED THE HOSPITAL ALREADY. NO NUNS!

She was liking this young detective already. DC Langdon was thorough, which was just as well while Hollie was distracted with so many things to learn and remember in her new role.

Hollie gave a slight nod for Jenni's benefit. She'd have to tell Mother Davies now. Where were those drinks? She'd rather they had Jenni's glass of water around before breaking the news.

'Mother Davies, have you listened to the news this morning?' Hollie asked, her voice gentle.

'We usually have Radio Humberside on after prayers,' she replied. 'But not this morning, due to our worries about Sister Brennan. We went out to see if we could find her. I thought she'd got lost again. I assumed she'd gone for an early morning walk.'

She looked at the two officers as if the penny had just

dropped. Hollie thought she heard a movement on the door handle, but she was mistaken. The drinks still did not arrive.

'What has happened to Sister Brennan?'

'I'm afraid she may have been involved in a tragic incident —' Hollie started.

Mother Davies's face blanched and she let out a little gasp.

'A woman we believe to be a nun was killed in violent circumstances late last night—'

Hollie took care with her words. She needed to let Mother Davies know what had happened, but she didn't want to shock the old lady any more than she had to.

'Oh no. Was there any violence?'

'Yes, I'm afraid it's a suspected murder. We can't yet confirm it is Sister Brennan but... but, the victim was dressed in a nun's habit.'

'Oh, dear God.'

'I'd have to stress that until we're able to ascertain the name of the victim, we can't confirm it is Sister Brennan. It might not even be a nun who was killed. We can't rule anything out at this stage of the investigation.'

DC Langdon got out of the chair while Hollie was talking, crouched at the old lady's side, and took her hand.

'It's going to be Sister Brennan, though, isn't it? I mean, what are the chances?'

'I think so,' Hollie replied. 'But we can't be certain just yet.'

'Will you need me to identify the body?'

She was made of stern stuff, this old lady. While she was wiping the tears from her eyes, she was still figuring out what had to be done.

'That would be helpful, thank you. If you feel you're up to it.'

The door handle twisted, and another nun walked into the room, holding a gaudy tray which looked like it had been bought from a jumble sale in the seventies. Hollie's drink was steaming in a bone china mug depicting the crucifixion. Jenni and Mother Davies had water in glasses similar to the ones Hollie remembered from primary school.

Mother Davies did her best to compose herself, then introduced the woman who had just joined them in the room.

'These are Detectives Turner and Langdon—' she started.

Mother Davies was still sharp as a tack; Hollie was not so sure she'd have remembered a couple of unfamiliar names like that.

'And this, detectives, is Sister Ursula Kay. We've got some very sad news about Sister Sophia, I'm afraid. You'd better take a seat.'

ELEVEN

Hollie struggled to work out how the two women had taken the terrible news. They appeared to be coping very well, considering the macabre nature of the death, but she assumed they must be shocked inside. Sister Kay seemed the most agitated, but she was doing a good job of hiding it.

'I must reiterate that until we identify the body, we cannot be certain the victim was Sister Brennan—'

'But it is, isn't it?' Mother Davies repeated.

'I fear it will be. But there is still a little hope.'

'When will we know?' Sister Kay picked up. She'd seemed relatively unmoved by the news of her colleague's death, but she was hanging onto every word they said. Still, Hollie had seen over her years in the job that people react in different ways to bad news.

'It's difficult to put a time frame on it,' Hollie answered. 'If you're certain you'd like to identify the body—'

'I am. It's the least I can do for the poor soul.'

'Then it could be as soon as the end of today.'

Hollie thought about the state of the body. There wouldn't be a lot to identify. It might even go to dental records for a second opinion, depending on how much had been retrieved. She'd seen some amazing cosmetic jobs on suicide and road victims, but there was only so much that could be done to make a body in that state presentable for viewing by a close friend.

'We'll try and spare you the ordeal of that if we can. Did – does – Sister Brennan have any other family?'

Hollie still reckoned things might play out in Sister Brennan's favour. She had sufficient air miles in the job to know the old woman's death wasn't a done deal until it was formally confirmed. Any number of scenarios could mean she was still alive, wandering the streets of Hull and wondering where she was.

'She has no other family,' Mother Davies confirmed. 'She was an only child, as far as we know. Her parents were dead when she joined us here. She was part of the Lord's family.'

'Of course,' Hollie agreed. 'Does she have any friends we could speak to?'

'Only Father Duffy, really,' came the reply. 'We find our companionship here at the Convent of the Sacred Heart of Mary. That and God's work are all we need in life.'

'Still, you must have spent time together?' Jenni queried. 'As friends, I mean. Don't you go out for coffees together and things like that?'

'Well, yes. But we fulfil our lives through our work. We enjoy each other's company. We live quietly here, detective. I wouldn't expect someone like you to understand.'

Hollie's phone vibrated and she checked the screen.

'Excuse me. I need to take this,' she said. 'Is it okay if I step out into the corridor for a moment?'

Mother Davies made a gesture which Hollie took as 'Be my guest.'

'DI Turner speaking. How can I help you, DCI Osmond?'

'How the hell did some damn blogger get a close-up picture

of that woman hanging from the bridge? Did you secure the area?'

It seemed DCI Osmond's open-door policy for nice little chats had just banged shut. It was straight down to business.

'Yes – er – yes. We secured the area. But it took a while to clear it. Besides, I arrived a little late on the scene—'

'Yes, I heard about that. Don't you have a satnav or something?'

Who had told him she'd got lost in Hessle?

'It was just a short delay. Besides, uniform had diverted the traffic and given the first response by the time any of the MIT guys got there. There's a lot of open-access land around the bridge. They could have been concealed anywhere. Besides, who's got this picture?'

DCI Osmond gave her a web address, and she typed it into her phone's browser, taking care not to cut off the call.

'Damn!' It was a full-page, sharp image of what was left of Sister Brennan hanging from the bridge. The only mercy was that they'd cropped the picture above the point where the torso had been torn away by the lorry.

'Yes, damn indeed,' came Osmond's voice. 'The DCC is on my back about it, which means I'm on your back. We can do without all this social media and citizen journalist interference. At least the newspapers know how to behave.'

'Look, I apologise, sir. But given the nature of the incident, there's very little we can do. It was a particularly difficult crime scene to secure. I'm sure you appreciate that, sir.'

She wondered if Anderson was right with the Crazy Horses jibe. The man seemed completely rattled. It was just another day in the shitstorm that was policing as far as Hollie was concerned.

Sister Kay exited the lounge with the empty tray. She made her way through to the kitchen at the end of the corridor. Hollie followed her course as she wound up the call with Osmond.

'I'll address it in the press conference this evening, sir, and appeal to the public for sensitivity. I'm not sure if it will do any good. I guess we might go for a contempt of court angle, but with no arrest yet, I think we just have to make an appeal to people's better natures.'

'Well, good luck with that!'

Osmond ended the call. Hollie had no intention of returning to the lounge. She could hear through the door that the ever-enterprising Jenni had engaged Mother Davies in conversation.

'Sister Kay?' Hollie called through to the kitchen. She walked through the open door. The nun was washing up in an old-fashioned sink, wearing a pair of pink rubber gloves. For some reason, it reminded Hollie of her mother.

The kitchen was sparse. A fridge hummed in the corner that looked so old it might have dated back to the fifties. There was no dishwasher, no coffee percolator and none of the usual modern kitchen accoutrements. The crockery in the dish rack was mixed, looking like a compilation of what remained from several decades of matching sets. The only item that seemed out of step was the Cliff Richard calendar hung up on the wall. She figured even nuns had to have their pin-up guy and who could be more wholesome than Cliff?

'Were you close to Sister Brennan?' Hollie asked. She picked up a tea towel off the worktop and started drying a cup. The soap suds crackled as she wiped them away.

'Sister Brennan kept herself to herself,' Sister Kay replied. She gave a glass a firm wipe with the dish cloth.

'Was she your friend?' Hollie pushed.

Sister Kay was silent. She handed Hollie the glass directly, rather than placing it on the draining board.

'It's unusual for people not to have a kind word for somebody who's just died,' Hollie continued. 'I get the sense she was tolerated rather than liked.'

'Sister Brennan was a difficult person to know,' Sister Kay said tersely. 'And what with the recent problems with her health, it didn't make life any easier.'

Sister Kay placed her hands in the soapy water once again, fishing around for anything else that might still be in the washing-up bowl.

'Why was she a difficult person to know?' Hollie pushed.

'She'd had a troubled past. She didn't make a lot of friends when we worked together at the mother and baby unit—'

Hollie turned to her, the tea towel still in her hand.

'You were there, too?'

'We both served there when we were much younger women. It was so long ago now.'

'Tell me more about this home at the Church of St Mary and the Angels. What went on there?'

'Unmarried and teenage mothers would stay there while they had their babies. It closed a long time ago. I wonder if that was what was troubling Sister Brennan. Many of the girls were very unhappy when their babies were taken from them—'

'Were you part of that?'

'I tried to offer comfort where I could, detective—'

'Do you think those girls might hold a grudge?'

'Yes, I do. They'll all be older women now, of course. There was a lot of anger and despair in that place, detective. Would they wait so long to get even? I'm not so sure.'

'And you were happy to work there?'

'As I've told you, I gave comfort where I could, detective. I was doing God's work, and I did it in the kindest way I could.'

'How about Sister Brennan?'

'She was not so pleasant,' the nun answered after a pause.

'Did she make enemies?'

Hollie couldn't believe this visit to the convent was proving so useful.

'I think any number of girls who passed through that place might have wished ill on Sister Brennan.'

'Anyone in particular?'

'It's a long time ago, detective. I really can't recall.'

The nun returned to her washing bowl. She seemed tense now, like these were uncomfortable memories.

'Would Sister Brennan have gone into a home had she become really ill?'

Hollie genuinely didn't know who cared for the nuns in their infirmity. From what she'd seen so far, they seemed to live to a ripe old age without much medical intervention.

'Ask Father Duffy about that,' Sister Kay scoffed. 'He gives the Church a lifetime of service and they shut him away in that horrible little flat. The Church doesn't really have a retirement plan, Detective...?'

'Turner.'

'Sorry, I forgot your name. I think they hope we'll do the decent thing and die on the job. We get our reward in heaven, of course.'

'You sound very bitter about your lot.'

Hollie let it hang there. Sister Kay emptied out the washing bowl, which was brimming with suds. She'd obviously given the washing-up liquid bottle too hard a squeeze.

'I'm not bitter. I just think Sister Brennan may have had what was coming to her—'

Sister Kay seemed shocked by her own words; Hollie could see it in her eyes. She'd broken off halfway through her sentence, like she'd only realised how terrible her words were once she'd heard them aloud.

'You can't think that in your line of work, can you, Sister Kay?'

'You forget, my religion is all fire and brimstone, Detective Turner. We're all sinners. Only some of us are bigger sinners than others.'

'What do you mean by that?' Hollie replied. 'Please don't hold back any information if you think it might help our investigation.'

'I've said too much,' Sister Kay answered guardedly. She wiped around the sink, squeezed out the cloth, and placed it behind the tap. Hollie noticed her hands were shaking.

'Thank you for your help, detective. Go and see Father Duffy. He's over at Stansted House on Bransholme. He knows Sister Brennan well. He'll tell you everything you need to know.'

With that, she was gone.

Hollie heard Mother Davies's voice coming down the corridor.

'Ah here you are. Oh, and you've cleaned up after yourself. We don't expect that kind of service from the local constabulary. Thank you.'

'Is there something we should know about Sister Brennan?' Hollie said. 'Something you're holding back?'

'I notice Sister Kay had a face like thunder when she was heading upstairs. What did you say to her? I hope you haven't upset her any more than she already is.'

'It sounds like Sister Brennan might have had some difficult relationships in her past.'

'I've told you what I know, detective, and now I'd appreciate some time to break this terrible news to the other sisters.'

'Of course, Mother Davies. You've been a great help, thank you. We'll need to follow up with further questions, and I'll also get somebody from the office to contact you about a possible identification. But now I think we need to pay Father Duffy a visit.'

'Yes, you do that,' Mother Davies replied. 'He'll want to know what happened. They were very close, you know.'

Hollie looked around the kitchen again, searching for evidence of any kind of modernity.

'We'll be on our way now, Reverend Mother. Thank you.'

Hollie and Jenni walked out of the kitchen and halfway along the corridor.

'I don't suppose you have the internet here, do you?' Hollie called back, mindful of the horrific picture she'd just seen on social media.

Mother Davies walked up to the kitchen entrance to give her answer.

'No, what would we want with something like that? It's the Devil's work, the internet.'

'It's a bloody good job,' Hollie whispered to Jenni as they made their way to the front door.

TWELVE

1974: MANDY'S STORY

Mandy couldn't believe her shoplifting activities were over before they'd even begun. Her hand moved under her coat towards the concealed item beneath her jumper. The game was up. He'd seen her and there was no point in playing daft.

His face was severe and accusing. Mandy thought she was about to cry. Then his expression cracked. He broke into a smile.

'I'm only kidding you. Look, I got you this.'

He pulled out an LP from inside his coat. It was a *Top of the Pops* compilation album. She took it instinctively.

'Here, I got some pick 'n' mix, too.' He grinned, pulling a handful of confectionery from his pocket. 'Help yourself.'

Mandy took a sweet and popped it into her mouth. She scrutinised his face, unable to work out what was going on.

'Here, have this,' he continued, taking a carrier bag from his pocket. 'If you're going to pinch stuff from the shops, you'll need to up your game a bit. I'll bet you haven't taken the Woolworths sticker off that record yet, have you?'

'No,' Mandy answered, sheepish, as if she'd just failed the first shoplifting test.

'If they come for you, you have to be able to deny it. Take the sticker off in the shop, that's my advice. Stick it to another record. That way, it's not on the floor at your feet if the security guys stop you before you've left the store. And always have a Syd's sticker with you to replace it. It throws them right off the scent.'

'But doesn't that mean you have to buy an album from Sydney's?'

'No. You go to Syd's first and peel off some stickers. Then you come to Woolies to load up with LPs. It's easy when you know how.'

He smiled at her. She relaxed a little. Her worst fear – that she'd been caught in the act – had proven unfounded. Now she wasn't quite certain what this man wanted with her. She studied his face further. He was just a young man, after all. He couldn't have been that much older than her. He was certainly old enough to have left school. Seventeen or eighteen, perhaps? Nineteen at the most. He was handsome, too. He had the smiling confidence of the pop stars in the teen magazines.

'I'm Terry. Pleased to meet you.'

He held out his hand and she shook it.

'Let me guess. You're skipping school?'

Mandy wasn't sure whether to admit that. Was he setting a trap for her?

'It's all right, I'm not a truant officer or anything like that. I'm at the art school. Only, as you can see, I'm not there today. I'm seeking creative inspiration in the surrounding environment.'

Mandy didn't know what he was talking about, and she guessed he could see that from the look on her face.

'I'm doing fine art, darling.' He grinned. 'I'm over at Queen's Gardens. It's very relaxed over there. Not like school. You'd like it. It's fun.'

'But you're skipping lessons, aren't you?' Mandy ventured.

'Ah, yes, but it doesn't matter that much. You see, I'm an artistic genius. You should come to my bedsit sometime and see. I've done loads of pictures. I'll bet you'd like it.'

Mandy hesitated a moment.

'How about I buy you a coffee in Hammonds and get you warmed up? You look cold to me.'

'Hammonds? That's a bit expensive, isn't it?'

The large department store was a place where Mandy's family went to look, but not touch. That was in the days when they went out together, when she was younger. It was a world apart from her life now. Even the prospect of going to the restaurant felt strangely exquisite.

'Why would I not take a special lady to a special place? Besides, we're partners in crime now. We know each other's secrets.'

Mandy felt a tingle she'd not experienced before. She liked this man. He was less of a man, now she knew him a little better, and more of a student. That felt like a more fitting description.

Terry got up and held out his arm.

'Come on,' he said. 'You can pick whatever you want from the cake trays, too.'

The prospect of a long day wandering the city's streets no longer felt like the most exciting possibility. Terry's invitation held the promise of something altogether more fun. She stood and placed her hand on his arm. He was so cheeky and upfront, it seemed like a natural thing to do. As her hand touched his arm, she felt how firm his muscles were underneath his clothing. It was exhilarating.

They walked along, each with a carrier bag of stolen goods in their hand, Terry taking her school bag. Mandy felt a million miles away from her crappy school days. This suddenly felt like the adult life she craved. What's more, she'd got away with stealing from Woolworths. The cocktail of new experiences made her giddy.

Terry had such an easy way of speaking to her. The boys at school were puerile, discussing stupid things which held no interest to her at all. The girls in her year had more interesting conversations, but they didn't like her anyway, so she never got to join in. Terry had so much to say. He knew about music, for starters.

'You should see my record collection in my bedsit. I must have at least seventy albums. I've lost track of how many singles I've got. Who do you like?'

'David Essex. Donny Osmond. David Cassidy. That sort of thing.'

'Well, I've got some of their records. And a lot more that I bet you've never heard of. You'd love it. I'll play you some of them some time, and we can expand your musical horizons. I'll let you choose one to take home if you want. Whatever you like best.'

They'd arrived at Hammonds already. They'd been chatting so comfortably that the time had flown by.

'Come on. We'll use the lifts.'

Terry led the way and Mandy followed, as much pulled by his tailwind as chasing after it.

As they joined the short queue in the restaurant, Terry invited her to pick whatever she wanted. Mandy eyed up the cakes; they looked delicious. Terry had pulled out a five-pound note from his pocket. She'd only ever seen her dad carrying that much money before; it seemed like untold riches for someone so close to her in age to be walking around with that much money.

'Have whatever you want. It's my treat. I can see you've got your eye on that Black Forest gateau. Here, it's yours.'

Terry took the neatly cut cake from the display shelf and placed it on the tray.

'I'll bet you'd rather have a Coca-Cola, too, wouldn't you?'

'Can I?' Mandy asked. They never had Coca-Cola at home. She'd had it once, at a kid's party when she was at primary school. The best she got at home was diluted orange juice.

'Sure,' Terry replied.

They loaded up the tray, Terry paid, and she followed his lead, taking a secluded seat in the corner of the restaurant. It wasn't too busy at that time of day, so they could relax and chat and not feel out of place among the pensioners. They took the day's spoils out of the bags and Terry demonstrated his trick with the price labels.

'Have you ever been caught?'

'Once,' Terry replied, a serious look on his face.

'Did you get into trouble?'

'No way. The opposite. I just showed them the Syd's label and told them they could walk around with me there and then and ask the people at Sydney's if I'd just been in the store. I acted all outraged that the security guy had challenged me and started causing a commotion.'

'What happened?'

'He apologised and let me move on. You've just got to show a bit of bravado. They soon back down.'

Mandy didn't know if she could manage that, but she was in awe of Terry for having the guts to go through with it.

She sank her spoon into the Black Forest gateau. It was moist and rich; it felt delicious in her mouth. Terry leaned forward and picked the cherry off the side of her plate. He popped it into her mouth, and she let him.

'Don't forget the best bit.' He smiled at her.

They stayed in Hammonds for an hour, chatting and laughing. Mandy felt at ease and relaxed. She couldn't remember a time when she'd laughed so much. Every now and then, he would touch her hand as it was resting on the table, and she'd experience a jolt of electricity sparking through her body. When he took it away, she'd feel disappointed, craving his touch

once again. In Terry's company, she was interesting and significant. She couldn't recall a recent time when life had made her
feel that way. So, when Terry stood and picked up his bag, her
heart sank.

'Well, I'd best be on my way,' he announced, abruptly
ending the conversation about his parents that had had her in
stitches. She could still feel the streaks where the tears had run
down her cheeks.

'Oh,' was all she could say. The prospect of killing time on
her own all afternoon was no longer as promising as when she'd
turned around before the school gates earlier that day.

'I really ought to show my face at college this afternoon,' he
continued, an earnest expression on his face. He paused and
looked at her, his face breaking into a smile. 'Only, I'd much
rather spend the afternoon with you. This is too much fun. I
have to drop something off at my bedsit first, though. It's not far
from here. Are you coming?'

An hour previously, Mandy would have been much more
cautious, heeding the stranger danger warnings she'd grown up
with on the TV. Only, Terry no longer felt like a stranger. He'd
made her laugh and bought her goodies they never had at home.
Besides, he'd offered to show her his music collection. She could
barely imagine what that many LPs looked like outside of a
record store.

'So, are you coming?' Terry repeated.

Mandy barely hesitated before replying.

'Of course I am. Lead the way.'

THIRTEEN

'I never got why this place had such a bad reputation,' Hollie said as Jenni pulled the car in at the kerb.

Stansted House was a seventeen-storey block of flats on the Bransholme Estate. They'd got the address details before leaving the convent. It looked to Hollie like it had received some modernisation to the fascia; she knew from her time as a student that the residences dated back to the sixties and seventies.

'It's like anywhere,' Jenni answered. 'Most people who live here are good, honest, and hard-working. It's just it has a higher headcount of scrotes than usual. That's what gives it a bad name.'

Every place had its troubled estates. Even her hometown of Lancaster wasn't exempt, despite being so close to Morecambe and the Lake District.

Hollie took out her phone and dialled. DS Patel was fast to answer.

'I've got some new intel on the nun and a couple of things I want you to check out—'

'No problem, ma'am. What's the latest?'

Hollie gave her the details about the mother and baby home

and the hints from Sister Kay that the victim wasn't well liked. The idea that she might have had a troubled past was intriguing, but Sister Kay had told her little that was useful. Sister Brennan appeared to be a closed book; it was up to her team to tease open the pages.

'So crack on with chasing all that, please. Make sure the DCs are on the case and kick them out of the office to knock on some doors if you need to. Try the local library or the city archive, I'll bet they have something we can use. I can't believe that nobody knows anything about that place. It's only been closed – what – a couple of decades? I want to know what went on there, where it was, who worked there, which girls passed through there – anything you can find. Oh, and is the building still standing? Can we take a look?'

DS Patel set to work; Hollie could hear her keyboard being tapped over the phone.

'One more thing. Someone will need to accompany Mother Davies to formally identify the body. We'd better put an experienced hand on it. Ask DS Anderson to accompany her, please, let's get that done ASAP.'

She ended the call.

'I hope the lift is working,' Hollie remarked as she pushed her car door shut. 'Fancy putting an old man on the fifteenth floor.'

'We've got to get in first,' Jenni reminded her. 'The cops aren't too popular around here.'

They'd managed to find a parking space directly in front of the high-rise. Somebody was playing loud music halfway up the building. They were kindly sharing the experience with their neighbours. Hollie wondered what Father Duffy would make of the Prodigy's 'Firestarter' as it blared out of the window. She guessed they didn't play that one in church much.

'I assume they all have doorbells,' Hollie suggested.

'Yes, if they're still working. If some little toerag hasn't busted them.'

A man stood by the small garden area beside the entrance to the flats. He smoked a roll-up and eyed them suspiciously.

'Good morning!' Jenni greeted him cheerily.

He nodded but said nothing.

The two detectives made their way to the entrance. To the right-hand side of the door was a metal-cased unit which housed the doorbells. It looked like somebody had splashed something unpleasant on it, maybe vomit. Hollie gave the situation the benefit of the doubt and hoped it was just curry sauce.

'What number was he?'

Jenni consulted the note she'd made on her phone.

'Floor number fifteen. Flat number four.'

Hollie pulled a tissue out of her pocket and placed it over the doorbell. She pressed it, but it seemed to be dead. She tried again.

'A lesser boss would have asked their junior colleague to do that.' Jenni smiled.

Hollie was warming to this woman. Now she'd relaxed, she was proving good company.

'A lesser boss only did that so she can send you up the stairs if the lift is broken.'

Jenni laughed. It was good to hear after seeing her so upset earlier.

'One more try,' Hollie said, pressing the button again. This time it gave out a tired, electronic buzz as if it were in the last ten minutes of a very long shift. There was no reply.

'He might be out, of course,' Jenni offered.

'I'm guessing an old priest who lives on the fifteenth floor doesn't go out unless he has to, but you never know. I want to be sure.'

She tried the bell again. It made the weary sound once more, but no reply came over the intercom.

'Right, we're going in.'

Hollie pulled at the door. It was locked.

'Damn. Electronic lock.'

'I don't know if it's keeping us out, or the residents in,' Jenni quipped.

'Someone's coming,' Hollie observed. 'And the lift's working. Look, it's a mother with a pushchair coming out. She'll let us in.'

'Oi!' came a shout.

It was the man with the roll-up.

'Yes?' Jenni beat Hollie to a reply.

'You should only go in there if a resident buzzes you in. We've had no end of trouble with yobbos in these flats.'

Hollie fumbled for her ID and held it out from afar.

'What are you doing? Delivering a sofa from DFS?' the man asked, amused at his own joke. He walked over and studied Hollie's card.

'Oh, I might have known. Police. You never show your faces around here when there's any trouble kicking off. But good to see you've got the time to pay us a nice social visit. I guess you've both got bored sitting in your offices, then?'

Jenni, posted at the door, prevented it from closing again once the mother and toddler had buzzed it open.

'Call the community team if you have any issues. I'm sure they'll be happy to help you.'

Hollie knew she was speaking bollocks, but did he really expect her to admit policing had been cut to the bone and they were lucky if a burglary was investigated these days?

She joined Jenni and they walked into the entrance area.

'This looks like Banksy on speed,' Jenni remarked as they surveyed the vandalism.

'It's more like the work of Banksy's failed apprentice,' Hollie retorted. 'Look at the state of this place. That poor woman is expected to bring her kid up here. What chance do they have?'

They walked over to the lift. It was engaged on floor six, so they waited and snooped around.

There were a couple of old community notices on a worn pinboard. Classes at the local community centre to learn IT skills. An embroidery group on Wednesdays at the church. Details of the food bank and eligibility criteria for accessing support. Just regular people going about their daily lives. Only, as Jenni said, they were plagued by scrotes and dickheads.

The lift made its gradual way to the ground floor.

'Jeez, take your time, why don't you?' Hollie scowled.

'That lift reminds me of a woman I used to work with,' Jenni added. 'She was so slow we'd have to check several times a day to see if she was dead.'

Nobody got out when the lift door opened.

'What the hell was that all about?'

'It was doing it to spite us.' Jenni smiled.

They walked into the lift, Hollie recoiling instantly.

'It smells of piss in here. Does nobody clean this thing out?'

'Looks like somebody couldn't wait to get home when they came back from the pub. I'm not so sure I could hang on for seventeen floors if I'd just had a skinful and I lived right at the top.'

For a moment, Hollie felt like she might have been back home in Lancaster. The banter was so ready and natural with Jenni, it was as if they'd been working together for years. It was a good sign.

Hollie pressed the button for the fifteenth floor. The doors thought about closing for a few moments, then finally got around to doing their job. Resentfully, the lift started its ascent.

'Mind you don't get whiplash,' Hollie warned.

It seemed to take forever to reach the fifteenth floor.

'I hope Father Duffy doesn't think my perfume smells of piss,' Jenni whispered.

That shook Hollie out of her downward spiral. She'd been

thinking about the kids while the lift laboured its way up the building. How were she and Léon ever going to resolve this? At best, they were living on opposite sides of the country. At worst, he was going to take them to France. Hull had its ferries, of course. It was still a hell of a long way.

'My perfume is so cheap it does smell of piss. I actually reckon I'll smell better after a ride in this lift,' Hollie joked.

They stepped out onto the landing.

'For fuck's sake—'

Spray-painted across the door of Flat 4 was an attempt at the word paedo. *Peedo.*

'Looks like we have an illiterate vigilante in our midst.'

Hollie wasn't entirely certain Jenni had noticed the misspelling. She refrained from judgement. These youngsters weren't so hot with their English, but they were a lot kinder than her generation. If they could save the planet, who was she to quibble over the occasional spelling error?

Jenni knocked at the door. It was a good policeman's knock. Hollie was pleased to see she'd got that mastered.

There was no reply, but as she banged on the door, it moved.

'Damn, the door's been broken in—' Hollie began.

She pushed it open and walked into the flat. The ceiling was so low she felt immediately claustrophobic. There was a walking stick on the floor. A patterned rug lined the dark hallway which led to a choice of four rooms. There was a kitchen to the immediate left and a bathroom to the immediate right. She assumed the bedroom was at the far right of the corridor and the lounge to the left.

The kitchen was a mess of undone washing up and food packets thrown out of cupboards. The bathroom was empty.

'You take the lounge, I'll take the bedroom,' Hollie instructed.

The bedroom was simple. A single bed, a chequered blanket, a dark wooden wardrobe, a set of drawers and a matching bedside table, and a simple crucifix on the wall. A book was sitting on top of the bedside table. She expected it to be the Bible but was surprised to see a Dan Brown book there.

'In here!' Jenni called.

Hollie tensed and rushed through to the living room. She knew that tone of old. She'd found something. As Hollie walked into the living room, she saw on the floor the body of a frail priest, his head soaked where it had, no doubt, been submerged in the fish tank to his right-hand side.

FOURTEEN

'He's still alive,' Hollie said, checking for a pulse in the priest's neck. A raw, red, bloody mark was visible just above his collar line.

'Call an ambulance. I'm going to start chest compressions. It looks like someone tried to strangle the poor guy, too.'

Hollie turned the old man over from his face-down position and began the process of CPR. Jenni put the call through.

'Get someone down from HQ. This flat will need to be checked over for prints and DNA.'

Jenni moved into the corridor, while Hollie went through the routine of pushing down on the old man's chest. He was a bag of bones through his clothing; Hollie had never touched a body that was so insubstantial before. It wasn't long until he'd coughed up the water and was breathing again, albeit shallow and weak.

'Okay, the ambulance is on its way.'

Hollie manoeuvred the priest into the recovery position. He gave no resistance; he was so weak it was like moving a scarecrow.

'My name is DI Turner,' Hollie began. She lowered her

voice. She'd been speaking as if he was deaf or stupid. They'd been warned about that in refresher training on stereotyping.

'You're in safe hands now, Father Duffy,' she continued. 'Are you able to tell me what happened?'

The priest's voice was hollow and reedy. She could barely make out a word he said.

'They... burst... in. I couldn't... stop—'

'It's all right, Father Duffy,' Hollie interjected. 'You rest now. You've been through a terrible ordeal. The ambulance team are on the way.'

As if they'd timed it specially, the siren could be heard in the distance as it raced through the streets.

Jenni walked over to the window.

'You'd best go down and let them in,' Hollie suggested. 'Careful not to touch or disturb anything.' She lowered her voice to a whisper. 'We'll get the old man seen to, then knock on some doors. This place will need to be secured once he's been attended to. This could have been a murder scene.'

'Any ideas what happened?' Jenni asked.

'Not a clue. It's likely the same person who killed Sister Brennan. I'll bet it's connected with that mother and baby home. I can't make much sense of what Father Duffy is saying. We won't get anything from him for a while. Let's get him seen to, then ask the neighbours if they saw anything. I'll see if I can find what was used around his neck.'

Jenni put her phone in her pocket and turned for the door.

'Oh, and see if they have CCTV on the landings or staircases. I'm sure I saw cameras on the way up.'

Jenni nodded and left. Hollie returned to check on Father Duffy. He was rambling and she still couldn't make any sense of what he was saying. He'd begun to shiver. She looked around for something to place over him, reluctant to further disturb anything in his flat which might provide evidence. She decided instead to lay her own coat over him.

The paramedics were up in no time, followed by a couple of uniformed officers and then Jenni. Hollie gave instructions to secure the scene as best as possible, given there was an emergency situation in progress. Support soon arrived in the form of the scenes of crime team and Hollie got their briefings out of the way. Within half an hour, Father Duffy had been stabilised and removed from the flat on a stretcher. The flat was secured, and Hollie joined Jenni out on the landing.

'I'll leave it to the SOCOs for now,' Hollie said as she joined her colleague at the landing window. She looked down to see Father Duffy being loaded into the ambulance below.

'Poor old bugger,' Jenni started. 'Do you think he'll make it?'

'I hope so,' Hollie replied. 'We still need to see if he can tell us anything useful about Sister Brennan. And I want to know what this paedophile thing is all about.'

'We still don't know if it is Sister Brennan,' Jenni answered.

'We have one murder and one attempted murder and absolutely nothing to go on. I'm going to check in on DS Anderson. They'll have had time to examine the CCTV on the bridge by now.'

Hollie looked around to ensure the landing was clear. It was. That was unusual. Most times, a crowd would gather if there was a commotion going on.

'Let me make this call, then we can start knocking on doors.'

Hollie dialled in and DS Anderson was quick to answer.

'Yes, boss?'

Hollie clocked that Anderson seemed to be the only member of the team calling her boss. It didn't concern her. She was happier being called boss or guv, but generally expected it to come after some time working a case together. She let it pass.

'Anything from the CCTV?'

'Whoever threw her over the side came along the footpath, as we thought. The bridge team confirmed that if he'd stopped a car along the road section, it would have caused a hazard and been flagged up to the bridge team—'

'So, they walked over? How about our hunch about using a wheelchair?'

'Bingo on that one, boss. That's exactly how he did it.'

'Really?'

'Yeah, we have a really terrible image from the CCTV, and it looks that way.'

'How did nobody see it?'

'People commit suicide from the bridge all the time. It's easy to walk over. Why would anybody be paying any attention?'

'But in a wheelchair?'

'It just looked like some guy taking his old mum on a night-time walk. Who'd look twice?'

'And there's no footage of how he threw her over? Anything we can use?'

'Sorry, boss. All we've got is some dark and grainy images of what looks like a man pushing an old woman in a wheelchair. And before you ask, you can't see him properly and her face is not visible either. She's slumped over.'

'Does she look like she's out cold?' Hollie pushed.

'Well, let's put it this way, she's not doing the macarena, I can tell you that much.'

'Okay, I'll take a look at the stills when I'm back in the office. How about the nun? Now we've got a name, we must be able to find out something about her. And let's get digging on the mother and baby home. Has DS Patel made any break-throughs on that?'

'She's hard at it, boss. Nothing so far, sorry.'

Hollie was about to curse, but a door had just opened along the landing and a young woman holding a sleeping baby was walking over towards DC Langdon.

'Look, I'll have to go.' Hollie lowered her voice. 'Are you all set to go with Mother Davies and get me that formal ID on the body? I need that before we do the press conference.'

'Just trying to organise it now, boss. I promise to show my sensitive side when I speak to the nun.'

Hollie paused for a moment, making sure she hadn't missed anything. It was like ticking off items on a shopping list.

'Oh, anything from the lorry driver yet?'

'Not that I know of. We're just back in the office now. I'll pull what we've got together so you're ready for your briefing later. We're still waiting for Doctor Ruane to give us more info on the body, too.'

'Okay, keep me posted. Thank you.'

Hollie ended the call. Jenni was talking to the woman now.

'That's a beautiful baby,' Hollie started. She pushed back thoughts of her own children. There was no time now; she'd deal with all that later. 'Does she always sleep that way?'

The baby was completely relaxed in the woman's arms. It hadn't a care in the world. Hollie wished she could sleep like that.

Jenni changed the subject.

'Apparently, this paedophile thing has been going on for a couple of weeks.'

'Have you seen anything?' Hollie asked.

The woman shook her head. 'The little buggers are all over these flats. They're like cockroaches. Look at what they sprayed on his door. How the hell can I be expected to protect my baby when all this is going on? The police can't do anything. These kids are out of control. And the CCTV doesn't work either—'

That was another of Hollie's questions answered.

'Is there any substance to the accusations?' Jenni asked.

'What, that he's a paedophile?'

'Yes,' Hollie confirmed.

'He's just an old man. What harm can you do at that age? I'm barely aware of him leaving his flat. He shuffles about and looks like the wind might blow him over any minute. I don't know. I think they just see an old priest and draw the wrong conclusions. You know what people are like.'

'Have you seen anybody else around? Somebody suspicious or who was out of place?'

The woman shook her head at Jenni's question.

'These kids come, and they go. You don't always hear them. I have the TV on, so I can't hear, anyway. It's lonely up here on your own. You just lock your door and hope you're not the next target. I did check the landing, but I didn't see anyone. Just that horrible message painted on his door.'

'Can you tell us anything about the kids?' Hollie ventured. 'This could easily have been a murder scene. It still might be depending on Father Duffy's recovery.'

'Everybody on the estate knows who these kids are,' the woman scoffed. 'Only, nobody does anything about them. If you want to know where to start, go and see Shane Hardy. That little toerag is bound to know something about all this.'

'Where do we find him?'

Jenni was writing the name in her notepad while Hollie was asking the question.

'He and his gang of idiots will be on Stroud Crescent. You'll know who they are when you get there. I'll bet he can tell you what's been going on with Father Duffy.'

FIFTEEN

1974: MANDY'S STORY

Terry had a stereo set up in his bedsit. It was built from separate units. For a Dansette owner like Mandy, it was the height of musical sophistication. She adjusted the controls on the treble and bass knobs, marvelling at the sound quality through the wooden speakers. Terry hadn't been lying. His records were stacked all along the floor with a speaker at either end to support them, an array of vinyl albums and singles. To Mandy, it was a treasure trove.

Terry let her rifle through his collection while he pulled out an album and carefully placed it on the turntable. Mandy heard the satisfying crackle of the needle finding its groove on the LP. It took her a moment to identify the singer. It was Barry White. He'd been in and out of the charts all that year, and Terry was lucky enough to own the album.

'I take it you like him?' Terry asked.

'Yes, of course. Who doesn't like Barry White?'

In Terry's company, Mandy felt like she'd aged two or three years. This was the freedom she dreamt about, a life away from her parents and that dingy school. It always seemed just out of reach.

Terry walked across the room to the kitchen area. Mandy noticed the dishes weren't washed. He opened a small fridge perched on the worktop. Mandy was more interested in the records than what Terry was up to. Moments later, he appeared behind her, holding something in his hand.

'Do you like wine?' he asked.

Mandy hadn't a clue whether she liked wine or not.

'It's Liebfraumilch,' Terry added, like it would make a difference.

Not wishing to appear foolish, Mandy held out her hand and accepted the glass. She moved it to her lips and took a large sip. It was nicer than she expected, but it still made her screw up her face at the taste of it.

'Sip it slowly,' Terry advised. 'It's an acquired taste, but I'm sure you'll grow to like it.'

He sat right at her side so their hips were touching. She didn't move. She liked it. She liked Terry.

'I'm sorry it's so hot in here,' Terry continued, removing his sweater. 'The heating goes a bit crazy sometimes. It's either boiling or freezing.'

Now he mentioned it, it was rather hot. Mandy removed her own jumper, throwing it over onto Terry's bed. He hadn't bothered making it, but then Mandy didn't particularly relish making her own bed in the morning. Lots of people were buying the new continental quilts. They seemed like so much less hassle to Mandy, but her mum and dad were happy to stick with sheets and blankets. It looked like Terry hadn't made the switch, either.

'So, why are you skipping school? Having a hard time of it?'

'Yes, something like that. It's not long until I can leave. I can't wait until I'm like you. I'll get a job, or maybe a place at college. I just want some independence.'

Mandy had never ventured towards the thought of college

before. She'd always assumed the academic world wasn't for her. She liked Terry's life; it looked good.

'I get that,' Terry replied. 'I couldn't wait to move out. My mum and dad were always rowing, but the house was too small. They were continually on my case about something or other. But here – well, as you can see, I do my own thing.'

Mandy scanned the bedsit properly for the first time. It was compact, but practical enough. Terry had a large Grundig radio next to the bed, its aerial sticking up high above his bedside lamp. Placed on a small bookcase were various literary classics, such as *Nineteen Eighty-Four* and *The Great Gatsby*. Mandy had never heard of the books, and she reckoned Terry must be really clever to be able to read them.

'You like the books?' he asked.

Mandy felt suddenly stupid. She wouldn't be able to read them even if she tried.

'Ooh, I saw your face drop then. I take it you don't like reading much. Well, don't worry. The books are just for show. I prefer my music.'

Mandy liked the posters on his walls. They were mostly music-related, but some seemed like exotic pieces of fantasy artwork. She'd never seen anything like it. All her mum and dad had by way of art was a picture of a crying boy procured from a jumble sale, and several turgid landscape images which were dark, heavily painted and indistinct. There were examples of his artwork all over. Mandy didn't know much about art, but he seemed to have a knack for it.

She reached out to pull an album from the stack and, at the same time, Terry moved his hand out, too. They touched and Mandy felt a thrilling surge once again. Terry held his hand there. Mandy thought about moving hers, but she didn't. Terry didn't seem too bothered by it, either.

'Well, seeing as we're here, we may as well hold hands, don't you think? You haven't touched your wine—'

Terry gently took her left hand while leaning over to pick up her glass. She took it with her free hand and had another sip, smaller this time. As she knew what to expect now, the wine tasted more pleasant. She took a second sip before she let Terry take it away.

They worked their way through the record collection, discussing what they liked and what they didn't like. Every now and then, Terry would draw out an album by an artist she'd never heard of, and she'd realise how worldly-wise he was compared to her. It would have been easier to unclasp their hands, but she didn't want the thrill to end, and Terry seemed in no hurry to break away either.

'You know, you look a lot older than a schoolgirl,' Terry said gently. 'You must be sixteen or seventeen, surely. It certainly seems the way.'

Mandy had been told that before, but usually by some relative who was exclaiming how she'd grown up since they last paid a visit. She felt her face colouring a little. She didn't set him right, in case he dismissed her as a silly little schoolgirl. Nobody ever said nice things to her.

'Your hair is lovely, too—'

Terry ran his hand over the side of her face. His hands were smooth, the hands of an artist. Her father's hands were rough, the penalty he paid for years of manual labour.

'Has anybody ever told you you've got beautiful hair? You could be eighteen when you wear your hair like that. You look incredible.'

Mandy was feeling things she'd never experienced before. Terry made her tingle all over when he spoke; it was like a gentle prickle of electricity dancing over her skin and making her heart jump and pound in her chest. She felt a little bit dizzy, but it was not an unpleasant sensation. Her head was spinning slightly, and she was more relaxed than she had been in a long time.

The Barry White album ended, and they let the needle click for several minutes before Terry pulled his hand away to change it over. The moment they broke contact, Mandy became desperate, wondering if they'd be able to find an excuse to sit so close together again.

She needn't have worried. Terry reached across and flipped the album over. He placed the needle on to the record, waited for the music to begin, and then held out his hand to her.

'Come on,' he said.

'What?' she replied. Was he proposing that they dance?

She took his hand, and he pulled her up off the floor. She was a little unsteady on her feet. That was the wine, she assumed. It was nice; she liked the way it made her feel. She liked the way Terry made her feel.

'Let's sit on the bed and talk,' Terry suggested. 'It's uncomfortable on the floor. It'll be much nicer up here.'

Terry flattened the sheets and blanket and tapped the corner of the bed. Mandy took a sip of her wine and joined him. This time, she sat up close to him. As the mattress dipped with her weight, Terry turned and ran his hand through her hair.

'You really are very beautiful—' he said as he leaned over to kiss her.

She didn't stop him. It was the most exciting feeling she'd ever experienced.

SIXTEEN

'I'm tempted to leave these dickheads to uniform.'

Hollie and Jenni had been watching the youths from across the road for five minutes already. In that time, she'd seen a story playing out as predictable as it was tragic. A group of lads – ranging from fourteen to nineteen or so years old. The young kids skipping school and in awe of the older youths. The older youths scavenging for what morsels of respect and status they could steal from the younger boys. Hull's future feckless fathers in training, perpetuating the circle of broken family lives and dashed hopes. It would have been Shakespearean in scope if the Bard had ever written about glue-sniffing, drug-running and underage drinking.

Somehow this group of feral tearaways had procured a motorbike and were churning up the communal grass area, performing skids and wheelies, watched on by the residents who knew better than to risk intervention.

'I'll bet you five quid that idiot is Shane Hardy,' Jenni offered.

'It's easy money. There's no way I'm signing up for that bet,'

Hollie answered. 'Right, let's do this. Steel yourself. It's going to get ugly.'

The two women got out of the car and walked over to the grassy area. It was streaked with brown, muddy furrows. The gathered youths seemed to sense they were being approached by a couple of police officers. They began to form a circle like predatory wolves as Hollie fearlessly approached the gangly, spotty youth on the motorcycle. It had no registration plates and looked like it had been retrieved from the scrapyard, such was the level of destruction to its paint and bodywork.

The young man on the bike gave Hollie the finger and pulled a skid to her side, turning the vehicle around and roaring off to the cheers of his mates. In her less composed moments, Hollie fantasised about giving kids like this a good hiding. Her socialised self knew they were the natural consequence of a failed political system, and she felt immediately guilty at the thoughts.

'Lovely titties, missus!' one of the younger boys called out to Jenni.

She'd left her junior colleague on her own. She knew from having studied Jenni's records that she was experienced enough in the field to hold her own, but she had no wish to throw her to the wolves.

'Give us a flash,' another one added.

Hollie cursed her negligence. Jenni was a good-looking young woman. Of course, this bunch of idiots were going to sexualise her in some way.

'Sorry, boys, I prefer women,' Jenni answered.

'Not after you've spent a night with me, you won't,' one said, laughing. He didn't even look capable of feeding himself, let alone carrying out his confident brag to Jenni.

'Is that your older dyke friend?' another added. 'Personally, I'd give her a miss.'

'Now then, lads. We need your help,' Hollie began. She'd never been more thankful for middle age. It meant she was sexually invisible to this group of cretins. She was more like their mother. Or, on that estate, their grandmother.

'You up for us filming you lezzing up?'

A boy whose voice hadn't even broken grinned at his mate, smartphone in hand.

Hollie ignored him and raised her eyebrows slightly. She drew out her ID.

'I'm DI Turner—'

'Is that police?' one of the youths asked.

'Yes,' Jenni replied. She held out her ID, too. The boy with the phone moved in for a selfie with her before either of them could prevent it.

'Have you got an OnlyFans page?' he asked.

Hollie observed Jenni's face colouring a little. How unpleasant for the poor girl; she'd end it as soon as she could.

'Who knows anything about Father Duffy?' Hollie pushed on, her voice steady and calm. She was determined not to be intimidated by these boys. If they smelled fear, it would fuel their bravado. She was keen to move this on. Without the attention of his peers, the boy on the motorcycle had lost interest in doing stunts on the grass. The motorcycle roared up at the side of the group. The youth who was riding it stopped the engine, his legs astride.

'That old paedo,' came a voice.

'Why do you call him a paedophile?' Jenni asked. 'Have you got any evidence?'

'They're all paedos, aren't they? Those priests. They're all at it.'

'He wouldn't fancy you, Scrogsy. I've smelt the farts that come out of that arse of yours. Not even that paedo priest would go near your ring piece.'

Hollie had lost track of who was saying what. It was a chorus of bullshit. She wished they had a mute button.

'Are you Shane Hardy?' Hollie asked.

'What's it to you?' the youth scowled. He had a scar down his cheek like he'd been cut by a blade. This one looked like a genuine tough nut. He was as skinny as a starving hyena and his eyes looked just as treacherous. He had poorly drawn tattoos up both his bare arms. They certainly hadn't been inked by a professional. It was a cold day, and he was putting a brave face on it by not wearing a jacket.

'We're investigating an incident at Father Duffy's flat this morning—'

There were stifled giggles, and Hollie observed much nudging among the group.

'It's about time someone had a word with these lads.'

An elderly woman had walked up, apparently noticing that someone in a position of authority was addressing the youngsters.

'Fuck off, grandma,' came a voice from the back.

'That's enough, lads,' Hollie interjected in her most stern mum voice. It appeared to work, too.

'DC Langdon, if you would?'

Jenni got the message and led the lady away from the already inflamed situation, gently explaining what was going on.

'In my day, you'd have all been doing National Service. That would have sorted you out.'

'In your day you'd have been eating dinosaurs for your dinner,' came the reply.

Jenni moved the old woman along more quickly.

'So, lads, back to Father Duffy.'

Hollie could see she was losing them. If she didn't strike fast, they'd miss their chance.

'Can you tell me anything about that, Shane?'

She saw it in his face, just for a moment.

'Why would I know anything about some paedo priest?'

His voice dripped with contempt.

'Somebody tried to kill him.'

Shane would be a terrible poker player.

'Look, I didn't kill no priest, right—'

'I'm not suggesting you did, Shane—'

'He's a fucking kiddie fiddler. He gets what he deserves.'

'Do you have any proof of that, Shane? Has he touched any of you?'

Hollie noticed some uncomfortable giggles.

'Shut up!' Shane shouted.

His command of the group was absolute.

'I wouldn't let an old bag of bones like that get anywhere near me. He's just a paedo, all right? They all are, aren't they? Them Catholic priests and that lot.'

'What about the graffiti on Father Duffy's door? Do any of you boys know anything about that?'

There was silence for a few seconds. A couple of the younger boys looked up at Shane as if awaiting their cue. Shane's hand moved on the motorcycle handle, and he poised his foot on the clutch.

'Would you mind coming down to the police station for a quick chat?'

The engine started on the bike. A cloud of black smoke belched from the exhaust. Jenni rejoined the group, having escorted the old lady out of harm's way.

'Screw you!' Shane shouted at her. 'I didn't do nothing, all right? He's just some stupid paedo priest. I don't know why you even care about him.'

'Shane, it's just for a chat. We don't think you were anything to do—'

Shane revved the engine, spun the bike, and roared away

from the group, mud flicking up from the rear wheel. Hollie tried to grab his arm but missed and slid in the mud. The group of youths sniggered at her mishap.

'Best get running, missus, if you want to catch him. If you're not too old, that is.'

SEVENTEEN

Hollie was up on her feet and after Shane. Jenni followed her lead.

'The little bugger's heading for North Point shopping centre,' Jenni began. 'He'll be a devil to find in there.'

Up ahead, Shane turned the motorbike and aimed it directly between the railings at either side of the zebra crossing. He pulled a wheelie as he crossed the road, but clearly hadn't seen a small white car coming. The car veered to miss him but clipped his back wheel. The motorcycle crashed to the ground, and Shane rolled along the road, thrown from his seat.

The woman in the white car screeched her brakes and leapt out to see if Shane was all right. Jenni and Hollie were nearing the roadside and could hear the exchange.

'Are you hurt?' the woman asked. 'You came from nowhere—'

'You stupid fucking bitch!' Shane screamed at her. It looked like he was about to physically assault her when he turned to see how close the pursuing officers were. Shane made an immediate turn, ran towards the railings, vaulted over them, and sprinted across the petrol forecourt towards the shopping centre entrance.

'That's the West Walk entrance,' Jenni panted. 'He has two more exits when he gets in there. One to the left, one directly ahead.'

'I don't know it,' Hollie replied, catching her breath. 'How come these kids can always run so fast?'

'Shane Hardy is innocent!' shouted one of the boys from the group. They were following en masse, seemingly excited by the prospect of a chase.

'Police brutality,' another called.

Hollie reflected that the mouthy kid would be the first one to get some if there was any brutality on offer.

'Are you okay, madam?' Hollie asked, remembering the motorist had just had a nasty shock and had been verbally assaulted.

'Yes, I think so. What a nasty piece of work. Are you the police? You look like police.'

'Yes, we are. We have to run, I'm afraid. Here's my card, it's got a contact number if you want to report him.'

Hollie's mind was on the fugitive. Once Shane got deep inside the shopping centre, it'd be hard to find him among the shoppers.

The two officers followed Shane's route across the petrol forecourt and pulled up by the doors.

'You take straight ahead. I'll go left,' Hollie instructed.

'Will do, ma'am,' Jenni replied.

They pushed through the doors. It was like any other shopping centre and, thankfully, only on one level. It was the usual array of stores, too – the chemist, a hairdresser, a charity shop and a couple of vacant units. She could see where the walkway widened to an open area up ahead.

'Nice place,' Hollie remarked. 'I didn't know this was here.'

'Yeah, it's one of Hull's hidden secrets. Look, he's skulking over there by the frozen food store. He thinks we haven't spotted him.'

'I'll go wide. You head straight for him,' Hollie suggested. It felt good to be in action. This was what she knew well – the cat-and-mouse chase, with a new idiot to pursue, full of excuses, never admitting culpability. It sure as hell beat pen-pushing and paperwork. Only, this wasn't about vandalism or burglary; potentially, Shane Hardy was a murderer.

A cacophony of shouting and mayhem sounded behind her. That's all they needed – his cronies following them into the shopping centre to tail the pursuit.

Jenni was almost upon Shane before he spotted her. Hollie laughed as he jumped out of his skin, like a cartoon character and just as ridiculous. His reactions were good, though. He launched himself from his spot, leaning against the freezer store window, and crashed into a woman who had set up a temporary stall in the square area. She was selling stuffed toys and her stock went flying into the air. Comically, Shane almost hit one of the pillars supporting the glass roofing above them, but he dodged just in time before committing to the north mall.

'There's only one Shane Hardy—' came the singing voices of his gang. 'Only one Shane Harrrdddddy.'

It sounded surprisingly tuneful, but Hollie could only guess how horrified the daytime shoppers would be.

As Jenni turned to continue her pursuit, Hollie winced in empathy as her right leg appeared to give way beneath her. She saw the grimace of pain on her colleague's face.

'I twisted something,' Jenni called over. 'Just give me a moment. I'll be right behind you.'

'Are you okay?' Hollie shouted over the approaching sound of the Shane Hardy song.

'Yes, get the little bugger. I'll be right behind you. I'll call for backup.'

Hollie was more out of breath than she ought to have been,

but she started at a trot and picked up her speed. It was lucky Shane was so lanky because she could clearly see him up ahead, towering over the silver-haired pensioners who seemed to frequent the place. This was Shane's home ground; he had her at a disadvantage. He was making for the exit.

She glanced behind to see if Jenni had recovered sufficiently to continue the pursuit, but she was nowhere to be seen. Hollie was on her own.

She exited the shopping centre and looked around. Shane was heading back into the housing estate. He was tiring, too. She could see him ahead, trying to catch his breath. It was a good job, as she was struggling to keep up. He ran over a patch of grass and entered an area of housing. It was just a standard estate, with concrete roads, patches of green for the kids and the dogs, and cars parked at the sides.

She glanced up and saw a street sign: Wilton Close. It was a cul-de-sac. Flat-roofed garages lined either side and six-foot wooden fences bordered gardens at the edges. So, it was going to be like this, then. Shane had given up running and he was going to conceal himself somewhere in this cluster of garages and houses. They were going to play a game of hide-and-seek.

'Come on, Shane. This doesn't have to be difficult,' Hollie shouted.

She surveyed the cul-de-sac for movement. Nothing.

'I just need to talk to you, Shane. Some nasty stuff has been going on. If it was a prank that got out of hand, you can tell me. I can help. This doesn't have to mean big trouble for you.'

'Yeah, sure!' came a voice.

It was to the right, behind the row of garages. This was ridiculous. If she went to the rear of the units, he'd just sneak around the front to avoid her. It would have been all right if she'd been playing with her kids, but this was not a game. Her family flashed into her mind. She couldn't go there. Not now. Shane might be dangerous. She was no use to her children if he beat her up. However feckless he might be, she had to stay on her guard. Cornered animals were always the most dangerous.

'I mean it, Shane—'

She began to walk around the back of the garages. She had to flush him out somehow. If only Jenni was with her, they'd be able to corner him here.

'You don't strike me as the kind of guy who'd want to hurt someone like Father Duffy. This doesn't have to be a big deal, you know.'

He'd disappeared around the far end of the garages as she'd been speaking. Hollie ran to the end, thinking she might catch him. He wasn't there.

In the distance, she heard a now familiar sound. It was a rabble of youths – Shane's friends – making their way along the street. And that bloody motorcycle was back. She could hear it revving. Fate would have done the entire estate a favour if the lady in the white car had trashed it.

When his gang arrived, it would become more difficult. Shane would need to show bravado in front of his mates. Life could get tricky. Hollie had circled the row of garages now, and Shane was nowhere to be seen. She heard a grunt to her side. She couldn't see him, but it was enough to tell her that he'd now crossed to the garages along the other side of the cul-de-sac. The revving was getting louder, and the baying audience would be joining them soon. Where the hell was Jenni?

'One last chance,' Hollie called, walking over to the middle unit on the opposite side. It was padlocked. They all were, except the unit at the far end of the concrete garages, where it looked like somebody had built a lean-to. She hadn't noticed at first, but there was a sixth unit in this row.

Shane's gang turned into the top of the street.

'Shane!' one of them shouted from some way off.

The kid named Scrogsy was now on the motorbike. He was far too small for its weight, yet he managed it successfully, gently revving the engine and balancing the vehicle at a slow speed.

'If you want to talk, come on up.'

It was Shane. He was on the roof.

Hollie stepped back. He was just above her, peering off the garage's flat roof.

'Do we have to do this?' Hollie asked.

'If you want to talk to me, we do it where my mates and all the people in these houses can see. That way there's witnesses if there's any police brutality.'

'Damn it, Shane. I'm old enough to be your mum. How do you expect me to get up there?'

'If you want to talk, find a way.'

Scrogsy had revved the motorcycle and pulled it up at her side. They didn't care. They couldn't give a shit about authority.

'Your lezza friend hurt her leg,' Scrogsy informed her.

'She's not my lezza friend—' Hollie began. She wasn't playing that game.

'Lads!' Shane shouted to his mates, who were now gathering around Hollie. She'd been silly and careless, rushing ahead before backup arrived. If this was Jenni, a young woman surrounded by youths like these, she'd give her a good ticking off for exposing herself to danger. If these kids turned on her, it could all go pear-shaped quickly. Then again, backup was taking its time to arrive, and she couldn't afford to let Shane get away. She hoped support wouldn't be far behind.

Hollie walked along to the end unit, choosing to ignore the group rather than be intimidated by them. The lean-to at the end was a ramshackle wooden affair. She guessed it wasn't endorsed by the local council and was unlikely to have been anywhere near a planning department. It was open at the back and appeared to be used now as a covered area for wheelie bins rather than a shelter for a vehicle. There were two bins inside; that would give her the height she needed. Hollie wheeled one of the plastic bins to the rear of the fifth garage unit. The group of youths had followed her around, giving a constant commentary of taunts, offensive remarks and jibes. She placed her hands on top of the wheelie bin and attempted to pull herself up. She failed completely and the surrounding group laughed their heads off.

'Looks like you need to go on a diet,' one said.

'You need to get yer leg over,' said another.

'Well, one of you be a gentleman,' Hollie replied. 'You might at least give me a leg up.'

The youths seemed stunned by the request, but after a moment of silence, one got down on his knees and formed a platform for her to climb up on top of the wheelie bin. From there, it was easy enough to pull herself up onto the flat roof.

'What a gentleman!' Hollie smiled.

She turned and sat on the roof first, then stepped up gingerly, checking it would hold her weight. The five garage roofs seemed secure enough, but the lean-to at her rear was constructed from rotten wood and torn roofing felt. She turned to face Shane, who had moved closer to her. He cackled along with his mates, who were urging him to do something stupid.

'Sort 'er out, Shane. Show 'er what we think of the cops round 'ere.'

'Now, Shane,' Hollie began. 'It's just you and me, like you wanted. Ignore your mates. Look at me. Talk to me.'

Shane seemed uncertain, looking between Hollie and his gang below.

'All I want to know is if you hurt Father Duffy. Even if it was by mistake—'

'I didn't hurt that fucking priest,' Shane shouted. 'All we did was paint paedo on his door.'

'Did you see Father Duffy? Did you speak to him?'

'No, I swear. We sprayed his door, then we ran off down the stairwell—'

'Why did you run down the stairwell?'

'Coz the lift stopped on his floor and this bloke got out.'

'Did he live in one of the flats?'

'No.'

'How do you know?'

'Coz he was heading for the priest's flat.'

'How do you know?'

'Coz there's glass in the door to the staircase. I looked back to see if he'd seen us.'

'Had he?'

'No. I don't think so.'

'Can you describe this man?'

'He was wearing a red cap. And who wears a red cap? It's right gay.'

'Is that all?'

'Are you accusing me?'

Hollie's attention was drawn by the sight of a new group entering the cul-de-sac. It was Jenni and she'd brought a couple of community officers with her.

Shane followed her gaze.

'Do one!' one of the youths shouted.

Scrogsy revved the motorcycle and they all disappeared down a path at the side of the houses, which Hollie hadn't even realised was there.

When she turned, Shane was pointing a knife at her.

'Jesus, Shane, put that thing away. I can't ignore a knife—'

'Shut up, you bitch. Yer just trying to pin this on me. Yer don't care who goes down for the paedo priest. Well, it's not gonna be me—'

Shane lunged at her with the knife. It was some ninja thing with a metal hoop at its end. She'd seen them in knife amnesties. Its blade looked sharp and deadly.

Hollie dodged and Shane pulled back, regrouping for another attack. He glanced behind him, checking on the progress of the other officers. Hollie was braced for another lunge, but instead, Shane backed up, then began running at her at some speed, screaming. There was no sign of the blade now. It seemed he'd cut his losses and was making a dash for it.

The moment his foot struck the lean-to's wooden roof, Hollie heard the old supports groan, then crack as the entire structure buckled under his weight. There was a great crash of wood and splinters as Jenni and the two PCSOs pulled up to her side on the pavement below.

Hollie looked down to assess the damage. Shane lay on the concrete base, blood pooling at his head, his leg contorted in a direction nature had never intended.

EIGHTEEN

1974: MANDY'S STORY

Mandy hurriedly pushed her hair behind her ears and thrust her head into the toilet bowl. It was a good job the bathroom fan rattled; her retching was so deep her mum would have heard it while packing up her sandwiches downstairs in the kitchen. She prayed the chatter from the local radio station coming out of the old radio on the worktop would help to drown it out. She'd never known a feeling like it before. It was nausea that came from nowhere. She'd been sick as a younger child before, usually due to eating something she shouldn't have and occasionally due to illness. This wasn't like those times.

She'd been feeling different, too, in a way she couldn't put her finger on. And her period hadn't come. It had arrived with ruthless regularity since they'd started, usually at school at the most inconvenient time possible. She had coping strategies now; she wasn't getting caught in that embarrassment again.

The wave of sickness passed. She flushed the toilet, washed her hands, and checked her hair in the mirror to make sure there were no giveaway signs. She pulled the lid down and sat on top of it.

'Are you all right in there?' came her mother's voice, following a cautious tap on the door. 'You'll be late for school if you don't get a move on.'

Mandy knew things were getting bad. She'd skipped the last two days of school, posting herself outside Terry's flat, desperate to catch him if he came back. He'd disappeared completely and she was out of her mind wondering what was going on.

She'd worked out that if she registered at school in the morning and then sloped off in the morning break, it postponed the inevitable moment when the school contacted her parents about her absences once again. But she was desperate. She had to talk to Terry. They had things to discuss. They'd been so close; he'd told her he could easily fall in love with her. He wouldn't just disappear like that.

Now steady enough on her legs to go downstairs, Mandy checked one last time in the mirror, put her hair up, unlocked the door and made her way downstairs, grabbing her bag as if nothing had happened.

'You promise me you're still going to school?' her mum asked.

She was pretty certain her mum knew she wasn't, but there was no way she would escalate things to a full confrontation. Her mother would wait until the heat was turned up so high, she would be forced to jump out of the saucepan.

'I promise,' Mandy replied, not looking her in the eyes. However ineffectual her mother was as a parent, she still didn't want to hurt her.

After getting herself registered, Mandy waited it out until the first break, then sneaked through the gates in the mayhem of classroom changeover. She pulled off her school tie and made her way directly into the city centre. She wasn't going to spend another day waiting outside Terry's place. Instead, she was heading to the library first.

As she neared the city centre, Mandy realised she'd been completely preoccupied, barely noticing her surroundings as she walked. She couldn't unseat the feeling that had been sitting in her stomach since her encounter with Terry.

Mandy didn't know much about pregnancy, but she'd gleaned enough from sniggered conversations at school to have got the gist of how it happened. And now, after spending the afternoon with Terry – and with the strange feelings she'd been experiencing – she wanted to put her mind at rest. Hull's Central Library would supply the information she wanted. There was no way she could ask her mum.

Before entering the building, Mandy took out her hairband so she looked as unlike a truanting child as possible. She strode in confidently, keen not to draw attention to herself. As one of the few warm and free places to hang out in the city, she knew the library was a favourite haunt of school truants. She had no intention of getting caught there by the attendance officer.

It took her a little while to figure out the sorting system on the shelves, but eventually, she pulled out the book she was looking for.

She studied the black-and-white line drawings, confused by the complicated names and overwhelmed by how uncomfortable it all looked. As she flicked through the pages, it became clear to her what she and Terry had actually done that afternoon. The way the girls talked about sex seemed horrible and disgusting. What she and Terry had done was nice. He'd been kind and gentle; she hadn't thought it was sex because it was nothing like the kids at school described it. But the more she read the book, the clearer it became to her what she'd done that day. So, by the time she came to a page listing the symptoms of pregnancy, she knew what was going on with her body before she read the words for herself.

Mandy ticked off the symptoms. Nausea, yes. Sickness, yes. A funny feeling in her breasts, yes. An odd sensation in her stomach, yes. But the book said those symptoms weren't usually as early as she'd experienced them. She hung on to that. The chances were she was imagining it. It was way too early to be feeling the way she did. But then her period hadn't come yet. She flicked back in the book, checking the pages on menstruation, relieved to see most women were not as regular as she had been to date. By the time she'd finished reading, Mandy had convinced herself she was mistaken. It was probably just a stomach upset as a result of being so anxious about Terry.

A female library assistant came up to her. She'd been reshelving, but Mandy hadn't taken any notice of her.

'Is everything all right?' the woman asked.

'Yes,' Mandy replied, closing the book.

'Only, you look quite young to be reading a book like that. I just wondered... do you need any help?'

'Oh, it's fine.' Mandy spoke as nonchalantly as she could manage. 'It's for a school project. Biology. The books at school aren't much use.'

'Shouldn't you be in school now?'

The woman was gentle; she wasn't accusing her of anything. Mandy thought she was kind.

'Yes, I've got permission to do this research. I've got a note from school if you want to see it?'

She hadn't, of course, but she hoped the library assistant would not call her bluff. The woman did not look convinced.

'Well, look, I can help with your project, perhaps. If a woman became pregnant, like in the book, she could get some help to get her questions answered. You might be able to do some project research there. They're called family planning clinics. You don't have to go to your doctor. They might be able to answer some of your questions. For your project, of course.'

Mandy pushed the book back onto the shelf and made sure

its hardback spine was perfectly aligned with the books on either side.

'Thank you,' Mandy began, 'but it's only for a project. I've found out what I was looking for. I won't be needing one of those clinics. I'd best get back to school now.'

NINETEEN

Once Shane was loaded into the ambulance, well sedated and his neck braced, Hollie confirmed the uniformed officers had it all under control and reminded the two PCSOs who'd been on the scene to make sure their records were meticulous in detail about what had happened. She was covering her arse. She knew how this would play out, but she was confident about this one. He'd lunged at her with the knife, he'd stepped on the insecure roofing of his own accord, and he had only himself to blame for what had just happened.

'Can I have the car keys?' Hollie sidled up to DC Langdon.

'Are we leaving already?' Jenni asked.

'You are. Let's get Shane's knife bagged up and then I want you to take it back to HQ and get it logged. Then I want you to take some weight off that ankle.'

'It's just an old war wound. A hockey injury from my school days. It plays up occasionally, but it's nothing serious. Nothing that stops me from catching the bad guys.'

Just for an instant, it occurred to Hollie that perhaps Jenni might need to be withdrawn from duties that required her to be fully fit. It was her management head doing the reasoning. She'd monitor the issue, but Jenni's injury might be a problem. She was a good detective – she'd seen that much already – and Jenni would not thank her for consigning her to light duties. She'd keep her thoughts to herself for a while and see how it played out.

'Still, give it the afternoon to recover. We're better safe than sorry.'

'Sure, boss,' Jenni said, digging out the car keys and handing them over. 'What next?'

Hollie sighed.

'I think we're screwed for now. Until we can get some sense from Shane, I'm not sure if our wild goose chase moved anything forward. I want to know more about Sister Brennan and get a sense of who she was. I'd like to know more about that mother and baby home, too; there has to be some public record or local history buff who can fill us in. Liaise with DS Patel when you're back at your desk, keep her in the loop. Would you catch a lift back with uniform and I'll see you at the office? It'll save you the long walk back to the car.'

Hollie started to retrace her steps to the shopping centre. She checked the time. Better not be late for the press briefing. She'd have to get herself fully up to speed before then, too: there was a large team of detectives working the case, and new information might emerge at any time.

She glanced at her phone. There was a voice message from Doctor Ruane. Could she get over to the morgue ASAP? He'd got some interesting information about the nun's body.

At last, some progress. She upped her pace, annoyed now that they'd abandoned the car so far away. Shane's group of merry men had made themselves scarce; she just hoped they weren't busy removing the wheels from her vehicle. That would really screw her for time.

As she was walking past the shopping centre, skirting

around it this time rather than cutting through it, her phone rang again.

'Hello, boss, I've just come off the phone to DC Langdon.' It was DS Patel. She went on, 'You don't hang around, ma'am – you were at a convent last time we spoke, now you're picking fights with the local youths. Is everything okay at your end?'

Hollie stopped a moment and leaned on a street sign, which was just the right height for her.

'I'm about to head over to the mortuary to get the latest from Doctor Ruane. How's that research coming on, any more on the home yet?'

There was a pause at the end of the phone.

'Sure, I've been onto the archive and the library like you said. I've got a lead at the local council, too, and the guy there promised to get back to me. Everybody's been cut to the bone, they're so tight on staff it's difficult to get people to work at the speed we need. If we're lucky we'll get some newspaper cuttings from the library, which should give us a bit of background. The archive people are seeing what they have on the building and the church. It's just lots of promises and maybes so far, I'm afraid.'

Hollie felt a surge of frustration, but she kept it to herself. She knew what it was like; sometimes, the early stages of an investigation could be a pain in the arse. There was a downpour of useless information from the public and a trickle of useful stuff that could be used. And it all had to be filtered as it came in. There was always the chance that something important would be missed, too. DS Patel appeared to be the thorough type; Hollie was pleased she was managing the office.

'I'd like to find out everything we can about Sister Brennan. Unfortunately, our best bet was Father Duffy. But the nuns at the convent will be able to help. Sister Kay and Mother Davies know more than they're letting on. We need to handle it sensitively; they have just lost a colleague, but I think we should send over a couple of DCs and do a bit of probing.'

'Yes, of course. There's one thing I'd like to ask, ma'am—'

DS Patel sounded more nervous than she had been previously. She'd immediately struck Hollie as a straightforward, easy but professional detective, but now it sounded like she had something on her mind. It was a first ask for the new boss.

'I'm feeling a bit overwhelmed here – is there any chance of an extra pair of hands?'

Hollie thought Patel was more than likely expecting a *get stuffed*; they were all sick to death of too much work and not enough officers. Apparently, according to the home secretary, more officers were being recruited and were on the way. The rate new staff were coming through, she reckoned the new officers were being grown from embryos. But she was pleased that she could give DS Patel a positive response on this rare occasion.

'Just for you, DS Patel, I've sent Jenni back to the office. Did she say what had happened?'

'No, did I miss some gossip?' Patel replied, her interest clearly piqued.

'I'll let her give you all the dramatic details, but I want her off her feet for the afternoon. You can use her as an extra resource. The sooner you can pull up some background for me, the better. I've got this press conference, and it would be nice if I didn't look completely clueless when I have to face the media. See if between the two of you, you can have a nice surprise waiting for me when I get back.'

'Great, I'll get Jenni directly on some phoning around jobs when she comes in to land. Are you off for lunch now, ma'am?'

'Not quite,' Hollie answered, standing up from her leaning position on the street sign. 'I've got the remains of a dead nun to look at now. I really must try to get myself some nicer pastimes.'

TWENTY

Doctor Ruane reminded Hollie of a TV medic. He was old enough to be in the retirement zone but still had the gleam in his eye that suggested he loved his work. He had a well-trimmed, grey beard and small, circular glasses that made him appear studious. He shook Hollie's hand with enthusiasm.

'Good afternoon, DI Turner. It's nice to see a member of the Murder Investigation Team in more welcoming surroundings.'

Hollie was annoyed and embarrassed that she'd been too late to catch him on the carriageway of Clive Sullivan Way the previous night. It was hardly a picture postcard scene by the time she arrived. Then again, the mortuary wasn't really more welcoming surroundings.

'I'm so sorry we didn't get the chance to chat properly before a case dropped on my lap,' Hollie said. 'I was rather hoping I'd have time to meet more people informally before I got stuck in.'

'Well, there's no better way of getting to know your team than in the heat of an investigation.' Ruane smiled. 'Are you ready?'

He held out his arm, indicating the direction of travel.

'It's pretty gruesome, as I'm sure you've already guessed,' he continued. 'I can talk you through it if you prefer. And I sent over my report via email just before you got here.'

Hollie had long since stopped flinching at the sight of dead bodies. She was so confident in the reliability of her stomach that she'd snatched a sandwich while driving over to the mortuary. Unfortunately, she'd had no opportunity to consume it.

The body was laid out already. She knew what was coming, but the violence of the nun's death was still shocking.

'So, what can you tell me?'

'There is some useful news in all of this,' Ruane began.

Hollie raised her eyebrows.

'I don't believe she was dead when she was thrown over the side of the bridge.'

Hollie let out a breath.

'Oh, the poor woman.'

'The killer tried to suffocate her,' Ruane continued. 'With a cushion or something like that. There were fibres in her mouth and lungs. It's unlikely the cushion would have finished her off, mind you. They just show you that on the TV. It's easy enough to grasp a breath if someone tries to kill you that way. I think it likely that she was still breathing when she was thrown over, though she might not have been conscious.'

Hollie was pleased that her instincts had been right. It didn't make sense that the nun was fully conscious – surely she'd have put up a fight.

She looked at the head, which was set at an angle to the torso's side. There wasn't much left of it.

'Do you think the killer wanted us to think she'd died at the bridge?'

Ruane smiled.

'Well now, detective, that's very much for you to discover in your investigation. If I were a guessing man, I'd speculate this was meant to shock. It's certainly caught the attention of the press and social media, I see.'

'Can we get her formally identified today?' Hollie queried. 'I've asked DS Anderson to get it sorted.'

'Yes, he's coming in shortly with the Mother Superior. I'll present her body as sensitively as I can.'

Hollie looked at the remains. She screwed up her face.

'I wish there was another way. Is there anything we can do to spare Mother Davies that ordeal?'

Ruane surveyed the torso laid out on the table and shook his head.

'Cases like this are very tricky. Most of the time, it's railway suicides that create these messes. It's the first time in my career I've dealt with something like this.'

'We've not recovered any ID in the clothing? There's no Bible with a name scrawled in it, a bank card or anything that might give us an earlier confirmation of her identity?'

'Nothing. Whoever killed her must have been wearing gloves at the time, too. So, they knew enough to take precautions.'

'Anybody who watches *Midsomer Murders* knows what to do these days.' Hollie frowned.

'And the bad weather took care of the rest,' Ruane confirmed.

She sighed.

'Feeling the pressure of the job?' he asked.

'All I've got are dead ends. A nun whose identity we haven't even confirmed yet. A priest who was half-drowned—'

'I didn't know about that development,' Doctor Ruane said. 'He's connected with the nun in some way, I take it?'

'Yes, if the nun is who we think she is. We believe she's a Sister Sophia Brennan from the Convent of the Sacred Heart of Mary. The priest is in hospital as I speak. In fact, I'm due a condition report on him. Oh, and I had an altercation with some yobbo from Bransholme Estate before I came here.'

'What did he have to say?'

'He's just been rushed to hospital with a broken leg, dislocated arm and who knows what else.'

Ruane laughed out loud.

'That's not very sympathetic,' she remarked.

'I'm sorry,' he continued. 'It's just that in some cases, events conspire against us. It's quite a body count for such an early stage in an investigation.'

He didn't have to tell her that. It was a terrible start to a new case.

'Are there any other scraps you can offer me, Doctor Ruane? I'll try not to resort to begging. But I'm close to it.'

'One more thing.' He smiled. 'I don't know if this will have any bearing on the case or not. She has a little tattoo on her arm—'

'I'm getting a strong sense that this woman has had quite a past. One of the nuns – Sister Kay – suggested it to me earlier. I've got DS Patel and DC Langdon working on it back at HQ. It's starting to look like she might not be quite as innocent as we're all assuming. I've heard she wasn't a particularly nice woman, either.'

'Yes, well, I suspect she might not be who we think she is. There's scarring on her arms, too.'

'Can you show me?'

'See for yourself while you're here. It's all in the report.'

Hollie stepped up to the table, so she was directly above the body parts. The damage to the old woman's flesh was substantial and she could see where bones had been splintered and crushed by the lorry's impact. But at the top of her left arm was the tattoo Ruane had been referring to. It was only small, a modest affair, and it was old. The ink had faded and had become indistinct through time; it had lost some of its definition as the victim's skin had aged. Hollie also noticed some evidence of faint and long-healed markings along both arms.

The tattoo was simple and amateurish. It was made up of the letters *KT*.

'Any theories?' she asked.

'Again, I'm not the detective,' Ruane reiterated. 'As you said yourself, she wasn't born a nun. She might even have become one later in life. We don't know anything about her history. Whatever it is, it was significant enough for her to get a tattoo. And those marks on her arms are evidence of historic self-harming.'

'We need to get this body formally identified,' Hollie resolved. Mother Davies would just have to do her best in the circumstances. Hollie needed a name.

'As I've said, I'm not a detective—' Ruane began, interrupting her train of thought.

'Go on, doctor,' Hollie encouraged.

'Well, there is one thing that struck me. It's all circumstantial, of course.'

'Carry on. I can't stand the tension.'

'Well, how the victim died is very different to what we thought.'

'What are you suggesting?'

'You saw how the body was disposed of on the bridge. That takes some level of physical fitness to accomplish. If I were speculating, I'd guess it was done by a man.'

'I'm really not certain what you're suggesting, doctor.'

'She was suffocated initially, using a cushion or something similar. That's quite a domestic way to kill. It doesn't require physical strength, particularly for a frail victim of this age. Many relatives of people with dementia or incurable diseases opt for that method. It's as much used as a mercy killing as a violent death. It suggests that the suffocation took place in a familiar or comfortable environment.'

Hollie nodded, but she still couldn't see where this was leading.

'Maybe the killer needed to make sure the victim didn't call out. A cushion would certainly do that job.'

'Yes, but consider this: what if there were two people involved? One, perhaps a woman or older person, who suffocated the victim. And then, perhaps, an accomplice. One with much greater physical strength. Most likely a man, I'd say. One who had the strength to manoeuvre a lifeless body over the side of a bridge. They're two very different ways of inflicting harm. I'm suggesting you might be looking for two killers, detective.'

TWENTY-ONE

1974: MANDY'S STORY

By Thursday morning, Mandy had had enough. She'd die if she couldn't see Terry. She had a feeling deep in the pit of her stomach, a longing and aching which would only go when she saw him again. Why hadn't he contacted her? He could have met her outside school.

First, she headed for the city centre, taking the side streets for much of the way to avoid anybody she might know through her parents. As she walked, she tore off her school tie and shoved it into her bag. It had already become an oppressive sign to her, the badge which marked her as a child rather than an adult. She didn't want to be a child anymore. She hated it. She wanted to be with Terry.

Mandy raced to the front door of Terry's building where a man wearing a worn donkey jacket had just exited.

'Can you let me in?' she asked as she ran up the weed-ridden path.

'Sure, luv,' he replied. 'Are you seeing someone inside?'

'Yes. Terry.'

'Is that the geezer on the second floor? You might be out of luck, darling.'

Mandy didn't wait to find out why. She pushed through the front door, barely stopping to say a thank you. She rushed up the stairs and took a moment to get her bearings. Terry's door came after the one with a deep scratch in it, like someone had scraped a heavy piece of furniture against it when moving in.

She was about to bang on his door, but a piece of paper was taped on it. She unclenched her hand and, with some difficulty, read the words at the top.

Eviction Notice (*Notice to Quit*).

The door to Terry's bedsit was half open, so she gave it a push. It seemed like he'd got half of his stuff, then broken off halfway through. Perhaps he'd had to do a runner from the landlord. It didn't matter; he was gone.

A woman stepped out further along the landing. When she spoke, it made Mandy jump.

'Are you all right, sweetheart?'

Mandy looked up to see who was speaking. She blinked to clear the tears in her eyes and couldn't see properly through the blur. It was the woman from along the landing. She was looking down sympathetically.

'Is Terry around? Have you seen him?' Mandy asked.

The laugh that followed was not a good sign.

'Terry? He's a fly-by-night, that one. He hasn't paid his rent for months. No wonder they've thrown him out.'

'Is he still going to the art school?'

Another laugh.

'I think he went there once. To pick up his money. It wouldn't surprise me if he's gone already. He knows how to dodge trouble, does Terry. He's got a sixth sense for it. He's best taken at face value. A pretty face, and a nice body, but not much else. He's fun, though, I'll give him that. And his taste in music is excellent.'

Mandy had noticed a twinkle in the woman's eye as she'd said those words and she wondered if she was friends with Terry.

'Wait, you're not...? How old are you? No wonder he's done a moonlight flit. Jesus, Terry, you're playing with fire.'

Mandy hadn't quite grasped what the woman was talking about, but she got the gist of it. But after the things Terry had said, there was no way he'd just disappear on her. The woman must have been mistaken. He'd be back. They had something special.

'Why don't you come round to my bedsit and have a hot drink? How does that sound?'

Mandy sniffed and nodded.

'And while we're here, it doesn't look like that bastard Terry is taking his LPs, so we may as well help ourselves. The landlord will only throw them out. Terry has done a moonlight flit.'

The woman sat on the floor and swiftly sorted through the albums. She made two neat piles while Mandy pulled herself together.

'There, my darling. I'll bet you like most of the bands in that pile, don't you?'

Mandy watched as she sorted. The second pile was much more adventurous than her musical tastes; she knew that one wasn't hers. But the first pile was packed with chart artists, most of whom she loved. She nodded, not confident yet of speaking without her voice faltering.

'I reckon you've earned these, don't you?'

She held out her hand and helped Mandy up off the floor, then placed the first pile of LPs into an empty box and passed it over. She then picked up her own pile of albums and led the way out of Terry's room.

'Good riddance, I say.' She pulled the door shut. 'He was a right waster, was Terry.'

Mandy followed her along the landing and walked with her

into the bedsit. It was completely different from Terry's. It was much more homely, with potted plants all over, shelves of books, and pictures hung on the walls. The kitchen area was spotlessly clean and had a full herb rack on the wall. Mandy had never seen one of those before. The bed was made too. A bright crocheted cover lay on top of the blankets.

'Take a seat, my darling. I'll get the kettle on. I take it hot chocolate is okay with you?'

Mandy nodded, placed the box of LPs on the small table next to the window, and sat on the compact sofa as instructed. That, too, had a crocheted cover thrown across it.

'I'm Laura, by the way. Pleased to meet you.'

Mandy said nothing.

'You're supposed to tell me who you are now.' She smiled.

'I'm Mandy.' She sniffed. Her voice was holding out fine. She was ready to talk again.

'I heard him here earlier from across the landing. His mum came to help him clear out. She sounded pissed off and told him he had more stuff than would fit in her car. I take it you just broke up?'

Mandy didn't know how to answer. Had she and Terry broken up? Were they ever together? She didn't know how to describe what had happened between them.

'If it makes you feel any better, he did the same to me. That record collection of his is like a beacon. Nobody can resist looking at it. He can turn on the charm, can Terry. I slept with him. Twice. I wised up after that. Terry's not relationship material. You're best rid of him.'

Laura busied herself at the small kitchen worktop. Eventually, she walked over with a steaming mug. The smell filled the small bedsit.

'There you are. There's not much a hot chocolate won't sort out.'

Mandy held it close to her mouth and blew on the drink. They sat in silence for a couple of minutes.

'So, tell me all about it. What's Terry done now?'

Mandy didn't know what to say. Laura helped her out.

'Where did you meet him? I'll bet you've not even left school yet, have you?'

Mandy shook her head.

'No, I'm playing truant. If my dad finds out, he's going to kill me.'

Laura looked at Mandy as if she were assessing her.

'I'd say your dad will have more than playing truant to worry about.' Laura grimaced.

'What do you mean?'

'You look to me like you're pregnant. I'm a student nurse. You're not showing yet, but you've got that look about you. And I know you weren't round Terry's just to listen to music. It's never just about the music with Terry.'

'I've researched it at the library. I don't think I'm pregnant. I don't know how I can be.'

'Did you use contraception? Rubbers? The pill? Anything like that?'

Mandy hadn't got a clue what she was talking about. Some boys at school had once waved things around they called rubber johnnies, but they were blowing them up like balloons and she wasn't entirely sure what was so funny about it.

Laura walked over to Mandy, put her drink down on the small side table by the sofa, sat next to her, and took her free hand.

'Oh dear, Terry really has taken advantage of you, hasn't he? How old are you? Please tell me you're sixteen, at least.'

'My sixteenth birthday is coming up in a couple of days. Why does it matter?'

'Believe me, it matters for Terry. Have you ever had sex before?'

'No. I don't even like boys. Not the boys at school. I... I just liked Terry. He was nice. He was kind to me. We kissed. We just drank some wine.'

'That sounds about right.' Laura frowned. 'That's just like Terry. I'm guessing your favourite album was playing at the time. And I'll bet you felt drunker from the wine than you should have?'

Mandy didn't know what Laura was talking about. She'd never drunk wine before that day anyway, so she didn't know how it was supposed to make her feel.

'If you ask me, he slips something in it. Terry's not normally my type, but I went to look at his record collection, just like everybody else does. He's a nice enough guy. He's friendly and he's funny. And I did casually fancy him. Well, I liked his body, let's put it that way. So, I was surprised when I woke up the next day in his bed without any clothes on. I just figured we'd got carried away and I'd had too much to drink. I assumed it was my own fault and that I'd let my guard down. The second time it happened, I knew something wasn't right. I can't prove it, of course. And if I said anything to anybody, they'd just tell me I'm a slapper and shouldn't be so quick to let men into my knickers. But it didn't feel right, you know?'

It sounded to Mandy like Terry might have done a similar thing to her.

'You didn't tell me – did you use contraception?'

Mandy looked at her, not knowing how to answer.

'It looks to me like Terry's got you pregnant. Have you been to the doctor yet to check?'

'I don't think I am—'

'Have you missed your time of the month?'

Mandy was still embarrassed to talk about her periods, but she nodded anyway.

'How long?'

'Maybe two weeks now.'

'If you're lucky, it will come late. If you're not, you'll have to decide quickly.'

'Decide what?'

'If you're going to have an abortion.'

Laura was approaching the conversation like she was working through a checklist. Mandy had heard her parents use the word abortion, usually when there'd been a story on the news about it. She didn't know much about it, but her father was dead set against it, whatever it was. It was yet another thing that made him angry.

'I don't know what that is,' Mandy said, embarrassed by her lack of knowledge.

'It means you're going to have to decide if you want to get rid of the baby.'

'Do you mean kill it?'

'Yes. It's called an abortion. My goodness, you are young, aren't you?'

'I couldn't kill a baby. Besides, how can I be pregnant?'

'Let me guess. You played music. You drank wine. You woke up later and your clothes weren't on, but you're not quite sure what happened. You weren't hurt. You hadn't had to fight him off, yet it didn't feel quite right?'

It was almost as if Laura had been in the room. That's exactly what had happened. They'd kissed, and Mandy had wanted the kissing – it was nice being kissed by Terry. But after that? She just didn't know.

Laura squeezed Mandy's hand.

'We're going to have to have a good talk,' she said gently. 'You need to decide what to do. I'll help you. But you can't let this drift. You're going to have to face up to what's happened.'

TWENTY-TWO

'How's that ankle?' Hollie asked, pulling up a chair next to DS Patel and DC Langdon. It felt good to be back in the office after the drama of the morning. And with DS Anderson away at the mortuary with Mother Davies, she expected to have her formal ID on the body at any time.

'Better, ma'am, thank you,' Jenni replied. 'I'd forgotten all about it, actually. We think we're onto something here.'

DS Patel was tapping away at her keyboard. She'd barely looked up when Hollie joined them. She scanned the desk for clues about her colleague's life. There were no husband or boyfriend photos and no evidence of children. Patel's desk was clear, organised, and professional. It even looked like she tipped the crumbs out of her keyboard. In office terms, that was sheer class.

'What have you got?' Hollie asked, her interest immediately piqued.

'I've found something on a local history website,' Patel updated her. 'It might be something, it might be nothing.'

Hollie got up off the chair and rolled it back to the empty desk where she'd found it. The upholstery was becoming unpicked at the back. Damn police and their tight budgets; it looked like something you'd rescue from a skip.

She stood behind DS Patel so she could get a better look at her screen.

'I'd better close down Tinder if you're standing behind me, boss—'

For a moment, Hollie thought she was being serious.

'Too soon?' Her colleague smiled. Jenni obviously found it amusing but was waiting to see how it was received by her superior.

'You'll probably find most of Hull's most-wanted on that website,' Hollie retorted. She was pleased that DS Patel was calling her boss now. When DS Anderson said it, the words sounded contemptuous, from DS Patel's mouth, it made her feel like she was back on familiar territory in Lancaster. It might take the DCs a little more time to catch up.

Jenni and Amber exchanged a smile; they were sounding her out. She'd expect nothing less from a room full of coppers.

'So, talk me through it,' Hollie said, settling herself in. She loved being out in the field, but a bit of well-targeted web surfing could sometimes save a lot of leg work.

'Me and Jenni were chatting over a brew—' DS Patel began.

'Some of the best police work is done in the kitchen,' Hollie chipped in. 'Don't ever think I'll be looking down my nose at you if you take five minutes for a kitchen break. It's those snatched conversations with colleagues that help fill in the blanks. Just remember to make me a drink while you're there.'

DS Patel smiled and carried on.

'We figured there's got to be something online about this mother and baby home. You know what local history buffs are like, they can't resist setting up websites about these things.'

'Did you find anything useful?' Hollie prompted.

'Not at first,' Jenni picked up. 'There's more information about the church that it was next to. I can give you a list of every priest who led services there from when it was built to when it closed. But there's very little about the home. As far as we can tell, it became disused sometime around 2010.'

'Okay, that's useful background. I wouldn't mind seeing the priests either side of Father Duffy's tenure, as we may have some overlaps. They'll be retired or dead, I'm guessing, but it's worth seeing who's still around and could give some background info. Let's also confirm Father Duffy's dates so we can firm up our timeline.'

Hollie was about to leave when DS Patel stopped her.

'Wait, ma'am, we wouldn't drag you away from your interminable paperwork for such measly scraps. I haven't got to the pièce de résistance yet.'

The use of a French phrase made Léon's face flash into her mind and, for one brief instant, she ached for him and his touch. Then she remembered what a dick he was being, and the glowing emotions were swiftly washed away by anger, frustration, disappointment... and yes, embarrassment. It was difficult to admit, but Hollie felt embarrassed and ashamed by their split. She felt like she'd failed in some way. Léon's head would not have been turned if she'd been more present – more available, perhaps. She pushed it away. Work always helped her shove anything too painful out of sight and out of mind.

Hollie's phone rang. It was Caitlen. Why was her friend from Lancaster calling now? A feeling of panic gripped her. Surely it wasn't Léon and the kids. She felt immediately guilty about thinking Léon was a dick.

'One moment, I'll need to take this,' she said.

'Hi, Caitlen. I'll have to be brief, I'm up to my ears—'

'I know, I've seen the reports on the TV. I'll make it quick – Phoebe has been called in at ridiculously short notice for an interview at Hull University. Can she stay with you overnight?'

'Brilliant! Send her my congratulations. Of course she can

stay. I might not be very good company, though; I've got my hands full here.'

'Lovely, thanks so much. Don't worry about having to entertain her, she knows you're busy. I'll get Phoebe to send over an email with her arrival times. Let's catch up some time, it feels like you've been gone ages.'

They exchanged a few snippets of news then Hollie ended the call.

'You've got my full attention now,' she confirmed.

'We found this letter from a couple of years back in the *Hull Daily Mail*. The local paper is great for memorabilia and historical stuff. Take a look at this article on the letters page. It's by some local councillor called Gilly Hodges.'

'She's got a real bee in her bonnet,' Jenni added.

Hollie moved in closer so she could focus on the print. She caught a faint hint of perfume from DS Patel. It was nice – subtle. She was about to remark on it but thought better of it. She'd get to know everybody better before relaxing with them too much. Perfume recommendations could wait.

Hollie read the headline:

Scars Still Run Deep Despite Intended Closure of
Controversial Home

There was a black-and-white photograph indented at the top of the page. It showed what appeared to be a Victorian building, with a massive, pillared entrance and balconies to the top floors. She read the caption.

The Controversial Mother and Baby Home at the Church of St Mary & The Angels.

'This is good, great work, that photograph is fabulous.'

'It gets better.' DS Patel smiled. Hollie could feel her glowing where the compliment had landed.

Drypool Councillor Gilly Hodges has hit out at Catholic Church representatives in the city after plans were announced to close and demolish the former mother and baby home in the city's Riverside area. The former home, which is adjacent to the Church of St Mary & The Angels, closed as a home for unmarried mothers in 1980, but the building continued to be used as an administrative base for several years afterwards. The Church has suggested that the land might, in future, be sold off for building land, but Councillor Hodges claims that will just continue an injustice to hundreds of local women and girls.

'Wow, this hits the mark,' Hollie remarked, looking up and turning to smile at each of her colleagues. She carried on reading, anxious to see what nuggets were waiting for her.

'I was one of the girls whose child was taken from them at the home,' said Ms Hodges. 'I thought I was going there to have my baby, then return home. While I was there, I signed paperwork which I was too young and naive to understand at the time. I gave those people permission to take my child away from me. I can never forgive them for what they did to me and hundreds of other local mothers. Our only crime was that we'd had babies out of wedlock. Now the Catholic Church wants to close the site and bulldoze over it. They've never apologised for the harm they did and if this building gets demolished, it will cover up the terrible things that went on there.'

Hollie looked up again.

'This is powerful stuff; you can almost feel this woman's anger dripping off the page. We need to speak to this councillor as soon as we can—'

'We're already on it, boss,' Jenni confirmed. 'We're trying to find an address for her. Even if she isn't involved in the murder, I'll bet she can give us some brilliant insight into what went on in that place.'

'There's one more thing – did you read right to the end?' Patel asked. 'The text is wrapped around the photo badly; you might miss it if you don't look carefully.'

Hollie examined the page again and saw that DS Patel was right. There was a bit more background about the home, then a final quote from Gilly Hodges.

'I was one of the lucky ones, I was eventually reunited with my son. But many of those mothers died before they found the children that had been taken from them. Others are still blocked from contacting their children by ridiculous privacy rules or misplaced paperwork. The people involved in that mother and baby home have a lot to answer for. What they did to countless young mothers in this city was pure evil.'

'Hang on a moment,' Hollie said, urgent now. 'What did that sign say that was hung around the nun's neck?'

Jenni and Amber smiled across the desk at each other, like their friend had just got the joke.

'Exactly!' said Patel. 'Pure evil. That's exactly the phrase she uses in the newspaper.'

TWENTY-THREE

'Damn, we're really tight on time,' Hollie cursed. 'How well do you know your way around the city?'

'Well,' DC Gordon replied, 'I've lived here all my life. I know the rat runs, if that's what you mean.'

'You're driving again, then,' Hollie instructed. 'I do not want to be late to my first press briefing. I got too caught up with what DS Patel and DC Langdon discovered. It serves me right.'

They got in the car and Hollie started reading the latest briefing notes to make sure she was fully on top of all the latest intel in the case. She saw that the formal ID had come through and made a catch-up call to DS Anderson to find out how it had gone.

'So, it's definitely her?' Hollie confirmed.

'Yes, boss.'

'How did Mother Davies take it?'

'As you'd expect. The doc had done a good job with the body, I'll give him that. What a bloody mess.'

'Is someone with Mother Davies now?'

'I've run her back to the convent, and I made sure there was someone with her before I left.'

'Great, thanks for that, DS Anderson. I'll catch up with you shortly. Thanks for handling that, it's never an easy task.'

'Is that the victim identified, ma'am?' DC Gordon asked.

DS Anderson continued speaking before she had time to answer.

'Did you send DC Langdon back to work in the office?' His voice was terse.

'Yes, she's sustained a small injury. Why?'

There was silence at the end of the phone.

'Is there something you want to say, DS Anderson?'

'No, boss, that's your choice. We're waiting for you at The Country Park. Shall I let them know you're on your way?'

'The Country Park? What's that? A hotel? I thought we were doing the briefing at The Royal Hotel?'

'No, boss, didn't I tell you earlier? DCC Warburton asked for a change of venue. She thinks it will help jog more memories if we're close to the bridge. It'll also be good for the TV people to have the bridge in the background—'

'For fuck's sake,' Hollie cursed. She turned to DC Gordon.

'There's been a change of location. It's at The Country Park now.'

'That's going to be cutting it fine. The traffic's going to be busy.'

'Can you get me there?'

'I'll do my best. Make sure your seatbelt is fastened properly.'

DC Gordon revved the engine and pulled out past a driver who was making a meal of reversing into a parking space.

'Sorry, mate, but we can't wait all day,' he called over as if the driver could hear him.

'Why didn't you tell me about the venue change when we spoke earlier?'

Hollie could barely contain herself. If she blew up at

Anderson now, she knew she'd be all over the place just in time for the press briefing. It would have to wait.

'Sorry, boss, I thought I had. My mistake. It won't happen again. And I've got some more bad news,' Anderson continued.

'Go on,' Hollie encouraged him.

'You know the kid who you threw onto the roof—'

'Who lunged at me and fell through—'

'Whatever—'

'No, not whatever!' Hollie snapped. 'It was his own fault he fell through the roof, DS Anderson.'

'Yes, boss. Well, the kid has some do-gooder solicitor representing him. They're claiming it's your fault. He's in quite a bad way, apparently.'

Hollie wanted to scream. She gripped the plastic side handle as DC Gordon threw the car around a corner, taking them down a narrow side street.

'What has DCI Osmond said about it?' she asked.

'It's difficult to tell with Osmond. He could have been angry. He may be constipated. Who can tell?'

'I'll remind you he's your superior officer,' Hollie scolded. This man was winding her up.

'Yes, boss. Sorry.'

Hollie took a couple of long breaths. They were seriously on the clock now. This battle would have to wait for another day, but she could feel it was coming soon.

She ran through the briefing notes on speaker phone with DS Anderson, trying to take note of their journey progress as she did so. She wished she knew the city better; she'd lost track of where they were. DC Gordon had taken them around a congested roundabout, but they didn't appear to have gained anything from it. She ended the call with DS Anderson when her phone cheeped, announcing a waiting call from Léon.

'Close your ears and concentrate on your driving,' she said

to DC Gordon as she ended the call with Anderson and connected with her husband.

'I need to know, Hollie,' he began. Not even a *Hello*.

'It's not the best time—'

'It's never a good time for you. This is why we are where we are. I need to know. We have to get the kids sorted out.'

'I'm just about to do a press conference, Léon. Can't this wait until tomorrow? Or later this evening, at least?'

'And then it'll be something else, won't it? This is why you can't take the children, Hollie. You know it. You just won't admit it to yourself.'

She felt her stomach tighten. Hollie thought she was going to be sick. Léon was right. She couldn't care for the kids. Not without him there. Not without someone to help. She ran the numbers in her head. Could she afford a nanny or something like that to cover when she was caught up in a big case? Hull was a cheap enough place to live. If she rented a nicer house somewhere, with a couple of spare rooms, she could make it work if the kids alternated between Lancaster and Hull. Couldn't she?

Hollie knew the answer to Léon's question, but she couldn't speak the words. Not yet. A crushing weight of guilt and failure threatened to suffocate her. A failed marriage and a failed mother. And she was barely managing her job. Her mind roared with doubt and self-loathing, a beast that wouldn't be slain.

'Can they stay with me before you go?' she asked quietly, trying her best not to plead. 'Once this case is sorted and things are a bit quieter, perhaps.'

She could sense DC Gordon absorbing every word. It would, no doubt, be reported back to her new team.

Léon sighed.

'If you can come and pick them up.'

'You know I can't do that. You've seen this case on TV,

haven't you? I'm in the middle of a shitstorm here. Another shitstorm.'

'Look, you'll have to come to Lancaster and collect them. What am I going to do in Hull?'

Then it struck her. Caitlen's daughter Phoebe was coming down for her interview. They could travel with her and kill two birds with one stone. Her best friend's daughter was the ideal person to chaperone the kids on the train to Hull. And Léon vaguely knew Phoebe, too, so that would help. She would check it out with Phoebe and see if she was willing to help out.

'Look, Léon, I've got an idea, but I can't discuss this now. I promise we'll sort it out tonight. I need to make a call, and then I can confirm everything with you. You can wait that long, can't you?'

He didn't say anything.

'Léon? Come on. You owe me that much.'

'Okay,' came his reply at last. 'But no more delays, Hollie. The children need to know what's happening. They need some certainty in their life.'

Hollie was about to remind him how it was he who'd created the uncertainty by taking up with a new woman. Instead, she asked him a question. 'Are they asking after me?'

Another silence.

'Léon?'

'Hollie, they're so used to you being at work, I think they've barely noticed. I know that's not the answer you wanted, but there it is.'

If he had cut her with a knife a hundred times, it might have hurt less. She ended the call. She would have fallen apart in front of DC Gordon if she hadn't.

Hollie had been so absorbed in the conversation she hadn't realised the car had come to a stop. She looked up and scanned the road. They were on the Clive Sullivan Way heading out of the city, and the Humber Bridge was looming up before them. But the traffic was at a complete standstill.

DC Gordon looked at her and shrugged.

'Sorry, boss. We're not going to make the press conference in time.'

TWENTY-FOUR

1974: MANDY'S STORY

Mandy's mother spotted it before she'd had a chance to reveal her secret. She'd been waiting for the right moment, but it never seemed to come. It had been three weeks since her chat with Laura in the bedsit.

Mandy had done a lot of growing up since that conversation. Laura recommended she seek out information about abortion. She'd followed the advice, her mind racing with the possibilities of what a pregnancy might entail. She'd disguised herself as much as possible before she went into the family planning clinic to consider her options.

The woman at the reception desk had given her a leaflet and sympathetically asked if she wanted to speak to somebody. Not yet. Mandy couldn't face anybody for the time being. If she was going to book an appointment, it would have to be at a time and place of her choosing.

Mandy found a bench to sit on, some distance away from the clinic. She read the leaflet slowly, several times, to try to understand what it was talking about. Why did they always use such long words? She didn't want to abort the baby, she knew that much. She was terrified of having the baby, too, but she didn't want it taken out of her. She tucked the leaflet into her coat pocket and made certain she was home at the usual after-school time.

That had been a waste of time. While she'd been at the clinic, two staff members from school had been around to the house with news of her continued and repeated absences. Mandy had promised herself she'd tell her mum about the pregnancy that night, but the fallout over her truancy had been so bad that neither of her parents could bring themselves to speak to her for several days afterwards. She'd thought her father was going to strike her at one stage in their row; she was safer hiding away in her bedroom, well out of his way.

Mandy was given an attendance sheet, which she had to get signed by a teacher at every lesson. When she got home after school, she had to show it to her mother, who had agreed to get in touch with the school immediately if there were any gaps. Her father would check it, too, when he was home, threatening all sorts of sanctions if she didn't comply. They'd even anticipated her forging signatures – each signature had to be given the school office stamp at home time. They'd locked her down. She had nowhere to move.

That gave Mandy endless hours in lessons and ample time to consider her situation. She couldn't see any further than telling her parents. Every projection about the future ended at that point. Until that was done, she hadn't got a clue how it would play out for her.

The teachers were building up to the mock exams after the Christmas holidays, warning them they'd be confined to the scrapheap if they didn't put the effort in with their revision. Her sixteenth birthday had come and gone, largely ignored by her parents who barely seemed able to tolerate her presence. One of the week's PE sessions was changed to a careers lesson. She'd thumbed through the cards in the prefab unit which claimed to be the school's careers information hub. As far as she could tell, they wanted the girls to be nurses and the boys to join the army or study for A levels. There didn't appear to be much choice in between. Every job sheet she looked at seemed completely irrelevant now. She'd be a mother soon, whatever that would entail.

'I washed your school coat today,' her mother began, that weekend.

Her dad was at the football and the house was quiet. Mandy had been hiding up in her bedroom, listening to the albums Laura had helped her procure from Terry's bedsit. She'd only nipped downstairs for a drink of squash.

'Oh good, thanks. It needed a freshen up.'

Mandy thought this was, perhaps, a sign that her mother was going to start chatting again. She poured the squash into a glass and turned on the cold tap.

'You seem to have a lot of LPs now,' her mother continued.

Mandy turned off the tap.

'Yes, I got a raise on my paper round,' she lied.

'I found something in your coat pocket before I took it to the launderette.'

Mandy sensed her mum was working up to something, but she was taking her time spitting it out.

'Thank you. That would have messed up the washing if it had gone in—'

'It was a leaflet about abortion.'

In those few seconds, Mandy realised the game was up. Fear came rushing at her; her body was paralysed by the terror of what was surely coming next.

'I can see it already. I thought you were touching your stomach a lot, but I told myself I was imagining things. It's true, isn't it?'

Her mother's voice was clipped and tense, her hands shaking, and her expression one of fearful apprehension.

Mandy hadn't realised she'd given the game away so readily.

She thought about the baby constantly; it was no wonder she subconsciously touched her stomach.

'How far gone are you? Please tell me you're not thinking of aborting it. Whose baby is it?'

Mandy had spent weeks denying each of these questions. Yet within one breath, her mother had put her finger on her predicament.

'Three months, I think. It's early days.'

'Oh, Mandy. What have you done?'

Her mother's face was white.

'I'm not going to have an abortion. I want to have the baby.'

For the first time in weeks, her mother came up and put her arms around her. Mandy couldn't remember the last time she'd felt any warmth or affection from her mother. She could feel her trembling. This hug was for her mother's sake, not for Mandy's.

'Who's the father? Is it somebody from school?'

'No, nobody from school.'

'Is this why you've been playing truant?'

Mandy nodded.

'Please tell me it's not one of the teachers?'

'It's not, Mum. It's a man I met—'

'A man?'

'A student. Something like that. He's in his late teens.'

'Does he know how old you are?'

She was saying it as if Mandy was still in contact with him. The last she'd seen or heard from Terry had been that day in the bedsit. Laura had made it quite clear she wouldn't be hearing more from him.

'He knew I was still at school.'

Mandy hesitated. Her mum seemed to sense it.

'Are you – in love? Does he want to marry you?'

'We're not together.' Mandy spoke quietly, barely daring to say the words.

'You mean he's abandoned you? Does he know about the child?'

'No, he doesn't know about the baby. He's gone. I don't know where he is.'

'Have you been with other boys?'

Her mother's eyes were haunted as if she'd already realised the problems this was all going to cause.

'No. And I liked Terry. He was nice to me. I don't even really know how I'm pregnant. We just kissed and things.'

'Well, you obviously did more than kissing, didn't you?'

She'd never seen her mum so angry and worked up. She thought all emotion had long been flushed out of her. If the situation wasn't so serious, she'd have been pleased to see it.

'I didn't, Mum. I swear. We had a little bit to drink—'

'You were drinking, too? No wonder you got pregnant, you silly girl. What on earth do you think you were doing?'

'I-I-I don't know, okay? It was an accident. It just happened.'

Her mother was sobbing now, wringing her hands as if Mandy's problem had just become hers.

'What are we going to do? What will the neighbours say? You haven't told anybody, have you? Your father will go spare when he finds out.'

'We're the only ones who know. And Laura, but I only just met her. She's not a friend or anything. She just helped me. She's nice.'

'Have you been to the doctor?'

'No. I still don't really believe I'm pregnant. I keep telling myself it's something else.'

'We'll need to make sure. We'll have to get you tested. You mustn't tell anybody else about this, all right?'

This was not playing out quite how Mandy expected. She thought there'd be shouting. She understood that they'd want to know everything. But her mum seemed more concerned about keeping it a secret. That hadn't even occurred to her as being the primary concern.

'This has to stay between me and you now, Mandy. Do you understand? You can't tell anybody at school, and you mustn't mention it to the neighbours. And we'll have to look at your school uniform. I can tell already from your stomach that things aren't quite right. We can't have anybody guessing. Nobody can find out. And for God's sake, don't tell your dad. If we're lucky, it'll either be a false alarm or you might lose the baby. But whatever you do, do not let your father know.'

TWENTY-FIVE

Hollie burst through the doors of The Country Park. Her legs were shaking from running, her face was red and sweaty from the effort, and she could barely catch her breath.

'Where's the press conference?' she gasped.

The receptionist looked at her like she was some sort of vagrant. Hollie pulled out her ID.

'I'm DI Hollie Turner from Humberside Police.'

'Oh, I'm sorry. I didn't realise. They're over there, far right-hand side.'

Hollie followed the directions through the foyer. A uniformed officer was standing at the door.

'Have they started yet?' Hollie asked. She held up her ID again. The constable stood a little straighter.

'No, ma'am, but they're just about to.'

'Have I got time to dash to the toilets?'

'If you're quick, ma'am, yes. They would've started, but they delayed it for the TV and radio programmes. Those press folk want to broadcast it live. I'd say you've got two minutes, maximum.'

'Thank you,' Hollie replied, her breathing now reaching a level of normality.

Hollie had seen the toilet facilities signposted as she walked over to the conference room. She rushed over and made straight for the sinks. She looked in a bad state. No wonder. She'd run alongside the Clive Sullivan Way, taken the slip road, and waved down a car to run her the last leg to The Country Park. Thank goodness she'd found a good citizen who was happy to give her a lift. For all she knew, DC Gordon was still stuck in traffic. It didn't look like it was going anywhere. She'd decided to cut her losses and made a run for it.

Hollie ran her fingers through her hair and pulled it tight with her hairband. She splashed water on her face, then dabbed herself with a paper towel to cool her flushed cheeks. She could feel the heat her body gave off. She'd have to deal with it; her time was up. She made one last check in the mirror, then dashed for the conference room. DCC Warburton was calling the room to order as she burst through the doors. DS Anderson sat at the table to the left of Warburton and there was an empty place to her right. One of the press team was just about to remove her nameplate from the table.

'No need to move that,' Hollie said. 'I'm here. I'm sorry, we got caught in a snarl up on Clive Sullivan Way.'

'Nice of you to show up.' Warburton sneered at her. The room was still bustling as the assembled TV crews, radio reporters, newspaper journalists and photographers settled in their seats.

The DCC placed her hand over the microphone that was positioned directly in front of her.

'In future,' Warburton continued, 'I'd appreciate it if my senior officer turned up in plenty of time, rather than me having to ship in another team member to cover for her at the last minute.'

Hollie was about to reply when the room fell silent. She took a deep breath to compose herself.

It was the usual affair. A table with white cloths. Microphones on stands in front of them. Three TV camera operators, the BBC and ITV regionals, plus one other. The nationals were there, too, since the story was big enough. There was a gathering of newspaper reporters, with pens and notepads in their hands, poised to scribble down anything of interest. She reckoned there were thirty or so members of the press in the room, so it was a good opportunity to appeal to the public for more information. She'd received the briefing email and skimmed it in the car before deciding to make a run for it. There was nothing new in there, and they'd held back certain details which would remain the knowledge of the investigation team for now. Normally she preferred to read from notes, but she'd have to busk this from the details on her phone. It all felt more intimidating to her this time. She didn't know the local press pack, and she figured that was the reason.

The DCC got things moving.

'My name is Deputy Chief Constable Rose Warburton and I'm joined by my colleagues DI Hollie Turner, who is leading the investigation, and DS Ben Anderson, who is part of the investigating team. We'll leave a short time at the end of this briefing for your questions.'

Hollie scanned her email. She'd be on after the DCC.

'At 10.07 p.m. last night, officers from Humberside Police were alerted to an incident on the Hull side of the Humber Bridge, close to where we are assembled now. A local woman, who we can now identify as Sister Sophia Brennan from the Convent of the Sacred Heart of Mary, was reported hanging from the bridge by a length of climbing rope.'

Hollie watched as the press, in unison, wrote down the victim's name. They were like jackals falling on carrion.

'Sister Brennan was seventy-one years old and a much-valued member of the small community living at the convent. I'll hand you over to my colleagues for more details of our investigation so far. But before I do, I'd like to say a word about the despicable imagery published on social media following this tragic incident.'

Hollie wasn't used to an intervention like this. A DCC laying into the smartphone brigade was unusual.

'I would seek to remind those members of the public that a poorly old lady who'd dedicated her life to the Church has died in this terrible incident.'

Hollie's mind flashed back to the tattoo and scratch scars on the old woman's body.

'I urge those who have shared horrific images of this incident to consider their actions. The public spectacle of Sister Brennan's death is unusual and unprecedented, but I would urge you all to reflect on how you might feel if this were your mother, daughter, or grandmother, and behave accordingly.'

DCC Warburton let that admonishment hang in the air for a moment. Hollie braced herself. She'd be on next.

'I'll now hand you over to DI Ben Anderson, who will bring you up to date with the details of our investigation.'

Hollie felt her face burning from the snub. To defer to her junior was a massive put-down, though only the officers in the room would probably notice that. Anderson was smirking. She composed herself. The TV cameras were on them, feeding the press conference live on TV.

DS Anderson started his briefing sounding like the cat who got the cream. Perhaps she was imagining it. She held her stare on her briefing notes, in an attempt to convey it had been the plan all along. Anderson ran through the public-facing details of the case. They didn't know much, and they wouldn't share any information about Shane Hardy or Gilly Hodges until they'd been questioned. They were keeping the attempt on Father Duffy's life under wraps, too. She needed something up her sleeve. Anderson and Warburton were shafting her on live TV, and there would be nothing left to say without making her look stupid by the time it was her turn.

Anderson was good, Hollie had to give him that much. He handled it well, didn't say too much, and maintained a steady and authoritative pace. Had it been a training session, she'd have given him full marks. As it was, she wanted to spit in his drink.

'I'll now hand you over to DI Turner, who'll be happy to take any questions—'

He had that smirk on his face again. The bastards were throwing her to the lions. She could tell from the DCC's body language that they'd planned this. She kept her face straight, but there was raging indignation bursting to get out.

'Thank you, DS Anderson. I'll take five minutes of questions, so be brief, please.'

This was her test. To give the press what they needed, but not too much. If she put her foot in it, she could blow the case. The press were like weasels; they had a habit of setting traps. Hollie went for an older man first. She didn't know any of these reporters yet, but he looked like he might be harmless.

'Yes, sir, if you'd like to ask your question first.'

'Good evening, DI Turner. Would you like to comment on the incident on the Bransholme Estate earlier today, in which it is alleged you assaulted a local youth you wished to question in connection with this case?'

TWENTY-SIX

Back at the flat and alone with her thoughts, Hollie began to churn over her earlier run-in with Warburton, immediately after the press had dispersed from the hotel. It wasn't the first dressing-down Hollie had received and she knew it probably wasn't the last. But it was never pleasant to feel like a rookie police constable, and she could have done without it so early on in her career with a new police force.

DCC Warburton had taken her aside after the briefing and made her feelings very clear in what was a full and frank feedback session. Why was a young man who could help progress the investigation now laid up in the hospital? Why was there a complaint against her already? Why was she so late for the press briefing?

The tone changed when Hollie mentioned the councillor's name and the article in the newspaper.

'Councillor Gillian Hodges?'

'Yes. Do you know her?'

The DCC paused a moment before answering.

'Yes. I know of her. She has the ear of the Police and Crime

Commissioner. The same PCC who diverted valuable funding to a safer-streets initiative.'

Hollie was about to question why that was an issue but was put off by the look on the DCC's face which suggested this was more of a one-way conversation.

'Take what Gillian Hodges says with a pinch of salt when you go to speak to her,' Warburton announced after giving it some thought. 'Her mouth is as big as her imagination. It's typical of her to write a letter like that to the local newspaper. She has some pretty crazy ideas about this city. She's always keen to get in on the action. She's the sort of rent-a-gob councillor who has something to say about everything. Dog shit on the pavement was the last bee in her bonnet. Can you believe she had local residents spraying turds on the pavement with pink spray-paint? That's the kind of woman she is.'

Hollie hadn't even met Gilly Hodges yet, but it was top of her list for the next day. She kept that to herself. The DCC operated in a different political sphere and that's why she may have held that opinion about the councillor. As far as Hollie was concerned, the fact that Gilly Hodges had been in the mother and baby home was a big leap forward. Still, the diversion had got the DCC off her back.

'You handled the questions from the press well,' she said begrudgingly.

'Thank you, ma'am.'

She was off the hook for now. It had been a very long day. She had to get home and deal with Léon.

Hollie called in at a chip shop on the way home. She was starving. The feeling of warm food wrapped in paper made her eager to get into her flat. It was only when she remembered it was empty that she felt deflated. Even those snatched moments with the kids – when she'd arrive home late and wake them from their sleep to give them a hug and tell them how much she loved them – they were times she treasured.

She'd had to park the car a little way from her building, but even from that distance, she could hear the neighbourhood drummer doing his thing. It was just past nine o'clock, not late enough to be officially disturbing the peace, even though he was quite clearly disturbing her peace.

Hollie knew how cases like that played out. It began with a complaint to the council. When they finally got their arses into gear, she'd be asked to keep a sound diary, recording the times of the disturbances. If it looked bad, they'd measure the decibels. The chances were nothing would be done.

As Hollie searched for her key, a couple opened the shared door to the flats.

'Oh, sorry,' the man said.

'That's okay,' Hollie replied, moving the key away from the door.

'Here, let me help,' the woman offered, spotting Hollie's hands were full.

'Smells lovely. The Avenues chippy?' the man asked.

'Yes, Cave Street was closed. I can't wait to get tucked in. I'm famished.'

'Well, the wanker on the top floor has laid on the evening's entertainment for you already.' The woman grimaced.

'Yes, it's a bit much, isn't it?' Hollie answered. 'Has anybody asked him to stop?'

'You'll just get a mouthful of abuse,' the woman answered, 'and the landlord doesn't give a shit. We're stuck with it, I'm afraid. Hopefully, he'll move on somewhere else soon. Either that or he'll be discovered dead up there with his drumsticks rammed up his arse.'

Hollie laughed out loud, as did the man.

'We're off out for a pint round the corner at the Banks Harbour. You're welcome to join us if you want?'

Hollie was tempted. Some non-police company was just

what she needed, and this couple seemed like they might be fun.

'I'll take you up on that another night.' She smiled back at the man. 'Thank you, both of you. And don't give me ideas about what to do with those drumsticks. If he goes on much longer like that, I can't be held responsible for my actions.'

The couple headed off into the night, and Hollie opened up her flat. It was cold; she hadn't figured out the timer on the boiler yet. She picked up an envelope and some flyers that had been pushed under her door and thrust them into her coat pocket. They could wait until the next day.

Her boxes were still scattered around the living room. She was living like a student, yet she was a middle-aged woman. She suppressed an overwhelming sensation of failure with a mindless TV show. A politician eating kangaroo foreskin was just what she needed after a busy day in the office.

She turned up the TV to drown out the sound of the drumming. What the hell was he playing up there? If someone had written a musical about migraines, that's what it would have sounded like.

Hollie tried to ignore it, focusing instead on the beautiful piece of fish she'd been served and the hilarious sight of a former cabinet member chewing what had turned out to be a formidable piece of meat.

As she finished her chips one by one, she checked in to see if Isabella had posted any social updates. There was nothing, except for a recent WhatsApp message which read:

I'm still alive! Stop worrying, Mum!

Isabella was twenty-three years old, and the worrying showed no signs of abating. Hollie had no reason to expect that it would any time soon. It was Isabella's decision to go off wandering the world after university. Hollie would have preferred it if she could monitor her kids 24/7, but she knew that was dysfunctional and that she had to let them take their own paths.

Disappointed by the lack of a detailed travel update, she texted Caitlen with a finger rendered grease-free by a quick wipe on a tissue.

> Big ask! Would Phoebe be happy to travel down with my kids on the train? Maybe stay an extra day or two as well? She can get a feel for Hull. NP if not. Sorry to ask!

Hollie wished she'd told Caitlen about Léon. It would have made this easier.

Caitlen was straight back to her.

> Of course. Phoebe says yes. She'll email you the train times. Missing you, C x

A sense of calm engulfed Hollie as she sat on the sofa. She couldn't be certain if she was comatose from her chips, or if it was the thought of the kids being with her again. She wondered what they were doing. It had stung when Léon said they'd barely noticed she was gone. She couldn't believe that.

As Hollie began to doze off on the settee, Shane Hardy suddenly came to mind. That cocky little shit. She wouldn't have wished those injuries on her worst enemy, but she was annoyed that she had landed herself with an investigation already. There were witnesses on her side, they only had Shane's word for it, and she was certain the problem would go away. Hollie made a note to sort out an early visit to Shane. It was time to move things along as far as he was concerned. She'd perhaps take DS Anderson with her to try to get a better measure of the man. Her phone vibrated. At least she'd remembered to silence it before the press briefing. It was Léon.

His intolerant face appeared on her phone screen. Talk

about a video nasty.

'I need your decision, Hollie. You said you'd tell me tonight.'

'And good evening to you, too. I want to see the kids before you go. I want to hear what they want. From them, not you.'

'But how? You're in the middle of this case. I saw you on the news earlier. You looked like you'd just run a marathon, by the way.'

'Thanks, Léon. Caitlen's daughter will bring them down on the train. I've sorted it out already. They can travel back with Phoebe, too.'

There was silence at the end of the phone.

'You know you can't look after them properly, Hollie. Who's going to watch them while you're chasing around after this nun killer?'

'Can I talk to them?' Hollie asked. 'Are they still up?'

Léon let out a slow and melodramatic sigh. He could be a bit of a dick when he was sulking after a row, but he'd ramped up the sighing to epic levels since announcing the split.

'I suppose so,' came the begrudging answer.

She heard him calling the children from upstairs. She could imagine them, in their bedrooms, Lily no doubt reading a book or doing her homework, Noah probably hard at work with one of his model kits. The thought of it took her breath away; would she ever see that again?

'Hey, Mum!' came Noah's voice as he grabbed the phone from Léon. He was joined by Lily who was already looking more grown up.

'How's school?' Hollie asked. It was lame, but that was the kids' world. She panicked at how nervous she'd become chatting to her own children.

'We made rockets today, Mum!' Noah exclaimed. 'Mine went second highest. The winner shot over the school roof.'

He was gone already, handing the phone to Lily. At ten years old, Noah was still a bundle of energy, living in the moment and a whirlwind of enthusiasm. He was always surrounded by a gang of pals at school, whereas Lily had always struggled with her friendships, electing instead to maintain a small group of very close companions. Where Lily would reflect and agonise, Noah was oblivious and carefree. Her kids were like chalk and cheese, yet they got on well and barely bickered.

'Hello, darling,' Hollie began. 'What are you reading?'

They were connected by amazing technology, yet they'd never seemed further apart.

'*Twilight*,' Lily announced, holding the book up to the phone.

Hollie wracked her brain, trying to recall if any racy bits were unsuitable for her thirteen-year-old daughter. Lily was studious and sensible, but she and Léon were still strict when it came to monitoring what TV she watched. She wasn't picking that fight right now, it was enough just to see her.

'Granny and Grandad say they want to come up and visit, but Dad says he doesn't want them here at the moment.'

Granny and Grandad were her parents; Léon's were referred to as *grand-mère* and *grand-père*, half in jest, half by way of easier identification.

'I asked you not to mention that to Mum,' Léon said, taking the phone back from her.

'Why can't the kids see my parents?' Hollie pushed.

'You know why they can't see them,' he snapped at her.

She saw him turn to the side to make sure Lily was out of earshot.

'We haven't even told the kids what's going on yet. Mainly because you're still in denial.'

'Screw you back, Léon. I'm not the one who had the affair. I'm their mother. I want to see my children. I want my parents to see my children. If you try to make this difficult, you'll have a fight on your hands.'

But Léon had ended the call already.

TWENTY-SEVEN

1974: MANDY'S STORY

Mandy stayed in her bedroom for the next three days, unless she was summoned to the living room by her father, who could barely stand to look at her. Her mum brought food up to her in a half-apologetic manner, but she, too, avoided looking at Mandy directly. She dared not play her music or make any sound. All the time, when her father was home, she would hear the deep thundering of his voice through the floorboards as plans for her future were made.

She didn't have to go to school either. Her mum had told her that the following day. She'd say Mandy was sick and wouldn't be in that week. They'd make a plan and figure out what to do. But whatever happened, her parents seemed most concerned that the neighbours wouldn't find out. This was ironic because her dad was shouting so loud on the night he discovered what was going on, the man living next door popped round to make sure everybody was all right. It was one of the worst nights of Mandy's life. She was called a tart, a whore, a slapper and a slut. She was told what shame she'd brought to the family. And all this from the man who, once upon a time, had called her his princess.

Mandy had a lot of time to think things over. She'd been on the receiving end of so much contempt over the past few days, but she didn't identify with the person they were describing. She felt no different from before, other than greater maturity now. The pettiness of school seemed so far away. She was beginning to imagine a life with the baby. It wouldn't be so bad, surely? She'd get herself a council flat. At least she'd have her own place. And the baby would be hers, somebody to shower with the love and affection she'd never received. It didn't seem so bad when she thought it through.

Terry's abandonment still stung. A part of her expected him to knock at the door, telling her that he'd been put up to it by his mother and that he was in love with Mandy and wanted to be with her. Terry never knocked at the door. But one day, a priest and a nun did.

She heard the knock and looked out of her bedroom window onto the street below. At first, she thought they were delivering leaflets or preaching at the door. Then her dad burst into her bedroom without knocking. He did that now. Since finding out about the pregnancy, it appeared she was no longer entitled to privacy.

'Get downstairs and make sure you behave.'

He was gone as fast as he arrived, his words dripping with contempt. Mandy put on her slippers and walked down the stairs, uncertain of what awaited her.

It was the biscuits she saw first. They never had nice snacks. But on the coffee table was a newly opened tin of Rover biscuits. The living room had been tidied, too. Sitting on one armchair was the priest. On the other was a nun. Mandy's mum was on one side of the settee, looking like she was just about to sit through the most terrifying interview of her life. Her dad had pulled up a chair from the dining table. His body language was tense and hostile.

'So, this is young Mandy. Hello, Mandy.'

The priest held out his hand for her to shake it. Shaking hands was something adults insisted on doing, so she took it, and he gave her a gentle squeeze.

'I'm Father Duffy and this is Sister Sophia Brennan. She's a nun at the Church of St Mary and the Angels.'

Mandy turned to the nun, expecting to see an extended hand, but she didn't bother with the pleasantry. Instead, she eyed Mandy up and down as if she were assessing her for something or other.

'Take a seat, Mandy.' Father Duffy gestured, directing her to the vacant place on the settee.

'So, Mandy, you've got yourself into quite a fix, I hear.'

He let the words sit there in the centre of the living room, and they hung like a vile stench. Mandy didn't know if that was a cue to say something. Father Duffy just looked around the room.

'It's a very nice place you have here, Malcolm and Lilian, a very nice place. This row of terraces is incredibly pleasant.'

Mandy followed his gaze. The furniture arms were worn, the coffee table stained with rings that wouldn't wipe out, and the wallpaper was beginning to peel along the edges where the adhesive had long since given up the will to live. It wasn't a nice place, and the Tyson family knew it.

'So, Mandy, we're here to discuss your future and what's best for you.'

The nun said nothing. She didn't need to. Mandy could tell from her face what she thought.

'She can't stay here,' Malcolm insisted. He almost spat out the words.

Mandy looked at her dad. He glared at her like he didn't even know who she was.

'She's not staying under this roof while that baby grows inside her. I'll never live down the shame of it.'

Her father's fists were clenched tight.

Mandy saw her mum's eyes reddening.

'Now, Lilian, I hear you have a sister young Mandy can stay with. Is that right?'

Mandy's mum composed herself and swallowed hard before speaking.

'Yes,' she whispered.

'Speak up, Lilian, for heaven's sake,' Malcolm snapped at her. She jumped in her seat.

'Now then, Malcolm, I understand this is a very difficult time for you, but there's no need to raise your voice.'

Mandy had never seen her father put in his place so swiftly. He accepted this priest's authority. Her parents were lapsed Catholics, but she knew her mother popped into the church to pray sometimes, usually sneaking away from her dad. She'd seen her once on her paper round. Her mum didn't know she'd spotted her.

Her mum cleared her throat.

'Yes,' she continued, louder this time. 'My sister lives in Bridlington. She's happy for Mandy to stay there while she – while...'

'Well, that's a good start, isn't it now, Malcolm? And you can both take the train to Bridlington and pay a visit, so that's all very nice.'

From the look on her dad's face, Mandy was not expecting many social calls. So, they were throwing her out while the baby grew in her belly. Auntie Caroline was okay; it might have been worse. She lived on her own and owned a Scottie dog. She also owned a small record collection.

'And what about after? When the baby comes?'

Her father wanted this done and dusted. It was like a perfunctory trial before execution.

'Well, Malcolm, as you know, we're always happy to welcome fallen girls at the mother and baby home adjacent to the Church of St Mary and the Angels. Mandy can move in when the baby is due, and she'll be able to rest there when it's born—'

'And after it's born? What then?'

He scowled at Mandy. There was a time when he'd loved her and shown affection, but she couldn't recall it now.

Father Duffy looked over at Malcolm and flexed his eyebrows. Mandy wasn't sure why, but she saw her father give the priest a small, terse nod.

'We can talk about that a little more when Mandy goes upstairs. Rest is so important for a girl in young Mandy's condition. So, Mandy, do you have any questions for us?'

She had a thousand questions, but it sounded to her like it was all taken care of. Auntie Caroline's for five or six months, then the home at the Church of St Mary and the Angels.

'What is the Church of St Mary and the Angels?' she asked. 'What happens there?'

'It's a place where we help young girls in your condition, Mandy. You'll get your own bed, and when it's time to have the baby, you'll be given all the help you need. Once you come out of the hospital, you can rest there with the baby while you're recovering.'

'When will I come home?'

Her dad, her mum and Father Duffy exchanged glances. Mandy noticed her mum was fighting back tears.

'There's no need to worry about all that right now, Mandy. We'll take good care of you, don't you worry.'

'What about school? I'm supposed to be taking my exams in the summer.'

'We've told the school you have a bad case of glandular fever and have gone to stay with your auntie. They're not expecting you back. There's plenty of time to discuss what comes next once the baby is born. We'll do whatever's best.'

Mandy was relieved about the exams. That was a burden off her mind. It was a failure waiting to happen, anyway.

Besides, she'd played truant so much of late, she already felt estranged from school life.

'So, Mandy, how does that sound?' Father Duffy asked.

It wasn't so bad. It would get her out of the house. She wouldn't have to go to school anymore. She'd have the baby, then get herself on the list for a council flat. It wasn't as if she had any friends at school anyway.

'What about my paper round?'

She knew it was a daft thing to say as the words came out of her mouth.

'It's over,' Malcolm declared. 'I told the newsagent you wouldn't be coming back. Your mother will take you to Bridlington first thing tomorrow.'

This was the end of her old life. She was losing control; they were taking everything away from her. She was being hidden away where she'd be out of sight and forgotten. They were painting her out of their lives. When she was delivering papers and earning a small wage, she felt she had some control over her life. She'd get another job when the baby was born. She'd work it out. It would be just her and her baby.

Sister Brennan stood.

'Shall I help you upstairs?' she asked.

Mandy looked at her dad and Father Duffy.

The answer was clearly yes.

'It's been lovely to meet you, Mandy, despite your current condition. We'll just chat through a few more details with your parents, but there's no need for you to hang around for this bit. You go and get some rest.'

Sister Brennan placed her hand on Mandy's elbow and gently steered her towards the stairs. It didn't feel so bad to Mandy. She wasn't certain what would happen next, but she was okay with this plan.

Sister Brennan guided her up the staircase and walked with

her into her bedroom. She was turning for the door when she glanced back at Mandy, a look of utter contempt on her face.

'We're used to dealing with young harlots like you, my dear. Don't worry, we know exactly what to do with your type at the Church of St Mary and the Angels.'

TWENTY-EIGHT

It was ridiculously early in the morning, but Hollie needed to do this alone. She didn't trust herself with her colleagues, not just yet. This case was too raw for her. She'd never shared the full story with her colleagues in Lancaster, either. She didn't really know what had made her drive over there when it was still dark. They'd got an address for the mother and baby home, and it was still standing, albeit abandoned long ago. She'd decided to take a look before the start of the new working day. It was something she felt compelled to do. She had to set her own mind straight first, before delving deeper into the case.

Sitting alone in the car, in the dark, with that empty, decaying building in front of her gave Hollie a sudden and overwhelming sense of vulnerability. It was as if the echoes of past events were all around her; the sadness, the isolation, the loneliness swirling around like wandering ghosts.

Hollie picked up her phone from the passenger seat and flicked through her most recent photos of Isabella. Her beautiful older daughter, she was so proud of her. She navigated through to a separate folder labelled *Izzy's Baby Pix*. Her daughter had no memories of ever living in Hull; she was a toddler when they moved back to Lancaster. Even though the earlier pictures showed them together in Pearson Park and the university grounds, as far as Isabella was concerned, her first childhood memory was walking in Williamson's Park in the shadow of the Ashton Memorial in Lancaster. She'd been with Hollie in Hull at too young an age to recall ever living there.

Hollie checked WhatsApp. Izzy was showing as online. That was an occurrence so rare, Hollie would have been less surprised if a flying saucer had whizzed overhead at that very moment. Her finger hovered over the phone icon, but she'd promised her daughter she would back off and leave her to her year out. The deal was that Izzy would check in regularly and let her know she was safe. That was nowhere near enough for an anxious mother, but she had to put a brave face on it; she didn't want to drive her away by smothering her. But it hurt so bad, knowing Izzy was out there somewhere in Vietnam, travelling alone. As far as Hollie was concerned, her daughter's post-university travel adventures couldn't end soon enough.

She looked out towards the mother and baby home. Hollie thought she'd caught a movement; was she just imagining it? She studied the cluster of shrubs to the side of the car and waited. No, her mind was playing tricks on her; it must have been a breeze.

She hadn't really known what to expect when she got here, but she shouldn't have been surprised. She'd driven the car up a long gravel drive, underneath old trees and onto a small area in front of the old house. There was sufficient light to see the eerie silhouette of the property and to make out its basic features. The old lamp posts which must have once lit the driveway no longer worked, and the house was set in extensive shrubbed grounds and surrounded by what looked like a sturdy wire fence, the sort that might protect a building site. She could see that most of the windows were boarded up, and there were warning signs attached to the fencing, making it clear that the building was unsafe, and nobody should attempt to enter it.

Something caught her eye, just beyond the car. Was it a bat, or an owl perhaps? She reached over to press the central locking button. As the locks slid shut, she felt a little safer in her cocoon. She half-expected a face to appear at her side, peering through the glass, trying to get in. She left the keys in place, just in case.

Had she been a little older, Hollie might have ended up in this place herself. Thank God, it was closed, and things had changed when she'd become a student in Hull, but a couple of decades earlier, that could have been her fate. Although her parents had always supported her with the baby, the social stigma of being an unmarried mother in the seventies might have been so overwhelming that her mum and dad succumbed to the pressure to have the baby adopted. It didn't bear thinking about.

She dialled Izzy anyway. She'd get a mouthful, or even worse, the call would be rejected, but at that moment she needed to hear her daughter's voice.

'Mum! I told you, I'm all right. This had better be an emergency.'

It was better than Hollie had expected.

'Hello, gorgeous. I'm sorry for calling. I just needed to hear your voice.'

A tear started its passage across her cheek.

'I'm just about to go out, Mum. I've met some guys on the road, we're leaving the hostel to do some exploring—'

Hollie wanted to say so many things.

Come home. Don't go with them. They might hurt you. How do you know they're safe? Stay with me, then nothing will happen to you. I'll protect you.

'I'm in Hull, Izzy. It just made me think about you when you were tiny. I'm missing you.'

'Look, Mum, we agreed that you wouldn't call me like this.

Please email me if it's important and I'll call you back if it's really urgent—'

Those boys are more important than a couple of minutes talking to me? You don't even know them. I've loved you for so long.

Her daughter seemed to sense that she needed a moment and softened her tone.

'Look, Mum, I've got a couple of minutes before I have to go. Is everything all right?'

Hollie knew she shouldn't have called, but seeing that home, and hearing about the girls, it had brought it all back to her. She had unfinished business in this city and, perhaps, that's what had drawn her to taking the job and disrupting her family life. One day, Izzy would know what it was like to be a mother.

'It's been so strange, seeing places where we used to go when you were tiny.'

'I really don't remember it, Mum.'

'I'm living next to Pearson Park at the moment. I used to push your pram around there. When you got toddling, we'd feed the ducks together. I was younger than you are now when I had you—'

Hollie couldn't believe now that she'd even considered an abortion. It had seemed like a disaster at the time; pregnant at nineteen and halfway through university. She considered having the abortion for a full week. She even took a taxi to the place where they'd do it. She couldn't go through with it in the end. She wasn't religious, she didn't hold any strong views about who should and who shouldn't terminate a pregnancy. She just knew that she couldn't let her child go. Every part of her urged her not to end the pregnancy, even though it was impractical, it would mess up her life, screw up her career and wreck future relationships. It had all seemed so serious back then.

She'd had Izzie anyway and never regretted her decision. The university and her friends helped with childcare at first.

The father was off the scene. When she decided to join the police, it made all the sense in the world to return to Lancaster, where her parents were delighted to share the childcare. It had seemed like the end of the world at the age of nineteen, but Léon had accepted Izzie and, when they'd started their own family, they'd had an older child to run after the younger kids. It worked; everything had sorted itself out in time.

Hollie looked at the abandoned home in front of her. In another time she might have ended up there with Izzy snatched from her arms. She'd felt no stigma when Izzy had been born, and despite the practical difficulties, things had worked out okay. Is that how those poor girls thought? They must have endured countless days and nights wondering what had become of their children, knowing as they got older that everything would have righted itself in the end.

Hollie heard a knocking at the door from the end of the phone.

'Look, I'm sorry, Mum, I've got to go. I'll come and visit you in Hull when I come back to the UK, I promise. You can tell me all about it then. Love you, bye!'

'I love—'

Isabella terminated the call.

Hollie felt suddenly alone and isolated. It seemed that all the people she'd brought into the world could now do without her. Was she becoming an annoyance to them?

Her confidence shaken by the call to Izzy, Hollie checked outside the car, turning in her seat to make sure nothing – no one – was out there. Apprehensive, she touched the central locking; every door was now open. She left the key in the ignition, thinking it better if she had to make a fast exit.

She switched on her phone torch and got out of the car. As the light came on, she thought she caught a shadow disappearing behind a tree. Her heart jumped and she stood still, listening, watching, alert to any sudden sound or movement.

She was in precisely the kind of place that she'd warned her daughter about so many times: dark, away from any thorough-fares, the sort of place unsavoury characters lurk. For a moment, she thought she'd caught a glimpse of light from the abandoned building, but she figured it was just the glare of the torch playing tricks on her eyes.

Hollie walked up to the fencing and gave it a shake. It was secure, there were no gaps to squeeze through. Standing there, the car behind her, the expansive grounds of the mother and baby home all around her, she felt exposed and vulnerable; perhaps she ought to have done with another member of the team after all.

She returned to her car and started the engine. As she switched on the headlamps and moved the gear stick, again she thought she caught a shimmer of light behind one of the wooden panels which had been nailed over the windows. She drove off, thinking she must be mistaken. That fence was sturdy, there was little chance of anyone breaking through it. But top of her list when she got into the office was to find out whoever was in charge of that fencing so she and her team could gain access to the building and take a proper look around.

TWENTY-NINE

The briefing room was packed by the time Hollie got back from the mother and baby home. Doctor Ruane was there, and she was pleased to see Jenni Langdon, too, walking without a trace of a limp.

'Feeling better?' Hollie asked, as she slipped into the room, relieved to have arrived punctually after her early morning detour.

'It feels as good as new.' Jenni smiled at her. 'Any time Shane fancies another chase, I'm well up for it.'

'I think I'll sit it out next time,' Hollie replied.

She walked up to the front of the room and the hubbub reduced to silence.

'Good morning, everybody. I'm delighted that Doctor Ruane has joined us this morning. Do you want to bring us up to speed with what you found on the body?'

Ruane nodded and walked to the front of the room, a small pile of photographs in his hand. He started going over the same information that he'd shared with her the previous day, but in more forensic detail. She was assembling her own thoughts for what was coming next when Ruane introduced something new.

'We've got an interesting development,' he continued, 'in that the priest – Father Duffy – had traces of fibres around his neck—'

Hollie looked up at him. This was hot off the press and unknown to her.

'I think the detectives who found Father Duffy were under the impression there was an attempt to drown him in the fish tank. He had markings around his neck, too. It turns out that there had also been a violent attempt to strangle him—'

'We think the killer was disturbed.' DS Anderson started speaking at the back of the room. He ambled up to the front like he was running the case.

'I'm sorry, DI Turner, I know this is new to you, but you were out of the office when we pieced it together.'

Anderson was smirking at her again.

'It looks like Father Duffy escaped strangulation, by what appears to have been a piece of climbing rope. Doctor Ruane has confirmed the fabric is the same as that used to hang Sister Brennan from the bridge. Not necessarily the same length of rope, but the same type, possibly cut from a different length.'

'There's something else, too,' Doctor Ruane picked up. 'The rope used to hang Sister Brennan had traces of saltwater embedded in the fibres. We've very few fibres to work on from the scarring around the priest's neck—'

'Is Father Duffy able to talk to us yet?'

'I put a condition check call in first thing,' came DC Gordon's voice from the side of the room. 'He's still out cold, but there was no serious damage done from the attempted strangulation.'

'We're working on the theory that your yobbo and his pals—'

'Shane Hardy?' Hollie confirmed.

'Yes, Shane Hardy, the one who's made the complaint against you,' DS Anderson continued.

They were heading for a showdown, she and Anderson. She'd pick her moment, or it would blow up in her face. At least things were moving on, even if he was being a prick delivering the news.

'To cut a long story short, we don't think Shane and his pals hurt the old man,' Anderson summarised.

'Yes, Shane said as much. At least that helps to confirm his version of events.'

It was the best she could do to wrestle it back for now.

'Let's bear in mind that if Shane Hardy was involved in the attack on the priest, that knife he wielded at me yesterday may well be a crucial piece of evidence. DS Patel, please ensure it is checked thoroughly for DNA and fingerprints.'

Doctor Ruane coughed and picked up where he'd left off.

'The key thing about the rope is it might suggest the killer is someone who works at sea, or potentially at the port. It could provide a useful lead.'

Or it might just be a coincidence, Hollie considered, but she kept it to herself. They were clutching at straws so far – anything which might point them in the right direction was welcome. She delivered her own update, sharing everything that they knew up to date, including the events and discoveries of the previous day.

'I'm interested in this tattoo that Sister Brennan had,' Hollie added. 'That suggests a previous life to me, that Sister Brennan hadn't always been the person she was in later life. I'd like somebody to talk to Mother Davies again if we can't speak to Father Duffy yet. DC Langdon, would you chase that, please, as you've spoken to her already and built up a relationship? I'd like to be in on that conversation, if I'm available; if not, don't let me hold you up.'

Jenni Langdon nodded. If only DS Anderson was as compliant.

'I think it's reasonably safe to assume the paedophile angle is wrong,' Hollie started.

'Why's that, boss?' Anderson asked.

'I think Shane Hardy was just putting two and two together and making five. We can't discount it fully, but I'm more convinced that it's connected to the mother and baby home.'

Hollie scanned the room. DCC Warburton wasn't there. It was probably a good job. Warburton might have little truck with Gilly, but for Hollie's money, that line of inquiry was much more interesting.

'DC Gordon, I'd like you to accompany me to question Councillor Gilly Hodges about that newspaper article on her time at the mother and baby home. DS Patel, keep on Father Duffy please, we need to speak to him ASAP. The same goes for the lorry driver – as soon as the infirmary give us the okay, we need to get an officer round there.'

She wondered if she should share details of her early morning visit to the mother and baby home, but decided to keep it to herself as it hadn't yielded anything useful. She'd have to work out how they could get through those barriers and take a look inside.

'Oh, and one more thing before we all set to it. We need to know much more about the home at the Church of St Mary & The Angels. The letter by Gilly Hodges is good for starters, but we need much more than that. Does anybody have any local knowledge to throw into the melting pot?'

There was a momentary silence.

'Do we have a local historian, anybody like that who might give us some context? When did it open, and when did it close? Were any records kept that we could access? I want chapter and verse on that place. If this murder relates to what went on in that home, we could be looking at a huge pool of potential suspects.'

'Do you think it's a former member of staff or perhaps one of the girls?' DS Patel asked.

Hollie considered it for a moment.

'Let's face it, it could be anybody. There would be a lot of people connected with a place like that who'd have a grudge. We've read Gilly Hodge's allegations about the place. We need to check that out and get it independently verified by more of the mothers who had their babies taken. It could be one of the parents who lost a grandchild. It might even be one of the babies that were passed on for adoption. For instance, if I'd been sent to an abusive family for adoption, I think that might make me pretty bitter about my life. It might even drive me to kill.'

THIRTY

1975: MANDY'S STORY

The taxi wheels crunched on the gravel drive as they approached the mother and baby unit. They came to a stop outside a sprawling old house. There were solid pillars on either side of the formidable front door. The rooms at the top had solid stone balconies. Huge, white-framed sash windows were set in weathered stonework, and there was little about the place to suggest what went on there. The building seemed cold and hostile like it was judging her and finding her wanting.

The sky overhead was dark and grey and the tall, leafy trees which were scattered across the grounds kept much of the light out. Set back from the road, the building was isolated and bleak. Mandy's stomach churned; this was it now, she couldn't pretend it wasn't happening anymore. The baby was due within the next week. She felt unprepared now; arriving at this place had made her lose her nerve.

'I'll leave you here,' Lilian said as the driver applied the handbrake.

'You're not coming in?'

There was no sign of her father when she arrived at the station. Not that she had expected it, but somehow, even the familiarity of his contempt might have made what was happening seem more normal. She'd never felt so ill-prepared and alone.

'No, I'll not go in with you. Besides, it will cost more if I leave the taxi running.'

'Oh.'

The taxi driver had got out to retrieve Mandy's case from the boot. He left it on the top step and returned to the car. Mandy struggled off the back seat and hauled herself out.

'Your father and I will visit soon,' Lilian said.

Mandy nodded and leaned in to give her mother a hug. Lilian turned away. Mandy wiped her eye and pushed the taxi door shut.

She gave a small wave to her mum as the tyres crunched over the gravel and the car disappeared along the long driveway. It felt like they were washing their hands of her, leaving her to sort out the mess she'd created for herself. When she turned, one of the nuns was waiting. Mandy just caught sight of two faces disappearing from an upstairs window. It seemed her arrival had caused some excitement among the girls.

'Welcome. You must be Mandy?' the nun said. 'Are your parents not staying for a bit?'

The softness of her tone was in stark contrast to the clipped tautness of her mother's responses. Lilian had barely shown an interest in how Mandy had been spending her time with her aunt in Bridlington. She just seemed to want to get it over and done with.

Mandy shook her head.

'I'm here on my own,' she replied, her voice faltering.

'I'm Sister Kay,' she said. The nun reached out and squeezed Mandy's hand. She had a Scottish accent; it sounded soft and kind. 'Come on in and let's get you sorted out.'

Sister Kay picked up Mandy's suitcase and led her through the huge wooden double doors into the pattern-tiled entrance hall. The doors were made of heavy dark wood, and their hinges groaned like it was an effort to let her come inside. Mandy looked at the massive central staircase. Its bannisters were fashioned from more dark wood, carved with ornate decorations that seemed like they belonged in another time. The lighting was insufficient to fully illuminate the entrance hall, so there were dark corners and heavy black shadows all around her. The slight echo created by the sheer size of the place made it feel hollow and empty like there was not enough warmth to fill it. The building was quiet; there was nobody around, it seemed.

'I'll need to leave you in the office before I take you upstairs. Sister Brennan will want to speak to you first. I'll wait outside for you; I'll be here when you're finished.'

Mandy tensed. She'd been dreading this second encounter.

They were standing outside an office; the door was slightly ajar. It was quiet inside.

'Go in and sit down,' Sister Kay urged. 'I'll tell Sister Brennan that you've arrived.'

Mandy walked into the dark, old-fashioned office. It was sparsely furnished with its heavy dark wooden desk, a couple of battered chairs and a couple of old grey filing cabinets pushed against the back wall. A crucifix was hanging on the wall. There was a stapler and hole punch on top of the desk and some paperwork concealed in a file.

Mandy didn't know whether to sit or stand. It felt like school, waiting in an office, exposed and vulnerable, not knowing what was going to happen next.

Suddenly, beyond the office door, there was screaming. It was a girl; the distress in her voice gripped Mandy's chest as a wave of anxiety engulfed her.

Nervously, she peered around the office door to see what was going on. A girl, about her age, was being dragged across the hall by one of the nuns.

'Leave me alone, you bloody witch!' she screamed, but the

nun drew back her hand and struck her across the face.

Mandy jumped, shocked by the easy violence of this woman. The girl became compliant, and Mandy watched, shaking, as the nun threw the girl into the room, her sobs stifled immediately as the heavy door was pulled closed. Mandy could only imagine how the poor girl felt; she wanted to rush over and comfort her.

From the opposite side of the hall, Sister Kay emerged, her face wracked with worry. She placed her finger over her lips and motioned to Mandy, who looked once more towards the girl's room, then returned to the office.

As Mandy stood there, her legs weak, her hands shaking, she heard a brisk, abrupt movement along the hallway. The nun walked in. They all looked the same unless you could see their faces, but this one was different. Her intimidating presence immediately filled the room, and Mandy jumped when she saw who it was. She felt small and worthless; this woman's intolerance oozed out of every pore.

The nun said nothing, barely acknowledging her presence. She sat at the desk, sighing heavily and opening up the folder. Mandy just stood there, watching, waiting and wondering what to do.

At last she spoke, slowly lifting her head and looking at Mandy as if she was a piece of rubbish.

'Here's how it works here,' she began, her voice sharp and abrupt. 'You're a disgusting slut and you're here because everybody is ashamed of what you've done. You're out of sight and out of mind, and that's how it will stay.'

She stopped and looked at the paperwork on the desk, shaking her head and tutting.

'All the nuns here have much better things to do than to waste their time on you. So, while you're here, you'll spend your time in your room and stay out of the way. You'll come downstairs at mealtimes, and you'll wash up your dishes and clear up your mess before you return to your room. Lights out is nine o'clock, after which we don't expect to hear a sound out of you. And we'll let you know if there are chores to be done. Understood?'

Mandy was still trying to take it all in. She nodded.

'Speak up, girl, has the cat got your tongue?'

'Yes—'

'Yes, Sister Brennan!'

'Yes, Sister Brennan.'

Mandy's knees felt weak again; she wasn't sure they'd carry her much longer.

'Sister Kay!' the nun shouted.

Mandy heard the swish of a nun's habit as Sister Kay made her way along the hallway. She appeared at the door, saying nothing. Sister Brennan didn't look up.

'Go!' she commanded.

Sister Kay opened the door wider, and Mandy stepped out. Gently, Sister Kay pushed the office door so that it clicked shut.

'You'll be in a small dorm with a couple of girls at first,' she whispered, 'but when the baby comes, you'll get your own room and privacy. Besides, you'll be feeding in the night, so you'll be grateful for your own space. I'll give you a quick tour.'

Away from the office, Mandy could hear the desolate sobbing of the girl elsewhere in the building. The nun showed her around the ground floor of the mother and baby home, her gentleness in sharp contrast with Sister Brennan's. Mandy heard the office door opening again and a bolt of fear shot through her, terrified that the woman would speak to her again. She didn't, and Mandy began to breathe again, soothed by Sister Kay's soft voice. They returned to the bottom of the staircase and retrieved Mandy's case. Sister Kay veered to the right at the top of the stairs onto a U-shaped landing, punctuated at intervals by more solid, dark-wood doors.

Mandy scanned the wide, open landing. It seemed to be

more like an old hotel than a home. The crucifixes on the walls and heavy religious artwork made it feel darker than it was. A stained-glass window at the top of the stairs subdued the light from outside, making it feel colder than it should.

On the far side of the landing, Mandy caught a movement. She wasn't certain what she was looking at initially, because the light didn't reach far enough. It was Sister Brennan; she was watching them. She stepped out where Mandy could see her clearly, staring, but saying nothing. She stood there and Mandy turned away, unable to meet her unwelcoming eyes. It felt like an icy wind had just blown through her life and turned all the leaves brown.

Sister Kay knocked at one of the doors, and there were giggles from the other side.

'Here's your new roommate, girls,' Sister Kay began, dropping Mandy's case inside the door. 'I'll leave you to introduce yourselves and get to know each other. The evening meal is at half past five, Mandy.'

Sister Kay disappeared quietly while Mandy surveyed the room. It was simple but functional. There were three metal-framed beds. Each had a wooden side table and a basic wardrobe on the left-hand side. Two girls perched on the middle bed. There was a simple, wooden cross at the far end of the room.

Mandy looked across the landing again. The nun was still there, staring at her as if she wished she was gone. She ducked into the room; the nun was frightening her.

'Hello, Mandy,' one girl said, smiling. 'I'm Theresa. Pleased to meet you.'

The other girl looked Mandy up and down. It was not at all obvious she was pregnant; she was much smaller than Mandy.

'Welcome to the home for sinning girls,' she said, a hint of contempt in her tone. 'I'm Gilly. Gilly Hodges. Pleased to meet you.'

THIRTY-ONE

They'd found Gilly Hodges's house easily enough, thanks to an obliging satnav and DC Gordon's prior knowledge of the location of Victoria Dock, to the east of the city. Hollie didn't have much hope that she'd be in during the day, but she wanted to try her luck anyway. As a local councillor, she'd been surprisingly easy to find online.

DC Gordon pulled in sharply.

'This is where she lives, ma'am.'

He secured the handbrake and switched off the engine.

DC Gordon locked up the car and they walked over to the house, Hollie half-expecting it to be a fool's errand. She tapped at the door. To her surprise, there was movement. Gilly Hodges opened up as if expecting a salesperson to be standing there. Hollie held out her ID. DC Gordon, a little slower off the mark, followed her lead.

'I was about to tell you to sling your hook,' Gilly began, immediately wary. 'I still might, depending on what this is about. You look like a couple of Bible bashers.'

Hollie kept it formal.

'I'm sorry to disturb you, but I'd like to ask you a couple of questions.'

'Is this under caution? Do I need legal representation?'

'No, no, nothing like that. It's just an informal chat. May we come in?'

Gilly seemed reluctant.

'I promise, it'll only take a couple of minutes of your time.'

Gilly opened the door fully, but she didn't look too pleased about it.

'It's a bit early for this, isn't it?'

Hollie ignored her remark. It wasn't the warm welcome she might have hoped for.

'Come into the living room, take a seat. I'd appreciate it if we could do this quickly, I've got a busy day ahead.'

Hollie walked into the living room, with DC Gordon following behind. There was a pile of what looked like council papers on the table. It reminded her that the case log would be waiting for her back at the office. DC Gordon took out his phone to record their chat.

'You know what happened at the Humber Bridge on Sunday night, I assume?'

'Yes. Who doesn't? It's all over the media. Is this being recorded?'

'Yes, it's only so we have a record of our conversation, it saves us from taking notes,' DC Gordon explained.

Hollie gave a nod to DC Gordon, who handed over a photo-copy of Gilly's letter to the *Hull Daily Mail*. She examined it, then looked up.

'And you think I did it because I wrote this letter? It's so long ago now, I'd forgotten I sent it to the newspaper. Do I need to contact a solicitor, detective?'

'As I said, it's just an informal chat. I think you may be able to help us with our investigation. Did you know Sister Sophia Brennan?'

Gilly's face gave it away.

'Perhaps,' she continued, wary.

'She was at the mother and baby unit attached to the Church of St Mary and the Angels in the seventies. You may well have been there at the same time as our murder victim. Were you?'

'Maybe. It depends on what kind of dates you're looking at. The home was operating for several years, you know—'

'If you know anything about Sister Brennan, it will really help if you could tell us now. It'll save me bringing you into the station for formal questioning. You appear to me to be a busy woman, and I'm sure you wouldn't want that inconvenience.'

DC Gordon's expression changed long enough for Hollie to see that he'd clocked what she was doing. She hoped he'd pick up a few tricks of the trade in the process.

Gilly sighed and sat down on one of the chairs that was pulled out from the table. Hers was a look of resignation that Hollie had seen many a time in her policing career. Faced with the prospect of a formal interview at the police station, most people acquiesced. Gilly Hodges looked like she was ready to play ball at last.

'Look, Sister Brennan was an old witch—'

Hollie was at once alert to what Gilly was saying. She hadn't been expecting such a strong start.

'Okay, so you didn't like her,' Hollie remarked. 'Was she enough of an old witch for you to push off the side of the bridge?'

'I hated the woman, but I didn't kill her. I certainly wanted her dead when I was younger. When I was sixteen, I got pregnant by my then-boyfriend.' She paused to look at them. 'How old are you, officer? Forty-something?'

She didn't bother addressing DC Gordon. Hollie nodded.

'This will be an alien world to you. And it'll sound like Victorian times to your colleague here.'

DC Gordon shuffled awkwardly.

'I was living at home with my mum and dad at the time, working in a cinema job. It was 1974 when I got pregnant; I was at the home in 1975. Can you believe you were ostracised if you had a child out of wedlock back then?'

She paused again for a reaction.

'I know it was taboo, but was it still an issue in the seventies?' Hollie asked. She could see the same rage surfacing that had been evident in Gilly's letter to the newspaper.

'It certainly was. I didn't even know I was pregnant. There was no internet in those days. I didn't smoke joints and watch X-rated movies with my parents like kids do nowadays. We didn't talk about sex back then. I was seven-to-eight months pregnant when my mum finally noticed. I wasn't showing much. I was slim when I was a teenager. You wouldn't believe it now, of course, but at seventeen I only weighed eight stone. You couldn't really see the baby.'

'What happened when your parents found out?' Hollie asked.

'They were more concerned about the family's reputation than my well-being,' Gilly continued. 'Can you imagine that? Anyway, my dad was furious. He drove straight round to my boyfriend's house and beat him black and blue. What's more, his parents didn't do anything about it, because they were so angry about what he'd done.'

'Did you keep the baby after it was born?' DC Gordon asked.

Gilly laughed and raised her eyebrows at Hollie.

'It wasn't as easy as that back then. My parents were very religious. Abortion wasn't an option for me. In 1975, the thing to do was whisk you off to a Church home before any of the neighbours found out.'

'Is that what happened to you?' Hollie said.

'Yes. Before I could draw breath, I was driven over to the

Church of St Mary and the Angels. The home there was where they took in' – she made air quotes with her fingers – '*fallen girls*.' She took a breath. 'I stayed there until I had my baby. I never saw the father again. He disappeared and his family transferred to a council house somewhere else in the city. And I never married after that. I've had relationships, of course, but nothing that stuck. It put me off for life.'

'What about Sister Brennan?' DC Gordon wondered. 'Was she around while you were in the home?'

'You bet she was, the old cow. All the girls hated her. She would call us harlots and sluts and tell us we deserved everything that was happening to us—'

Gilly suddenly choked up. She took a moment to compose herself.

'She would even shove us in the stomach when nobody was looking. She would tell us God despised our babies, and they didn't deserve a place in His kingdom.'

'Did you tell anyone?' Hollie asked.

Gilly snorted at that.

'We didn't have helplines in those days. Nobody would have believed us, anyway. You daren't speak up against the Church back then. No, we just had to take it and pray it didn't harm our babies.'

'What happened to your child?' Hollie enquired. 'In the end, were you able to keep your baby?'

Gilly's eyes teared up again.

'They were taken away from us for adoption,' she replied, her voice faltering. 'We got to keep them for ten days or so, then they'd be taken from us in the night. We'd be forced to sign the papers, and that was that. I didn't even know what I was signing, I didn't understand the wording. No woman would ever give up her child voluntarily. My baby was stolen from me. I would never have agreed to that. I took it on trust. It was all taken on trust. My parents told me it was for the best. Father Duffy—'

'Father Frank Duffy?' DC Gordon checked.

'Yes, that's him. He was always Father Duffy to us. Sister Brennan and that other one – I can't remember his name – they were like devils, both of them.'

DC Gordon and Hollie exchanged a glance.

'Can you say more about the third person?'

'He was a social worker. McCready was his name. A nasty piece of work he was.'

'Do you have a first name?' Hollie checked.

'Patrick. Patrick McCready. A horrible little man.'

DC Gordon made a note of the name.

Gilly took a few seconds to settle. Her words were laced with sadness and anger.

'My darling boy was taken away from me. He was only days old. I barely knew what was happening. I had no say in the matter. My parents despised me. To the Church, I was just a whore. I had no voice. It's why I do this now. It's why I'm a councillor. People need a voice. They need someone to stick up for them.'

Hollie reached out her hand to touch Gilly's arm. This was not the turn she'd expected the conversation to take. She knew a bit about what had happened to unmarried girls in the past, but it was just a story to her. It wasn't something that went on when she was a teenager. All her friends' mums had encouraged their daughters to go on the pill. She still remembered her own mother sitting her down to have an awkward conversation about contraception when she was a teenager. This might have been her with Isabella; she shuddered at the horror of it.

Gilly turned and looked at a black and white picture on the wall behind her.

'That's me, there, in the photograph.'

She pointed, then got up to take it down off the wall.

Even from that distance, Hollie could make out a very young-looking Gilly. The photo was of four girls in what looked like a dorm room.

'Most people who visit don't even bother to look at that old photograph, but it's one of my most cherished pictures. The girls that you're looking at in that picture are the girls who were in the mother and baby home with me. You're looking at Mandy, Violet and Theresa. That picture was taken in 1975.'

THIRTY-TWO

'May I take a snap of that photograph?'

'If you must. It's enlarged from the original Polaroid image, so it's a bit blurred.'

Gilly handed it over and Hollie took several shots on her phone, sending the sharpest image to DC Patel's work email.

'Can you give me the surnames of those other girls?'

Gilly sighed. Any resistance she'd put up at first was being fast worn down.

'Are me or the other girls under suspicion, detective? Do I need to get some legal advice?'

'No, that's not necessary, but I am going to look into this. That photo is incredibly useful to the investigation, if only to rule out that group of girls from our enquiries.'

Gilly turned to look at the picture, and she pointed to one of the girls.

'Well, that's Mandy Tyson,' she began. 'And there's Theresa Morgan. That's how I knew them back then, of course. They were in the same dorm as me at the mother and baby unit at the Church of St Mary and the Angels.'

'What about the other girl?'

'She's Violet. We were friendly with her, but she was in another dorm.'

'Are you still in touch with them?'

'Yes, but I haven't seen Mandy for some time. We keep in touch, though.'

'Does she still live in Hull?'

'Yes, she stayed here. She's still in the city centre.'

'Tell me about the other girls?'

'That's Theresa, Theresa Jacobs. Her surname was Morgan back then.'

DC Gordon was taking notes, so Hollie continued with the questions.

'She married the father?'

Gilly laughed out loud.

'No, DI Turner. None of us married the fathers of our babies. Mandy's disappeared, mine was a useless piece of shit, and Theresa thought she was in love, but soon found out her bloke was less interested when the baby came along. They tried, but they didn't make it. I had coffee with Theresa yesterday.'

'She's aware of what happened at the bridge?'

'Why do you think we met for coffee? We were having a gossip.'

'And what about the fourth girl?'

'Violet Farrow. She lives in Goole now. We still email occasionally. Violet wasn't in our dorm, but we got to know her. She was the fourth Musksluteer—'

'I beg your pardon?'

'It's what we used to call ourselves. Sister Brennan was always calling us sluts and harlots. It's how we coped. We turned it into a joke.'

Hollie caught a momentary glimpse of what life must have been like for the teenagers. She'd slept with guys at university in the nineties. One of them had fathered Isabella. If it had been two decades earlier and one of those casual relationships had resulted in a pregnancy, she might have found herself in the same position as Gilly and her friends. It was too frightening to think about how it would have felt to have Isabella snatched away from her. There were only twenty years between them, yet attitudes had changed so much.

'Violet has cancer, I'm afraid. She's probably not long for this world, though I hate to say it. It's such an evil disease. You'd think if there was a God up there, he'd decide that Violet had had enough.'

'You're not a believer, then?'

'No, DI Turner, I'm not. I wasn't back then either. What I experienced in that home put me right off the Church.'

'Could any of those girls be responsible for Sister Brennan's death?' Hollie wondered aloud. She knew it sounded ridiculous, and Gilly confirmed it.

'We're all older women now. We're in our sixties. We certainly have the motive, but none of us has the pelvic floor control—' She laughed at the thought of it. 'I can barely hold in my wee these days, let alone carry Sister Brennan along the Humber Bridge and throw her over the side.'

'And the others?'

'Come on now, DI Turner. You can't think it was one of us. Theresa wasn't sad Sister Brennan got her comeuppance, but that doesn't mean we'd actually kill her. She died in a manner befitting her hateful life.'

'I think she may have been seeking forgiveness at the time of her death—' Hollie suggested.

Anger flashed across Gilly's face.

'That's like Jimmy Savile coming back from the dead and saying *Sorry guys, it was all a mistake*. Some things you can't forgive.'

'She was that bad?'

'We were young girls!' Gilly exclaimed. 'We deserved support and empathy, not judgement and contempt. We'd all made simple mistakes. And for the main part, nobody seemed too concerned about the men who'd got us in the family way. They all got on with their lives and most of them never had anything to do with their kids. We were left to carry the can. It was brutal.'

Hollie could see Gilly was getting exasperated with her, so moved things on.

'So, I'll ask again, might one of the young women who stayed at the home have killed Sister Brennan?' Hollie asked gently. 'It sounds like Sister Brennan and this social worker were not very popular among the girls.'

'How many of us passed through that home?' Gilly answered. 'How many teenage girls spent their nights sobbing over the babies that had been snatched from them? Hundreds? Maybe more. I'll bet every one of those girls dreamt about strangling Sister Brennan. So, if you're asking who killed her, I'd say there are a fair few suspects to add to your list. You can add me for one, though I didn't murder her, of course. You can probably add the other three girls, too. I'll bet they thought about killing her more than once. But I can tell you, I smiled to myself when I saw the picture of that woman hanging from the Humber Bridge. She deserved what she got. Her God caught up with her in the end—'

THIRTY-THREE

1975: MANDY'S STORY

'Your waters have broken.'

'What?' Mandy answered, looking to Gilly for more information.

'That means the baby is coming,' Gilly added. 'I thought I'd be the next to pop after Theresa. It's so exciting! Looks like I'll be the last of the Musksluteers to drop.'

Despite the feeling of panic engulfing her, Mandy was still able to offer a giggle at Gilly's musketeer joke.

Mandy had only been at the unit for just over two weeks. And what a fortnight it had been with her two new friends. Now it was her time. The baby was early, and she wasn't quite ready for it. She wished she could buy herself a couple more days to get her head around what was about to happen.

Violet had gone to alert Sister Kay and a taxi was being called. Mandy's bag was already packed and waiting at the end of her bed. It had seemed ridiculous to get her things ready so soon, but the nuns insisted on it. It turned out they'd been right.

Since arriving at the unit, Mandy had realised how little she'd thought it through. Thankfully, the unit was all geared up for this eventuality. There was a small stockroom downstairs packed with donated Babygros, changing mats and laundered terry nappies, as well as all the paraphernalia required, such as safety pins, plastics, cotton wool and tiny mittens. Mandy loved the mittens; she couldn't believe a baby's hands could be so small as to fit them. She'd packed her bag with the basics and had made sure she had a couple of nighties in there, along with a dressing gown and her slippers. She hadn't seen her mum and dad since the day they'd come in to complete some paperwork in the office, but she had received a perfunctory call from them from the phone box. There was a heavy black phone in the office and the girls could use it under the supervision of one of the nuns.

Sister Brennan arrived with a mop and bucket.

'Yes, it's your time all right,' she snapped. 'The taxi is on its way now.'

She held out the bucket.

'Well, take it then. You don't think I'm going to clear up your mess, do you?'

Mandy looked at the small puddle of liquid on the floor, then at Gilly.

'That's all right, I'll do it,' Gilly said, moving toward Sister Brennan.

'No!'

The girls jumped at the severity of her answer.

'It was Mandy who got herself into this mess. It's Mandy who can clear it up.'

Mandy felt a pang in her stomach. She assumed this must be contractions. The doctor and her roommates had told her about these, but she hadn't really known what to expect. She took the mop and bucket and cleaned the floor.

'Now, take your bag and wait in the entrance hall for the taxi to arrive. Don't keep the driver waiting, it all costs money. You've caused quite enough trouble as it is.'

Sister Brennan snatched the mop and bucket from Mandy and left the room. Gilly moved in to give Mandy a hug.

'Good luck,' she said. 'You're lucky going first. You'll be able to tell me what it's like.'

Gilly gave her a kiss on her forehead. The girls had grown close in such a short time. Mandy loved being able to share her hopes and fears with girls similar to her own age. They would never have mixed at school, yet there they were already as thick as thieves.

Gilly hugged Mandy and picked up her bag.

'I'll take this down for you,' she offered. 'I'll wave you off at the door.'

Mandy changed her clothes and then the girls made their way down to the entrance hall. Sister Brennan was waiting there in her heavy black coat. She looked like a shadow in the doorway, dark and portentous.

'Isn't Sister Kay coming with me?' Mandy asked. 'I thought Sister Kay was coming to the hospital with me?'

'Sister Kay is busy,' came the curt reply. 'I'll be accompanying you to the hospital.'

'But—'

'It's okay,' Gilly tried to reassure her. 'The nurses will look after you when you arrive.'

'Is my mum coming?' Mandy asked, feeling suddenly anxious.

'Your mother will not be attending the birth,' Sister Brennan snapped. 'You'll be doing it alone. Perhaps you should have thought about that before you were so quick to jump into bed with that young man.'

Mandy could feel the tears forming in her eyes, but she didn't want to be weak in front of this spiteful woman.

'It's all right,' Gilly comforted her, squeezing Mandy's arm.

'I've got a cramp in my stomach,' Mandy said. 'I'm scared, Gilly, I don't know what it's going to be like—'

'You should have thought about that nine months ago, you stupid girl!'

Sister Brennan moved towards the door.

'Get a move on!' she called, terse and dismissive.

'I feel sweaty, but I'm cold. Is the baby all right? I feel strange—'

'Shh, it's okay, Mandy. The nurses will reassure you. It'll all be fine.'

Mandy held Gilly's hand until they reached the front door. The building had never felt emptier. Mandy knew that when she released Gilly's hand, she was on her own.

The crunching of gravel announced the taxi's arrival. The girls had a final hug.

'I'm so scared—' Mandy whispered into Gilly's ear, out of earshot of Sister Brennan.

'I know, I'm sorry, Mandy, I wish I could come with you. I'll be here when you get back. Try to be brave—'

They released hands. It reminded Mandy of the balloon that had drifted away from her when she was at Hull Fair as a toddler with her auntie. She'd cried her eyes out as she watched it floating away in the distance; that's how she felt about Gilly now.

Mandy gave a small wave and got into the vehicle. As the home faded out of sight through the back window, she felt alone and wretched. She had a sense that the baby was eager to come, yet she held out hope that her mother would soften and might agree to stay with her in the hospital. She was scared now, and desperately worried about how painful it might be. Sister Brennan sat tense and disapproving at her side; her last source of comfort and reassurance was now gone. Her mind raged with the fear of what was about to happen. She wanted it to stop, she wasn't ready yet, it was too much for her.

The taxi driver attempted to make polite chit-chat. 'So, it's an exciting time having a young 'un,' he began.

'I would prefer it if you kept your eyes on the road and the chatter to a minimum.' Sister Brennan shut him down.

He looked at Sister Brennan as if he was about to give her a piece of his mind, but the sight of her habit seemed to make him think again. They continued in silence until they arrived at Hedon Road. Sister Brennan paid the fare without a thank you, and she left Mandy to carry her bag.

'Good luck!' the taxi driver called over to Mandy. 'I hope it goes well. It's a magical time having your first.'

He was chased off by Sister Brennan's scowl.

Mandy followed the nun into the foyer. Sister Brennan seemed to know what she was doing. The nurses at the reception desk gave Mandy a sympathetic look. She could feel her body trembling, gripped by crippling trepidation. Her head was wet with sweat, and she was bent over because of the cramps. She thought about what was coming and she was scared. For so long, the birth had seemed so far away yet now, it was almost upon her. She wasn't ready.

While Sister Brennan supervised the paperwork, Mandy stood there on her own, lost and lonely.

One of the nurses sidled up to her.

'Don't worry, my darling. The nurses will look after you in there. You'll be all right.'

Everything seemed to have been organised. Mandy had signed some paperwork already, but she hadn't read it all the way through. It was far too technical for her.

Before long, she was in a hospital room, her clothes discarded and replaced by a gown. Mandy was now feeling the pains regularly and they were coming stronger. A midwife came into the room, closed the door, and announced she was going to examine her. Mandy did as she was told but felt embarrassed and uncomfortable as the midwife poked and prodded at her in a way she'd never been touched before.

'You're six centimetres,' she said.

'Pardon?' Mandy replied.

'Six centimetres dilated. That means it shouldn't be too long now. How are those contractions coming along?'

'I can feel them, but—'

Mandy stopped dead in her tracks. An overwhelming wrench in her stomach stunned her out of completing her sentence.

'That's good. If they're getting stronger, the baby won't be too long now.'

The midwife finished her checks, then left Mandy and Sister Brennan to their own devices, promising to check in on her at regular intervals. All the nun could do was scold her and tell her she'd brought this situation upon herself. Mandy desperately wanted a hand to hold for reassurance; she wished her mother was there.

Over the next ten hours, Mandy endured the most pain she'd ever experienced in her life. The contractions came strong and consistent, making her back ache. Mandy was shocked to be shaved; it was uncomfortable and the intimacy of it made her feel awkward. It felt like she'd left her right to privacy at the hospital reception desk.

It seemed to take an age until the midwife was happy with the progress of dilation, and Mandy began to wonder if she would have the strength to endure the birth.

As the number of people in the room grew, she begged for something to help with the pain.

'No, you don't get that,' Sister Brennan seethed at her. 'If you remember how much it hurts, maybe you'll think a little harder before you get pregnant again.'

Mandy could barely take in what was going on around her. Her legs were placed in stirrups, which she hated, but by that time all she could focus on was the severity of the contractions and the feeling of the baby inside her. It had changed position –

she could tell that much – and she wondered why it wouldn't just come out.

'She's crowning,' came a male voice from the far end of the bed. It was a student, as far as she knew. She seemed to recollect Sister Brennan agreeing to it on her behalf earlier in the day.

'In for a penny, in for a pound,' she'd said as the doctor had exited the room. 'You might as well let everybody have a look. You haven't been too fussy so far.'

The baby finally arrived after a painful, stinging push, which she'd been told not to give. There were positive sounds from the end of the bed and then a baby's cry. They cut the umbilical cord. She was asked to push one more time and the baby was whisked away for a few minutes. Mandy was dazed and confused but she was frantic to hold her baby and cradle him in her arms.

'She'll need stitching,' she heard the midwife say. 'That's the afterbirth clear.' And then: 'He weighs five pounds and seven ounces, my dear. Congratulations, you have a son.'

A beautiful scrunched-up baby wrapped tightly in a white blanket was handed over to her by the midwife as the medical team attended to the various jobs which needed to be done. She took him gingerly, terrified that she'd drop this tiny, precious thing that had just come into her life.

The baby made a small snuffling noise and she stared at his beautiful face, traces of vernix still on his dimpled skin. His tiny hands were clenched into fists, fierce and determined; his blue eyes were wide open, and alert and he appeared to be looking directly at her. She'd never known such an overwhelming rush of love in her life; this child meant everything to her, she would never let him go.

'Hello, darling,' she sobbed. 'Look at your lovely little hands and that tiny nose. You're so handsome and I'm so lucky.'

She put her finger in his hands, and he clenched it tight like he never wanted to let her go.

'Oliver,' she whispered to him, smiling and crying at the same time, elated that this incredible baby was hers to love and to hold forever.

Mandy felt somebody skulk up to her at the top end of the bed.

'Make the most of him,' Sister Brennan whispered, 'but don't bother getting too close.'

Mandy didn't know what she was talking about. She was sore and exhausted, but she wanted nothing more than to sleep with her tiny baby nestled into her chest. He was perfect. There was nothing that could spoil this for her. Nobody could ever separate them.

THIRTY-FOUR

'Who still uses a fax machine?' Hollie laughed.

'Apparently the archive service does,' DS Patel replied, 'though they warned me it's not getting replaced when the current model breaks. I hope you're not an eco-warrior, ma'am, this is taking up a lot of paper and it might result in the loss of a rainforest or two.'

Hollie had come directly back to HQ with DC Gordon, who was now processing Gilly's photograph of the girls in the mother and baby home and distributing it to the team. The top priority was tracking down the other three girls and pulling them in for questioning. That, and locating the social worker, Patrick McCready.

Hollie couldn't remember the last time she'd used a fax. It was almost unbelievable there was still a functioning model in the office. They'd found it underneath a pile of discarded brochures for some long-forgotten community initiative. Hollie read the title.

Counteract the counterfeiters! Shop a shop lifter!

'I'm pleased that the comms team do a better job these days. I'm not sure how a bit of dodgy word play is going to help us clear up much crime.'

'We mostly use those old leaflets as coasters,' Patel replied. 'I barely even look at them. I felt like an archaeologist finding that fax machine there, though. And it's still plugged in, too.'

The electronic chirps made Hollie recall a time when the internet took ages to load, and an online session could be swiftly curtailed by her parents picking up the phone. Much as she despised what technology had done to her attention span, she was pleased she no longer had to use dial-up.

'Let's get some of these pages torn off and start sifting. What's the name of this chap at the library?'

'Edward something,' Patel answered. 'He's a useful contact to have. The moment I mentioned what we were looking for, he was like a man with a mission.'

Hollie tore off a length of paper, even though it was still chugging out of the machine. She tore that in half and handed it over to Patel.

'Shout if you find anything useful.'

Hollie took a seat at the adjacent vacant desk. She'd had enough of case-related paperwork, she was ready to sink her teeth into a bit of hands-on detective work. So far, the local newspaper had been worth its weight in gold. But Amber and Jenni's discovery of the letter by Gilly Hodges suggested there might be better pickings if they dug a bit further back in time, to when newspaper archives were stored on microfiche rather than online. Edward, the helpful guy at the city's archive, had been happy to go searching on their behalf. It sounded to Hollie like someone else was seeking a distraction from boring admin work besides herself.

Hollie scanned the black-and-white imprints, each one cata-loguing something to do with the mother and baby home or the adjacent church. Edward had scrawled dates under each cutting, which was useful for context.

'These go back as far as the sixties,' DS Patel remarked. 'The number of local women who might bear a grudge about that place is ridiculous. That's before you count their adopted children. The scale of this operation is huge.'

'I know it seems vast, but we're looking for one little part of it. By all means check the old articles for titbits or background info, but we need to zoom in on the mid-seventies at the risk of getting distracted. Something will leap out, a minor detail or a name. Most cases are overwhelming at first, but when you get to the truth, it's usually something ridiculously simple. That's what we're looking for, it'll be in there somewhere.'

The articles were useful for background information, but they didn't throw any new light on the investigation.

'The problem is, the home was a place of shame back then,' Hollie remarked. 'It's not like they'd have fundraising fêtes in the grounds or open days for the public. Most of these articles relate to changes of use for the building or Church-related matters. We're not going to find pictures of the girls in here or get any names.'

'Look at this,' Patel cut in, handing out a sheet of paper which she'd neatly detached using a ruler to create a straight line. 'That's the priest, isn't it?'

The fax copy wasn't clear, and the images became stark when they rolled out of the machine.

'It looks like him. Damn, that's 1975. He'd have been a young man back then. Can you read that caption for me? It's a bit smudged.'

Hollie handed it over, and DS Patel used her phone to photograph the print and enlarge it. She held her phone up for Hollie.

'That's him with that guy from social services. It's some

social function, but it all looks very cosy. That's Patrick McCready, according to the caption. It's funny how the same names are coming up.'

DS Patel's desk phone rang again, and she placed her mobile on her desk. Hollie noticed it reverting to a screen saver while she was chatting to whoever it was on the phone. It was a picture of a cat; it looked like it might have been taken in her home. The wallpaper on her walls looked modern; it was tasteful but not something Hollie would have had the courage to use in her own house.

'Okay, thanks so much, I really appreciate it,' Patel said, finishing the call and placing the receiver back in its cradle. She immediately moved her hand to her mouse and reactivated the screen.

'We've got a bite from the council,' she continued, as much to herself as to Hollie. 'He's just sent me an email. You might want to pull up a chair.'

Intrigued, Hollie placed her roll of fax paper on the desk and scooted her wheeled chair over.

'What have you got?'

'Well, it was good news and bad news,' DS Patel said, continuing to click around her screen. Hollie could see she was waiting for a large file to open; it was taking its time.

'It seems like the Humberside Police IT system is in no hurry, so tell me the bad news while that file is thinking about it.'

'The council have had an initial search for records connected with the mother and baby home. They were all on paper, apparently, but that's only to be expected. If the home closed in 1980, you're not even going to get some dot matrix printing.'

'Okay, so how deep are the records buried?'

'The chap at the council reckons they could be in several

places. They might have been destroyed. The local councils have various places where old documentation is stored. He says he's having a devil of a job finding the adoption paperwork, but he's promised to carry on looking.'

'Was he able to say anything about adoption agencies?'

'Yes, he gave me a bit of technical information. Local councils, which have responsibility for social services, handle a lot of adoptions themselves. However, they also work with voluntary agencies—'

DS Patel checked the email.

'They're called VAAs – Voluntary Adoption Agencies – but they don't have children in their care.'

'And, of course, our case dates back to the seventies, so you can bet your life that's all changed since then. Okay, we need to do more digging. Why don't you try at the university? I'll bet they'll have some social services experts. And the easiest and fastest way to sort it out, of course, is going to be to get it straight from the horse's mouth.'

'Father Duffy or this Patrick McCready fellow?'

'Exactly,' Hollie confirmed. 'We need to get the smelling salts to Father Duffy and find out where this social worker is living these days. Or if he's still alive.'

The document finally opened on DS Patel's screen. Hollie could see it was a scan of a handwritten list. It seemed to have been extracted from an old record book of some sort.

'So, if that was the bad news, I hope you're going to tell me this is really good news?'

'I am,' DS Patel replied, scrolling up and down the pages. 'He did find a record of the girls and young women who stayed at the mother and baby home. It seems they used to sign them in and out like some kind of visitor's book. There's an entire record here from 1969 until 1978—'

'Bingo! We've got the time when our four girls were at the home.'

'Just look at all those names. There was none of this data protection legislation around back then. Any one of these girls might have a reason to kill Sister Brennan—'

'It must have taken him ages to scan all that.'

'He had a work experience kid working with him. I think he was grateful for the distraction; it kept this kid occupied for ages, he reckons.'

'Well, I'm pleased we could be of use. See if you can find the name of our councillor, will you? That seems like a good place to start.'

It took DS Patel a while to find the name, but it was in there: Gillian Hodges, entering the mother and baby home at the end of January 1975.

'They didn't keep them in there for long,' DS Patel observed. 'She looked like she was in at the same sort of time as Mandy Tyson, Violet Farrow, Theresa Morgan, Pattie Ross, Tina Logan... this is odd—'

'What is?' Hollie asked, leaning in to take a closer look. Gilly hadn't mentioned Pattie and Tina, but they may have been in the home at different times.

'Look at that,' DS Patel continued. 'A girl's name has been removed from the book. Somebody went through with a big black marker pen.'

'When was liquid paper invented? It might not have been around in the seventies, I don't know. Perhaps the girl left, she might have been homesick. Or maybe the baby came as soon as she arrived?'

DS Patel moved through the scan rapidly, examining the other pages.

'It's funny, that. There are no other names blocked out in that way. It's almost as if somebody wrote a name down and then decided it shouldn't be there.'

'Or,' Hollie suggested, mulling it over, 'that name might be somebody who we need to be speaking to in connection with

Sister Brennan's murder. Make me a copy, please, DS Patel. I know someone who can help us out. I'll bet Councillor Gilly Hodges will have something to say about that.'

THIRTY-FIVE

'You're with me, DS Anderson.'

'I am? Where are we going?'

'Shane Hardy. We're going to Hull Royal. We've just had a call to say he's in a fit state to interview.'

'I like a big shit before lunchtime. Looks like I'm getting what I wished for.'

Hollie gave him the benefit of the doubt. She assumed he was referring to Shane Hardy.

'Sort a pool car out, please. I'll finish off here and join you in the car park.'

'Righto, boss.'

There was something about the way he said *boss* that was winding her up. She'd dealt with old coppers like Anderson before. She knew his type. But this was different. He clearly thought she'd stolen a job from him that was rightfully his. Well, fuck him. She'd show him she was the better detective. Even though it didn't feel that way at the moment.

'Oh, Jenni, do you have a moment?'

DC Langdon was heading over to her desk, next to DS Patel's. She turned and smiled at Hollie.

'Is everything okay after yesterday?'

'Yes, honestly, it's not a problem. I was as right as rain when I woke up this morning. How about you? It was a bit of a shock what happened to Shane Hardy. I hope you're going to take him flowers and chocolates?' Jenni ventured a cheeky smile, and Hollie laughed.

'Let me know as soon as you've spoken to Mother Davies, all right? I suspect our victim has had an interesting past. I'll put money on it that she wasn't always a bride of Christ. Push her a bit, will you? Particularly about the tattoo and the self-harming scars. And I reckon Sister Kay knows more than she's letting on, too. See if you can turn up anything.'

'Will do!' Jenni promised as she turned and headed out of the door.

'DI Turner.'

It was DCI Osmond.

'Yes, DCI Osmond?'

'Are you happy with how things are progressing?'

'I think, bearing in mind how new the case is, it's going as well as can be expected. We need a suspect, though. The DCC is on my case about this. I don't know why she's taking such a personal interest. Do you know anything about DCC Warburton and Councillor Gilly Hodges? There doesn't seem to be much love lost between them. Not on the DCC's part, at least.'

Osmond shook his head. 'No, they've no history I'm aware of. But the DCC is adamant she doesn't want too much weight placed on what the councillor says.'

'What's your thinking, sir?'

'Keep your mind open. Gilly Hodges is a local woman who's lived here all her life. She knows everyone. By which I mean, she grew up alongside the great and the good. She'll have known many of them when they were kids. She'll remember stuff that goes way back. I know what the DCC said, but the case is more important than personal grudges. Just keep it on the QT.'

'Will do, sir.'

Osmond walked off. He was an odd man; she couldn't put her finger on it. It made sense he'd had mental health issues. There was a fragility about him as if he was still stress-testing his body to see how much it could withstand.

The journey over to Hull Royal was not at all relaxing. Anderson seemed oblivious to it, and he simply carried on as usual.

Hollie had always found time in the car useful with her own kids. There was something about sitting in the vehicle and chatting that made the children more forthcoming about what was going on in their lives. She had hoped the same would apply to DS Anderson.

'So, do you live in Hull?' Hollie began. It was as good a place to start the small talk as any.

'Beverley,' he answered. He was not nearly as attentive at the steering wheel as young Harry Gordon. 'I like to keep an arm's length from the clientele, if you know what I mean.'

'Any family?' she asked, then immediately scolded herself for the question. It was a comment laden with societal expectations, assuming he'd have a wife and kids at home. For all she knew, he might be gay. It was none of her business and she knew she shouldn't have asked.

'I live with my partner, Bruce—' he began.

She kept her poker face on and looked ahead at the road.

Anderson burst out laughing.

'Had you there, didn't I? Don't worry, I'm not one of them—'

Hollie bristled but said nothing. She had to be circumspect about how she dealt with this man. He could be poison to her.

'I'm divorced. I have one kid who won't talk to me. He reckons I'm a Neanderthal. My son goes on Pride marches and insists I use the pronouns *they* and *them*. I prefer to use the words *arsehole* and *prick*. To think he's half my genes. I blame my ex. All the shitty DNA came from her side.'

Hollie thought back to the tense conversation she'd had with Léon the night before. She didn't want to end up talking about him the way Anderson was talking about his former wife. She and Léon could do better than that. They had to, for the kids' sake. She checked her phone to see if Phoebe had confirmed the train times yet. She hadn't. It made her suddenly nervous that the trip wouldn't happen. Léon might still block it. She suppressed the wave of anger that rose at the thought of it.

'I'm as hackneyed as those cops you see on TV. Only, I don't have a drinking problem. In fact, I don't drink—'

Hollie turned to look at him.

'Didn't expect that, did you?' Anderson grinned. 'It's true. I never touch a drop. Everything about me is the middle-aged, world-weary cop. Only I still love the job. I've got the divorce and the estranged kid, but my liver remains in excellent shape.'

The drive to the hospital was quick, the morning traffic having cleared. They negotiated their way through the hospital's parking system, the reception desk, and the labyrinthine corridors until they finally found Shane Hardy's ward. A police constable was posted outside. He straightened up from a slouching position the moment he spotted them. It was a shared room with several other patients, of mixed ages. Shane saw them coming and leaned over to press the alarm to alert a nurse.

'Not so fast, sunshine,' Anderson said, pushing Shane's hand out of the way. His leg was in plaster, his right arm heavily bandaged. He had scratches and cuts all over his face.

'This is police intimidation—' Shane began.

'I hope you've come to give that kid a lethal injection,' said the man in the bed to the side of Shane's. 'He's been talking complete bollocks since he arrived in here.'

Anderson drew the curtains around the bed to give them what little privacy could be achieved in such a public place.

Hollie pulled up the high-backed chair at the bedside. Anderson looked around, then sat on the end of the bed. Shane flinched as the mattress sank under Anderson's weight.

'So, Shane, are you ready to tell us what was going on at Father Duffy's now?'

Hollie let her words hang for a moment.

'Fuck off, pig... urgh!'

Anderson had leant on his leg the moment the expletive was released.

'Sorry, Shane, my mistake.' Anderson smiled at him. 'But you are being very rude.'

It was some time since Hollie had seen an officer using tricks like that. She checked the curtain was properly closed. It was. It appeared to have calmed Shane down, and it was definitely borderline as to whether it had been a genuine mistake on Anderson's part. A lot of what he did seemed to be borderline. She gave DS Anderson the nod and he opened up the recording app on his mobile phone.

'Okay, okay.' Shane surrendered. 'Look, I'll tell you what I know then I want you to leave me alone, all right?'

'It depends on what you tell us,' Anderson replied, moving his hand close to Shane's leg.

'I want to know more about this man you saw on Father Duffy's landing,' Hollie started.

'I don't know him. His face was covered by that daft red cap,' Shane replied, his eyes on DS Anderson.

'Come on, Shane, you can do better than that,' Hollie urged. 'Bearing in mind you waved a knife at me yesterday, I was expecting a bit more effort from you. You need to convince me you had nothing to do with the assault on Father Duffy. I might even consider dropping the case against you for threatening a police officer. So, let's think again, shall we? What was this man's age? How was he dressed?'

The vacant look on Shane's face didn't hold out much promise.

'He was an old geezer. Your kind of age. His hair was going grey. He was wearing jeans and a shirt. He was just some bloke.'

'That doesn't help very much, does it, Shane? What colour was his shirt?'

'Blue, or grey, or a bit of both. It was one of them old man shirts with squares on it—'

'Okay, that's a bit better. What about his trousers?'

'They were jeans. You know, just normal jeans. They were blue if you didn't know that already.'

'What about his footwear?'

'Jeez, you bloody cops never stop, do you? He had trainers on. Cheap shite, I reckon – probably from Shoezone or some dump like that.'

How dare he knock Shoezone. She'd found many a last-minute pair of school shoes there when rushing to get the kids sorted out at the end of the summer holidays.

Shane's face suddenly changed, as if he'd just realised something. This is what Hollie reckoned indicated brain activity on Shane's part. They hadn't seen much of it so far.

'There was that woman,' he said.

'What woman?'

Anderson and Hollie asked the question at the same time.

'She was always visiting the priest. You'd see her walking with him sometimes when he went to the shops. They seemed to know each other. She was just driving away from the flats when we were larking around near the garages. I reckon she was paying him a visit. She doesn't live on the estate. It was an hour or two before we sprayed his door, mind you.'

'Come on, Shane, we need more than that,' Hollie urged.

Shane seemed to be reflecting. That must have been a first, she reckoned.

'She was older than you,' he began. 'Her clothes looked like she couldn't decide what her favourite colour was. She stood out a bit, if you know what I mean. She was a bit of a state.'

'Do you know her name?' Anderson asked. 'A name would help.'

'She's some interfering old cow from the council. She's a councillor, I think. Whatever they do. I don't know her name. But she knew the priest, that's for sure.'

'Can you describe her?'

'She looked like a bloke. She had one of those short haircuts that old women get sometimes to make them look like they're younger than they are.'

Hollie swiped her phone screen and typed a search term into the web browser.

'Is this her?' she asked, holding up the phone so Shane could see the photo she'd brought up on the city council website.

'Yeah, that's her. She looks like a lezza with that haircut. I don't know what she's called.'

Anderson looked at Hollie.

'Gilly Hodges,' she began. 'The woman you saw was Councillor Gilly Hodges.'

After wasting more time with Shane, they drove back to HQ. The information he'd given was scant, but it gave a couple of vague pointers.

On the drive back to HQ, it was one-on-one copper talk; Hollie's head was totally in the case.

'What do you know about Gilly Hodges?' she asked. 'I mean, how aware were you of her before all this happened?'

'Same as Shane, really. She's one of those gobby councillors you're aware of. You know, she's always being pictured in the local paper holding a big cheque at some charity event, that sort of thing. If there's something that needs opening, she's usually there. I don't know her particularly. And she was at the mother and baby home, too, as we've known since yesterday. That makes her a potential suspect, I guess.'

'Yes, we know she was at the home and that she despised Sister Brennan and the social worker. I didn't consider her a strong suspect when I spoke to her, but if she's spent time with the priest, I'm catching the whiff of a stink. When I spoke to her earlier, she didn't say that much about being pals with Father Duffy. We haven't issued a press release about the priest yet, but the media will pick it up at some point. We need to call her in or pay her another visit. I've primed her for it, I warned her we'd have follow-up questions. It just needs to be sooner rather than later. Like, today sooner—'

Hollie picked up her phone and reached DS Patel. She asked her to fix up a second visit to Gilly Hodges, reasoning she might be less hostile if she didn't drop in on her unannounced this time.

They exchanged details on the latest developments.

'DS Patel has some interesting updates on the rope, and the lorry driver has been released from the hospital,' Hollie relayed to Anderson. 'The DC who interviewed him said there's nothing new, just a middle-aged bloke who had his day ruined by a dead nun appearing in front of him on the road. Poor guy, I wonder if he'll ever drive again after that. It must have been one hell of a shock. He's not told us anything we didn't know already from Sunday night.'

Anderson said nothing, but she sensed him nodding at her side.

'What's your gut telling you?' Hollie asked. 'You know Hull better than I do. You've worked this patch. Who would kill a nun like that? Who would want to strangle the priest?'

'I'm more concerned about who might be killed next,' Anderson replied.

'Meaning what?'

'We know this much. This has to be connected with the Church of St Mary and the Angels. As we agreed at the briefing, there are a lot of people who are well within their rights to hold a grudge against that place. They took babies from young mothers for Christ's sake. This job has hardened me like a bucket of concrete, but even I can see how that would screw up your life. Imagine carrying all that anger. And what about the kids who were taken? You'd be pretty messed up by that, wouldn't you?'

Hollie pictured Isabelle again. It hurt too much to go there.

'We need to find out who worked there and get to them before the killer does. If you asked me to guess, I'd say someone with a grudge is working their way through the personnel file. It's like someone has a vendetta. We need to get a handle on who was running that place. I'd say this social worker might also be at risk.'

Hollie activated her phone screen and dialled the office again. Anderson looked interested as she conducted the call.

'DS Patel, I need the search for Patrick McCready to move up the priority list. Where are we up to with him?'

'We've got his home address and a couple of DCs have knocked on the door, boss. He's been out every time.'

'Can we get a phone number for him?'

She could tell from the pause on the end of the line what the answer was going to be.

'He's a difficult man to track down. There's no social media, the neighbours say he disappears for several weeks at a time, but there's no trace of him.'

'If you haven't already, try and track him through the council, see if they have a number for him. He may be at risk and he's sure as hell a person of interest in this investigation.'

'I'll get onto it, boss.'

Hollie sighed as she put the phone down.

'What is it?' Anderson asked.

'Patrick McCready is the invisible man. And Father Duffy is still out cold. I wish the priest would come around. They're always out cold when you need them most.'

DS Anderson smiled.

'You'll be asking them to resurrect the dead nun next,' he added.

'Well, bearing in mind what she did as a vocation, it shouldn't be too hard with a word in the right place.'

They shared the joke and returned to silence.

'You know DCC Warburton better than I do. What's she like?'

It was unusual for a DCC to stick her nose in over someone like Gilly Hodges. Hollie was keen to know why.

Anderson shrugged.

'She's a bit of a cold fish, but then aren't all the brass? She's relatively new. She transferred from a different force, much like you. I think the chief has an appetite for some new ideas. They're appointing from outside the force rather than from within. Which is why all the old buggers like me are left circling the few promotions that come up, like aeroplanes waiting to land.'

Hollie let that one hang in the air. She wasn't taking the bait. Considering him as a copper, she quite liked this man. It was just the personal stuff she was still getting to grips with.

'She knows the city of old, though, so the office gossip says. Not as a copper. She lived here once before, I think.'

It wasn't much to go on. They were back at HQ, and Anderson dropped Hollie at the entrance to the building and went off to park the car.

Hollie headed to the kitchen before checking on DS Patel. Her phone sounded as the kettle clicked off. It was Léon. She wanted to keep things civil. If she didn't, she'd end up like DS Anderson.

Hollie composed herself and picked up.

'Léon, hi.'

'I've had Phoebe on trying to make arrangements to pick up the kids. I'm not comfortable with this arrangement, Hollie. I don't want them to come to Hull.'

'I could do without this now, Léon, can't you just throw me a rope here?'

'I don't know Phoebe very well. How responsible is she?'

'I don't know Veronique at all; how responsible is she?'

'Piss off, Hollie, you know what I mean. She's still a teenager—'

'She's nineteen. Léon. That makes her an adult—'

'You're not an adult at nineteen—'

'I was nineteen when I fell pregnant with Izzy.'

Léon mumbled at the end of the phone.

'Yeah, and look how well that's going.'

'What do you mean by that?'

He'd hit a soft spot. A rage surged inside her. She knew it was no good falling out on the phone, but she refused to let it slide.

'That's a bit shitty, Léon. We're talking about the girl you raised as your own for years.'

'Yes, which means I know her as well as you do. And you drove her out of the house. She was so desperate to get away, she's gone to the other side of the world, so she doesn't have to deal with you.'

'You didn't have to say that, Léon. Don't you think I reflect on that every day?'

She felt him soften at the end of the line; it was a short intake of breath he'd always take when he knew he'd gone too far and was stopping himself before he hurt her anymore.

Perhaps he still cared if he was bothered enough not to give the knife a final twist.

'Please, Léon, I need this right now. Phoebe is totally responsible and it's too good an opportunity to miss. I don't know when I'll see the children next if I don't see them when Phoebe comes.'

There was silence at the end of the phone.

'I'll think about it,' he said. 'I'll let you know.'

THIRTY-SIX

'I know my browser history looks like I've been looking for Christmas presents, but it's good, honest police work, I swear.'

Hollie peered over at DS Patel's screen. There were several tabs open which related to outdoor activity equipment.

'It looks more like you're working through Bear Grylls's shopping list,' Hollie observed. 'I take it this relates to the rope?'

'Yes, boss. I never knew rope could be so technical. You might want to put a hard hat on, I'm going to bore you with some science.'

DS Patel opened up a digital image of a length of blood-stained rope.

Hollie grimaced.

'It never gets any easier to look at, does it?'

'It's horrible, boss. This is a close-up of the rope that was used to throw Sophia Brennan off the side of the bridge. I've been comparing it with other ropes online. Don't judge me, but I started on Amazon – you can make the pictures nice and big on their website—'

DS Patel clicked on the Amazon tab and demonstrated what she'd been looking at.

'I soon realised that the ropes are different, and they're made from a variety of materials,' she continued.

'Go on,' Hollie encouraged her. 'I'm finding this much more entertaining than I should. I need to get myself some new hobbies.'

'Get ready to have your mind blown then. There are dynamic ropes and static ropes—'

'You should go on *Mastermind*. I'm impressed.'

'Dynamic ropes have some give – or stretch – in them.'

A joke about knicker elastic was on the tip of her tongue, but Hollie restrained herself. Professional credibility first, the gags could come later.

'However, static ropes are not supposed to have much give in them. Are you following me so far?'

'Yes, I'm assuming this is all leading somewhere useful?'

'It is. Next, I checked the manufacturing materials. Polyester is used for static ropes, because it has low stretch, whereas nylon is strong and stretchy, so makes better dynamic ropes.'

'I feel like I'm waiting for a magician to pull something out of his sleeve.'

'Take a closer look at that photograph again, ma'am. What's that made of?'

'Is this a test? I feel under pressure now. That's nylon, isn't it?'

'Yes, nylon. Dynamic rope. Which means it's used for climbing.'

'How do we know it's not used in boating?'

'Well, I think the saltwater angle threw us off the scent. It's not out of the question that somebody with a very light craft, or an amateur, might use a dynamic rope to tie up a boat.'

'This is good research, DS Patel, well done—'

'I've got more, ma'am. Do you see the flecks in the rope? That's pretty distinctive, isn't it? I started hunting for similar ropes on various websites. I found a few, too. Take a look at this. What do you think?'

DS Patel opened up an image that she'd saved to her PC, then moved it so it was side-by-side with the image of the rope that was used to suspend the victim from the bridge.

'That's an exact match, isn't it?' Hollie checked.

'I'd say so. The rope the crime scene guys retrieved is well used, and there is some blood residue on it. But I'd say that's a match, wouldn't you?'

'I'm impressed, DS Patel, that's a great use of the internet. Where is it sold?'

'Nowhere that I can find locally, I'm afraid. And not on Amazon. It appears to be a bit more specialist than your average length of climbing rope—'

'What about the saltwater?'

'I thought you might ask that.' DS Patel smiled. She clicked on a website tab which showed numerous photographs of climbers attached to ropes hanging from sea cliffs.

'Ta-dah! Climbing rope and saltwater.'

'Brilliant, make sure you share this with the rest of the team. Great work, DS Patel, keep it up.'

The phone rang at her desk. Hollie waited while her colleague dealt with the call. She watched as Patel scrawled some notes on her pad.

'Good news, boss. Father Duffy has come round and is talking. The hospital called to say we can speak to him now, so long as we keep it short and sharp.'

'Thank God, something positive at last. I'll go and see him now. I'm going to be on first name terms with the staff there at this rate. I'll use my own car, no need to book one out. Have you got a ward number for him?'

'I'll give you the info the hospital handed over. I'll text it to you.'

'Oh, by the way, how are you getting on with that list from the mother and baby home?'

'It's vast, boss. There are so many names. It's difficult to know where to start.'

'Well, you've got DC Langdon for as long as it takes for me to see her walking properly on that sore ankle of hers, despite what she keeps telling me about being fully recovered. That should help to cut through it a bit faster. Oh, and start with Sister Brennan's years at the home and work out from there. In fact, photocopy that list of names for me around 1975 when Gilly was in the mother and baby home. I want to speak to her about that when I pay her that second house call.'

Hollie took a moment to scan the incident room; everybody was on the phone, examining CCTV images, scanning photocopies of newspaper articles and any number of other tasks which formed the backbone of an investigation. She wanted to chat with the priest herself. DS Patel handed over the photocopy of the list and sent the text with Father Duffy's ward information.

Hollie stepped out into the car park and pointed her key fob at her car. It was raining. She wasn't dressed for it; she only had a light coat on. She stepped into her car and took out her phone. It was a message from Léon, in a more conciliatory tone.

> OK, it's all sorted with Phoebe. But no more than three days. I've got in touch with a family mediator in Lancaster too. We need to work out the details.

She was angry with herself for even considering a three-day visit from her own children to be a victory, but she exhaled in relief. It would be good to see the kids. It would be even better if she cleared up the case before their visit and the pressure cooker environment eased a bit. She tapped into her phone, erasing the first few messages she typed because she considered them to be too passive-aggressive.

Great. Thanks Léon. Can't wait to see them.

That's what their marriage had come to. Visits from children resembled hostage exchanges. There was the looming threat of family mediation. Hollie wondered if they'd be better off sorting out the finer details with a cage fight. She still loved Léon, which was the hardest part. They were on different tracks. He was imagining a new future with his younger French lover, but she was still scrambling to catch up.

THIRTY-SEVEN

Hollie drove back over to Hull Royal Infirmary with a mind buzzing from the case. They'd got some names to be working with now, and they needed to speak to everybody in the photo ASAP. She also wanted to hear what Father Duffy had to say about it; there was nothing like an old photograph to jog a reluctant memory.

She hit the jackpot by finding a parking space after only two circuits of the car park. The rain had upped its game and she was wet by the time she stepped into the hospital foyer. She checked DS Patel's note and repeated the ward details to herself a couple of times. The woman at the reception desk gave her directions, but Hollie was unable to retain them, having no source of reference in the building. It had been easier getting to Shane's ward; it had helped that DS Anderson was so well acquainted with the building after so many years working in the city.

Fifteen minutes later, after an informative but frustrating tour of the hospital's upper floors, she found Father Duffy's room, with a single police officer parked outside, just like at Shane's ward. He looked bored out of his mind but became lively and alert the moment he saw Hollie making her way along the corridor. She didn't know the PC, so she guessed he'd seen her on the TV briefing.

She checked in at the nursing station and showed her ID to the officer; it didn't seem like he was primed to ask her for it. Hollie tapped at the door, then stepped inside.

Father Duffy looked frail. She saw the markings around his neck straight off and they now seemed worse than when they'd found him lying on the floor. His hair was silver-grey, his eyes pallid, and the skin on his face looked like it was hanging on for dear life. It was shocking to see such an old man so bruised and badly grazed after his ordeal. It was a wonder he had survived the attack. She drew in a breath and got her head in the zone to question him. Surely he'd have something useful to offer them?

'Good afternoon, Father Duffy. I'm DI Turner,' she began.

Father Duffy began to reply, but his mouth was apparently so dry he could barely manage to get his words out. Hollie pulled up the chair at the bedside, noting the electronic beeps from the medical monitoring machines punctuating the silence in the room. She was facing him, her back to the door. There was a plastic cup filled with water on the bedside table. She lifted it up. Seeing him make no effort to take it from her, she held it to his mouth and let him drink.

'That's better,' he croaked. 'The nurses leave you so long in here. I'd rather be in a ward where I have some company.'

'Well, you're here for your own safety, Father Duffy. You've had a nasty shock, too. I'm here to ask you some questions about what happened. Is that okay?'

He nodded.

A nurse entered the room.

'Is everything all right, Father Duffy?' she asked.

She was officious and marking her territory. Hollie's presence was being tolerated rather than welcomed.

Father Duffy hadn't had time to answer properly before

she'd given the monitoring machine a quick once-over and topped up his cup from the jug at its side.

'Be brief, please, detective. Father Duffy has had a shock. I don't want him put under any strain.'

Hollie gave some reassurances, and the nurse left the room. Hollie opened up the recording app on her phone and explained to the priest what she was doing.

'I want to talk to you about Shane Hardy, Father Duffy. What can you tell me about him?'

'He's one of the ne'er-do-wells on the estate.'

Hollie moved closer. It was difficult to hear him; his voice was weak and reedy.

'He's got it into his head I'm some kind of child abuser.'

'Has he ever hurt you or threatened you?'

Father Duffy shook his head.

'He calls out to me when I'm walking to the shops, and they sprayed those words on my door. When was it now? Was it yesterday or the day before? How long have I been in here?'

'It was yesterday. My colleague and I found you in your flat. Do you know who tried to kill you? Did you get a look at them?'

Father Duffy looked down. Hollie wasn't sure if he'd fallen asleep on her. Moments later, he looked up again.

'I've been thinking about this a lot,' he began. 'And I'm certain of it. There were two people in my flat. And I'm as sure as I can be that neither of them was Shane Hardy.'

'So, let me get this straight. You're certain Shane Hardy did not break into your flat. Is that correct?'

He seemed to be working something over in his mind. She couldn't tell if he was trying to figure out what happened or coming up with some off the cuff nonsense to throw her off the scent. The old man's act was beginning to wear a bit thin.

She thought back to Shane's comment about the man with the red cap. He'd come out of the lift as Shane and his mates were making their escape down the stairs.

Somewhere in that cloud of confusion – or obfuscation – was a clue, and she was desperate to find it.

'Do you recall a man wearing a red cap?'

Father Duffy hesitated before he answered.

'Perhaps.' He struggled. 'It was all a blur. I opened the door with my walking stick in my hand, ready to shake it at those yobbos and chase them away. There was nobody there when I opened the door. As I was closing it, somebody pushed it open, and I fell against the wall. They put something around my neck and began to pull at it. It was a belt or something like that, I think. They were strong, I can tell you that.'

Father Duffy took another sip of water, reaching for it himself this time.

'Yes, he was wearing a red cap. And a blue and grey chequer shirt. Oh, and jeans and trainers, rather than slacks and shoes. He was an older man, I think.'

Shane deserved a medal for his observational skills; he'd actually got it right. But perhaps that meant Shane was involved in some way; perhaps his description was so good because he knew this man.

'How old? Did he say anything to you?'

'I was a bit preoccupied at the time. Fifties, I'd say. He was angry, I know that.'

'Any idea why?'

Father Duffy's head sank.

'Father Duffy, do you have any idea why somebody might want to kill you?'

He shook his head. He had a look of regret in his eyes.

'I'm an old man now, DI Turner,' he started. 'I've had a long life and the world has changed around me, sometimes for the better and sometimes for the worse. Have you done things in your life that you regret?'

Hollie could think of one or two off the top of her head. There were probably a couple of people out there, in jail, who wouldn't mind doing her some harm. But she was a copper, not a priest.

She gave a noncommittal nod.

'Some things happened at the Church of St Mary and the Angels which I'm not so proud of now. The world has changed. You have to remember that. What was right back then is not right now. I could have, perhaps, shown a little more forgiveness.'

'What do you mean by that?'

The old man needed a nudge. It was a bit like shoving coins along in the Penny Falls, only they were all bunched up with lots of promise, but none of them were dropping where she could make use of them.

'Everybody keeps telling me things weren't quite right at the mother and baby home, but you're all scant on detail. I'm not a mind reader, Father Duffy, I work with facts.'

'Not everybody had sympathy with the young mothers in the home,' he continued, looking like he'd just been chastised.

Father Duffy appeared to be choosing his words carefully.

'Many of them were very young, all of them came to us pregnant. The world is much more sympathetic now than it was then. Many people did not like how we were helping those young ladies. I think, perhaps, I was too hasty to judge back then. I regret that now.'

'Why were you hasty to judge?'

'I might have given those girls a little more sympathy. Don't get me wrong, I was never unkind. But they were often shunned by their families and all alone. I should have been more understanding, I can see that now.'

'What can you tell me about Sister Sophia Brennan?'

The priest tensed and his right hand began to shake.

'Well, she's a dear friend and a dedicated servant of the Lord.'

The priest didn't seem to know she was dead. Perhaps

nobody had told him. Either that or he'd forgotten what happened to her. She hesitated a moment, uncertain of whether to break the news or not. All she needed was to have him distracted. He'd just survived a massive shock. She decided to break the news. It would be tough on the old man, but she wanted to see his reaction.

'I'm sorry to tell you, Father Duffy, that Sister Sophia Brennan died on Sunday night—'

'Oh.'

She'd expected a little more than that.

'She was the victim of a murder. We suspect the same person – or persons – tried to kill you.'

'Poor Sophia. She didn't deserve that.'

Hollie knew a retired priest would have been exposed to death during his career in the Church, but she'd expected something different. She wasn't sure what, but it didn't feel right.

'How do you feel about that?'

He paused and then made a big deal out of taking another sip of water.

'It's very sad. But we're all getting very old now, detective.'

While she felt Father Duffy couldn't possibly have killed the nun, she'd expected a bit more emotion. Perhaps he was in shock.

'Is there anything Sister Brennan might regret in her life?'

For the first time, Hollie noticed a little colour in Father Duffy's cheeks.

'Only human frailties, I'm sure,' he replied. 'She devoted her life to the Church.'

'Sister Brennan had a small tattoo on her arm, and some scratch marks on her lower arms. What do you know about her past life, before she was a nun?'

He shook his head.

'Very little, I'm afraid. She was very damaged when she came to us, and very vulnerable. But with our help, she salvaged her life. She never spoke about where she came from or what happened to her before she found the Church. She was fiercely private about that part of her life.'

'Do you have any idea why somebody might want to harm you or why someone would want to harm her?'

'It must be because of our work at the Church of St Mary and the Angels. Most of the girls were distraught when their babies were taken. Some of the parents were very upset, too. And then there were the boyfriends and partners. But I honestly thought we were doing good and that it was for the best. Now, I'm not so sure. If I've done any wrong in my life, I'll soon find out what God thinks of me.'

'I need more than that. What wrong have you done in your life? And might it have come back to bite all these years later?'

'I just mean that there were a lot of mixed emotions in that mother and baby unit. Not everybody saw things the way the Church did. I'm certain some people might feel... angry or hostile, even after all these years.'

'Did you ever wonder if people might want revenge?'

'Perhaps. They were emotional times.'

'Why would someone wait all these years, though?'

'I suppose someone might. Perhaps someone who'd found out what happened later in life.'

'Anybody in particular you can think of?'

'No. Nobody in particular.'

'What about Patrick McCready?'

His face froze at the mention of that name. It was momentary, but enough for Hollie to notice.

'We worked together a long time ago.'

'Is he still alive?'

'I'm sure he is.'

'Does he live locally?'

'He travels abroad a lot... I think. He may be in Hull; he may be elsewhere.'

Hollie was in danger of throttling him herself. She moved on, that line of questioning clearly going nowhere.

'You said there was a second person in your flat?'

'Yes, I think so. I was confused. It might not have been in my flat.'

Hollie was alert again. Father Duffy thought it over.

'Yes, that's right. I remember hearing some activity out on the landing. I thought I was about to pass out. It was the nice lady with the child in the next flat. I think she'd heard something and was coming to investigate. Whatever it was, it must have disturbed the person who was trying to hurt me. They removed whatever was around my neck and pulled me into the living room. They picked me up and pushed my head into the fish tank.'

'How did you get away? Were they disturbed?'

'I sank to my knees and played dead.'

'Really?'

'Yes. I was almost passing out already. But as my head was thrust into the fish tank, I took a deep breath and held it in. After a short while, I let my legs collapse and slid to the floor. They left after that.'

'And the woman inside your flat? Who was she?'

'I thought it was Councillor Hodges at first—'

'Gilly Hodges?'

'Yes, she visits me sometimes. I thought it was her, but it wasn't. It was a man, I'm sure of that. I used to know Gillian in the old days, of course. She was just a young girl back then. A sparky thing she was. Still is, actually.'

'Why does she visit you?'

'I helped her to find her son. In fact, her son found me first. I was able to track her down because she's a councillor and she was easy to find. They were reunited. It made me feel like I was doing some good again. She was so happy when she found him. We kept in touch.'

'Does Councillor Hodges's son live locally?'

'Yes, he never left the city. I don't know what he does for a living.'

Hollie put her hand in her pocket to draw out her phone. It was time to give the priest's memory a helping hand and show him the picture of the four girls.

'What do you know about her son?' Hollie continued.

'He's a nice lad—'

The nurse returned to check over Father Duffy.

'His pulse is racing. What on earth have you been doing to him?' she asked impatiently.

'Is he all right? I've just been asking some questions. He has had a bit of a shock, I'm afraid. I had to break some sad news.'

'He'll be fine, but he needs some rest,' the nurse answered. Hollie was clearly an annoyance to her.

It was time to try him on the photo of the four girls. She located the sharpest picture from the batch.

'Do you know these girls?' Hollie asked Father Duffy as she handed him her phone. 'And if so, might one of them have a motive to kill Sister Brennan?'

'I need my glasses,' he replied. He was becoming more flustered by the minute.

The nurse was hovering, watching what was going on.

Hollie handed Father Duffy her phone.

'I don't know if I can do this—' he stuttered.

The monitoring machine made a beep, and the nurse checked the console.

'I'm going to have to ask you to let Father Duffy rest now,' the nurse warned.

'Just a couple more questions, please?' Hollie urged.

The nurse tutted, but Hollie pushed on.

'You know that's Gilly Hodges, right? Even I can see that. What about the other girls? Can you confirm their names or tell me anything about them?'

'Okay, that's enough now,' the nurse said. 'You can chat to Father Duffy again tomorrow morning. Get one of your officers to call in at the nurse's station and we'll let you know if he's okay to receive visitors.'

'But—' Hollie began to protest.

'It won't look good if you kill the old man, will it?' the nurse whispered to her. 'He needs his rest. I'm sorry. I know it's frustrating, but he's an elderly gentleman who's had a huge shock.'

Hollie exhaled. The nurse was right. Sometimes witnesses and suspects couldn't work to the police timeline. It was as frustrating as hell, but she did not want a priest's death to deal with alongside the complaint from Shane.

'Okay, okay, fine.'

Hollie could have screamed. The pressure of the DCC breathing down her neck was weighing on her.

She held up her phone again.

'Take a good look at that picture, please, and try to remember the names of those girls. I'll send an officer around to speak to you tomorrow morning. It would really help us if you could remember—'

'Officer!' the nurse snapped.

Hollie returned her phone to her pocket.

'I'm so sorry you had to hear about Sister Brennan like that,' she said.

'Do you detectives never get the message? I'd like you to leave the room now, thank you.'

'I can always make this a formal interview, you know,' Hollie threatened, immediately wishing she'd kept her mouth shut.

'Knock yourself out, officer. But patient welfare trumps that for now.'

Hollie apologised to the nurse and made her exit, feeling a little ashamed of her attempt at rank-pulling. She walked along the corridor to find a spot to tuck herself out of the way. She called the incident room and asked to be handed over to DS Patel once again.

'Are you heading back to the office after you've called in on Gilly Hodges?' DS Patel asked. 'Or, God forbid, going home at a half-reasonable time? We've got flash flood warnings on the roads and flood warnings in the lower River Hull area, too. It's chucking it down. Have you seen?'

'I'm just about to head into it now. I'll be back in the office tomorrow for the briefing. I suspect I won't make it back tonight. Email me over anything new I need to look at overnight.'

'Will do, boss. Mind how you go out there.'

Hollie could hear the rain smashing against the hospital windows. There was no way she would make it back to her car without getting drenched. It had grown dark, too, in the time she'd been speaking to Father Duffy.

She headed down to the ground floor and waited at the entrance to brace herself for a dash. The large raindrops struck the car park's asphalt, bouncing straight up again, creating a blur of spray. She found her car keys, placed her finger on the remote button, and then ran for it. By the time she reached her vehicle, she was dripping wet. Her hair stuck to her face, her feet were soaked through, and her clothes were heavy. She pulled the car door shut and used her hands to wipe the water away from her face. The words drowned rat came to mind. But there was one more call she wanted to make before calling it a day. One woman's name kept cropping up again and again: Gilly Hodges. It was time to make that second house call.

THIRTY-EIGHT

Hollie was pushing Gilly's patience making two visits in one day, but she couldn't wait until tomorrow, and it was an easy detour to make on her way home. Besides, DS Patel had rung ahead this time.

The weather was no better by the time she reached Gilly's house on Victoria Dock. Hollie knew the city had flooded badly in 2007 but couldn't recall which areas had been affected. Being so close to the estuary, she figured the modern development on Victoria Dock must have borne the brunt. She wondered how many nervous residents were anxiously looking out of their windows that night.

It was fully dark by the time she reached Gilly's house. From her parking spot on the road, she could see the towering, illuminated structure of the city's floodgate up ahead. Somehow it seemed more imposing at night.

Her clothes had absorbed so much rainwater already that they were heavy and clammy against her skin. As she stepped out, she thought she caught a movement over by the small play area opposite Gilly's house. Something made her pause for a moment. She couldn't see anything; it was probably just a dog walker. In weather like this, they deserved her sympathy rather than her suspicion. She ran up to Gilly's front door and rang the doorbell. She heard movement inside the house, and then the door opened.

She was pleased Gilly seemed to be a little more forthcoming when she answered the door. She still didn't know what to make of the woman. Perhaps she herself might have been evasive if questioned about the circumstances surrounding Isabella's birth. It was more than two decades ago, and she'd put it all behind her. She'd be prickly if someone wanted to rake over the past.

'Hello, Gilly. It's DI Hollie Turner under this bedraggled hair. May I come in?'

Gilly gave her the once-over.

'You look drenched, DI Turner. Come on in. I'll get you a towel from upstairs.'

Gilly left Hollie standing on the length of carpet that extended along her hallway. It gave Hollie a moment or two to snoop, unobserved. She peeled off her wet shoes and looked around. There was a photo on the wall, a large one, of Gilly and a man who looked like he was in his forties or fifties. She'd missed it the previous day. Hollie did the maths in her head. It must be the son. They looked delighted to be in each other's company. Hollie couldn't bear to consider the prospect of being separated from her own children. It was bad enough the two youngest being in Lancaster and Izzy... well, who knew where Izzy was? She was glad Father Duffy had been able to reunite Gilly with her child.

'Here you are,' Gilly said as she walked down the stairs. 'I'm not being rude, but I'll put a blanket down on one of the armchairs so you can sit down. Something has got to absorb all that moisture.'

Gilly walked Hollie through to the living room.

'Take a seat. I'll get the kettle on. You do want a drink, I take it?'

Hollie sat on the blanketed armchair, grateful for this sanctuary. Gilly returned with a cup of hot chocolate.

'You're not vegan or anything, are you?' she asked.

'Not a chance when there's a hot chocolate on offer.' Hollie smiled.

The living room curtains were still open, and Hollie caught a shadow cast across the living room wall from out on the street. The rain was still beating against Gilly's window.

'You didn't tell me you were pals with Father Duffy,' Hollie called through to the kitchen.

'To be fair, you didn't ask me,' Gilly said, poking her head through the doorway. 'Why, is it a problem?'

'I didn't realise you made social calls after he helped you to find your son. That's him in the photograph in the hallway, I assume.'

'I'd prefer it if you didn't snoop in my house, DI Turner.'

'I saw it while I was waiting.'

Gilly sighed.

Hollie took out her phone to start recording.

'Yes, that's my son. Father Duffy helped us reunite. I see him occasionally. I have mixed feelings about Father Duffy, but he was never cruel to us. And if it wasn't for him, I might never have seen my boy again. So call it begrudging gratitude if you must.'

Hollie pulled out a folded sheet of paper from her pocket. She'd still got the items in there that she'd picked up from her doormat the previous night. It was all damp from the rain.

'I'd like you to take a look at this list if you would,' Hollie said, unfolding the photocopy that DS Patel had given her. Gilly found her reading glasses and studied it.

'This is old,' was her first response. 'Look at that neat handwriting, you don't see that very often these days—'

She stopped.

'What is it?' Hollie asked.

Gilly seemed choked up.

'Where did you find this?'

'The local council dug it up in their records. You've seen your name, I assume?'

'Yes. Look at us all there; Mandy, Violet, Theresa... those other girls were either coming or going by the time I arrived. They've written my name as Gillian. My God, it's like travelling back in time.'

'Have you any idea who that blanked-out name might belong to?'

'Not a clue,' Gilly responded, perhaps a little too quickly.

'Think about it,' Hollie urged. 'I know it's a long time ago. Who might that have been? Was there a girl who came and went? Perhaps her baby came on the day she arrived, something like that?'

Gilly looked back at the old picture on the wall. She'd hung it back on its hook after Hollie's previous visit.

'There's an innocence about that picture that I love. We looked after each other. That's all we had back then. We were so isolated in that home, it was horrible.'

She continued looking at the picture, her mind seeming to be distracted by the memory of it.

'Unless—'

'Go on,' Hollie urged.

'The girl who took that photograph. It might be her.'

'Do you recall her name?'

'I was seventeen by the time, detective. Do you remember what happened almost half a century ago? You're not even fifty yet, are you?'

'If you can't remember her name, what can you tell me about her?'

'She kept herself to herself. She was very young, probably about Mandy's kind of age—'

'How old was Mandy?'

'Sixteen years old when she had the baby, but only just. She was fifteen when she got pregnant. Still a child.'

Hollie thought how common it was to see young girls pushing babies in prams. Modern-day teenagers seemed so much more sophisticated than the girls in that photo, and it was sometimes difficult to remember that they were only kids.

'Why might her name have been blanked out?'

'She was the daughter of someone important, I think. I'm guessing they didn't want her name in that book. Until you showed me that photocopy just now, I'd never seen that before. I reckon anybody on that list might want Sister Brennan dead. Good luck in finding your killer!'

Hollie was distracted by the shadow again. It was coming and going as it was cast against the living room wall. She got up and walked slowly over to the window ledge, peering outside but attempting to keep herself concealed.

'Is anything wrong?' Gilly asked.

'I think you might have somebody lurking outside near my car.'

'It'll just be dog walkers or teenagers. Probably dog walkers on a night like this. They let their dogs crap over there on the green patch next to the park. I sometimes run out there and challenge them if I see them doing it and not bagging up. Not tonight though. Their dogs can have a free shit on me. I'm not going out in that rain.'

'I'm not so sure,' Hollie replied. 'Have you had any trouble since Sister Brennan died? Has anybody reached out to you?'

Gilly's face was blank.

'No. But I'm a local councillor, so I'm not hard to find. My home address is on the council's website. If anybody came looking, I'd be the easiest to locate.'

A loud thump rattled the front door. Hollie jumped at the force of it. The shadow moved away from the house, disappearing from Gilly's wall.

'What on earth was that?'

Hollie didn't answer. She was already halfway over to the living room door. She entered the hallway, where her shoes had been discarded on the doormat. An envelope had been thrust through the letterbox.

'You've had a visitor,' Hollie said, grabbing at her shoes and cursing that they weren't still on her feet.

'Where are you going?' Gilly asked. She seemed alarmed at Hollie's sudden movements. She picked up the envelope and studied it. There was something small and hard inside.

'It's got your name written on it—'

Gilly put her hand in the envelope and pulled out a cheap mobile phone.

'I'm going to check who's out there—'

Hollie forced her feet into her sodden shoes. She grasped the door handle and looked out into the night. Leaving the door wide open, she ran along the path so she could look up and down Gilly's road.

To the right, it was all quiet. But to the left, making his way towards the cycle path on foot at some speed, was a man who clearly had no intention of hanging around for a pleasant doorstep chat.

THIRTY-NINE

'You can't go out there,' Gilly called to her.

'I don't have a choice,' Hollie shouted out, the rain whipping against her face. She glanced back briefly to see Gilly examining the envelope from the shelter of her doorway.

For one moment, she considered calling for backup. In the time that it would take her to put a call through, he'd be well away, and she'd stand no chance of catching him. No, it was only early evening, the area was well-lit, she'd chance it. It wasn't as if they were in an unpopulated area.

Hollie hadn't a clue where he was leading her. Victoria Dock was still being built when she was a student in the city, and she'd had no cause to be in that part of town. The cycle lane was lit, at least, and the well-lit floodgate was nearby. If her geography was serving her correctly, they'd be coming out close to Myton Bridge.

To the right of her were bushes, and to the left, more open ground. The man was staying on the pathway. He looked like he knew where he was going. Up ahead were some iron posts to prevent cars from taking a cheeky shortcut out of the estate. The path curved after the posts, and she lost sight of him.

'Bugger it!' she cursed, pushing herself harder to keep up with him. She reached the end of the path. She'd expected it to bring her out alongside the flyover, but she was wrong. They were below it. To her left was some rough parking ground. A couple of campervans looked like they might have been pitched there overnight. It was open ground that way. She didn't think he'd have run in that direction. Directly ahead of her, in the distance, was the tidal barrier. He had to have run towards the flyover. It was the only option that made any sense. There were bushes and overgrown brambles to the right of the path; he'd be a brave man to hide in there.

Hollie ran towards the thick concrete pillars which supported the flyover, the traffic thundering overhead. As she ducked under the bridge, it gave her blessed relief from the rain. It was dark there, and the concrete structure extended quite a way out to her right. Some cars were parked there. Was he hiding among them, or had he run ahead?

She scanned the area ahead of the bridge. He wasn't that far in front when she'd started chasing him. He couldn't possibly have got away from her. She took a chance and veered right, taking the path that provided gate access to the small parking area. She wasn't moving as fast as she wanted to, her sodden clothes preventing her from progressing at any kind of pace.

Then Hollie spotted the giveaway. Whoever this man was, he had also got a soaking in the fierce rainfall. He'd left a trail along the canopied ground underneath the flyover. Hollie took out her phone and switched on its torch. Although the bridge area benefited from street lighting on either side of it, there was still much in shadow underneath. Hollie realised how vulnerable she was at that moment. If it had been Jenni Langdon in the same situation, she'd have given the young detective a good dressing-down. It still wasn't late, just dark and overcast, and there should still be people around at that time of night. Though she couldn't actually see any at that precise moment.

'I know you're there,' she shouted out. There was a touch of an echo, not much, and underneath the flyover the traffic was muted, more of a dull rumble. She shone her torch into the distance, but it wasn't much use. She heard a foot crunching on gravel.

'I just want to talk. Please, we don't have to go to the police station.'

'Are you all right, luv?' came a voice behind her. It was a man heading towards a white van just up ahead.

Hollie pulled her ID out of her pocket.

'When you go, will you point your headlamps over the far end so I can get a good look?'

'Are you sure you're all right down here on your own? Aren't you guys supposed to call for backup?'

'Something like that,' she answered. 'But right now, you can help me to flush someone out. I'm not in danger, I promise.'

'If you say so, luv.'

The bit about being in danger was a guess, but the man was running, he didn't look like he was going to attack her. She had to rely on her instincts. She thought about the kids; she had no intentions of leaving them without a mother. There were still people around – if it looked like she might be exposed, she'd call for backup.

The van driver started the engine, gave her the thumbs up, and then switched his headlamps on full beam. He floored the accelerator, spinning the van around. The beam swept across the car park and illuminated right up to the far end.

Hollie was dazzled momentarily, but she caught a shadow at the tail-end of one of the cars parked behind the second row of pillars. The van driver exited the car park behind her, but Hollie kept her gaze directly ahead, blinking away the multi-coloured array of flashes from her eyes.

'I know you're there,' she called out again, hoping he'd stay still long enough for her to regain normal vision. He didn't. He made a sudden rush for it but seemed to instantly realise his mistake. The far side of the car park was lined by a sturdy wire fence, about five or six feet high. He tried to scale it, jumping up and attempting to pull himself over, but he couldn't do it. Hollie slipped her phone into her pocket and ran at him. He was making a second attempt at pulling himself over the fence, but he still couldn't manage it. There was a lower wooden barrier just inside the wire fence, and he'd worked out that if he stood on it, it would give him the clearance to leap over to the other side. Hollie saw what he was doing and grasped at his right leg before he could raise his left one. The two of them crashed to the ground, the man falling on Hollie and knocking the wind out of her. She gasped for breath.

The man had pulled up a snood to conceal his face, and she reached out for it, desperate to get a full view of him. She could see he was an older man now; this was no youngster. He seemed reasonably fit, but he clearly did not have endless supplies of energy. He pulled himself up off the floor, Hollie still dazed by the weight of him falling on top of her.

'Are you all right?' he asked, not breaking his movement.

'Yes,' she managed to answer. As she spoke, he looked towards her, allowing her to grasp at his snood. She reached out and caught the top of it with the tip of her finger.

A birthmark. He had a birthmark on the side of his neck. It would be easy enough to hide with a shirt or a scarf, but it was there, an easily identifiable marking.

He pulled the snood back up over his mouth and made a third leap for the wire fence, this time using the lower wooden barrier as his launch pad. It was clear to Hollie he wasn't used to such displays of athleticism as it was an awkwardly executed move, but he made it, and he was away.

Hollie glanced over, still too winded to pull herself up. He looked like he was about to run up the road towards the Premier

Inn, but as he stepped off the path, a car narrowly missed him, and the driver angrily sounded his horn. He switched direction, passing what looked like a dilapidated electricity substation, and he ran into a gravelled parking area.

Finally, Hollie caught a proper breath and forced herself up off the ground. Something had fallen onto the floor in the scramble. It was protected in a small plastic bag. She picked it up and pushed it into her pocket; it would have to wait for now. She avoided the wire fencing, running along a little way so she could use the small gate, all the while fixing her gaze on the man she was chasing.

Hollie was tired now. The moment she came out on the other side of the underpass, the rain beat against her face. It seemed more exposed there, too. She scanned the area. It was a rough gravel car park. There were still one or two cars uncollected by their owners. Along the far end was the River Hull, at the point in the city where it flowed out into the Humber Estuary. She could hear the water from that side of the flyover; it sounded furious even from that distance. There was nowhere for him to hide. He could try to outrun her, but she could see he was also worn out now.

The man looked around desperately. He must have realised the same thing. He stood at the end of the short road, the traffic on the flyover thundering to his left, the River Hull directly in front of him, and a long rough car park to his right. For a moment, Hollie thought he would try to outrun her. Instead, he rested his hand on the side of the waist-high barrier erected alongside the river to prevent accidents.

'No, no—' Hollie shouted.

Placing his other hand on the barrier, the man kicked out his leg and climbed over. Extending out into the river, a series of wooden posts formed an access pathway or barrier of some sort beneath the underpass. It looked like some kids had left a plank of wood or something similar, making it possible to access the structure without jumping. Gingerly, the man set off along the wooden walkway, out into the flow of the river.

FORTY

'I'm not who you're looking for, DI Turner—'

'It sure as hell feels like you're my man,' Hollie screamed at him as her eye caught the fierce grey water below. His timing could have been better. The torrential rain seemed to be sending every water source in the Yorkshire Wolds out via the River Hull and into the Humber. If he slid on the wooden posts, he'd be washed out beyond the tidal barrier.

'Now please, let's talk about this. This doesn't have to end with either of us getting injured.'

The man looked down. He was assessing the situation, just like she'd done. She'd already worked out for herself that there was no way either of them could fight that current if they fell into the water. The best chance of success would be for the lifeguard to recover their bodies from the estuary. Worst-case scenario, they'd end up as food for the fish.

Hollie struggled to hear him over the wind. She had to turn her head one way to catch his words in the gale. Her clothes were so wet and heavy now, she felt completely weighed down. He was going to make her pursue him across the wooden walkway, she could tell.

'Why leave the phone? Why not just speak to me directly?' Hollie shouted over to him. Damn, he was about to walk further out across the river. She was going to have to step out there with him.

'I can explain that to you. But not now. I can't let you take me into custody. I'll call you on the phone when I'm ready. You won't be able to trace it. Just leave it switched on. I'm sorry, DI Turner—'

Hollie had spent years dealing with scoundrels. She'd met psychopaths, petty thieves, people whose mental health issues led to extreme behaviours, evil killers and worse. This man did not seem like the type. Everything about his body language told her he could not be the man who threw Sister Brennan over the side of the bridge. Or who held Father Duffy's head in a fish tank until he collapsed and fell lifeless onto his living room carpet. He wasn't built for the physical struggle, for starters. And from the look on his face, he was as shit-scared as she was at the prospect of crossing the river via that wooden structure. But it had to be this guy – if not, who the hell was he?

A surge of water washed over his feet, and he stumbled momentarily. Hollie wondered if she'd have the courage to jump in after him. No way. He was on his own if he fell. She'd have to call the coastguard; she was not rescuing a potential killer to leave her kids motherless.

He steadied himself. Hollie could feel her heart pounding. She'd just missed one of those moment-of-truth events that coppers hate. He hadn't fallen into the water, so she didn't have to make the call about whether to save him.

'Just come in off the walkway,' Hollie urged. 'We can talk. I haven't called for backup yet. It's just you and me. Tell me your side of the story.'

'Sorry, I can't chance that,' he called over.

'You dropped something,' she chanced, hoping it would

make him pause. 'It was in a plastic bag. Is it something you need?'

From the look on his face, it was something he'd rather still have in his possession.

'For Christ's sake,' she heard him curse.

He was assessing the remaining path. Did it cross underneath the full width of the bridge? She didn't know. Did he? Would he just get stuck out somewhere in the middle? She put her hand in her pocket and felt for her phone. She'd work on him just a little longer. The moment he saw a blue flashing light, they'd lose him. If he got washed away in the Humber, she might never find out why Sister Brennan's life ended.

The man walked further out, away from the bank. The water splashed up all around him. There were times when it looked to Hollie like he was actually walking on the surface of the river. She was going to have to follow him.

She stepped forward. She had to treat it like a tightrope: never look down. If she did, she'd panic with the swirling wash just beneath her feet. She closed her eyes, centred herself, and stepped forward, onto the small plank of wood which created the bridge between the car park and the walkway.

'I'm going to have to risk this,' the man called over. It was almost impossible to hear him now. 'Sorry, DI Turner. As soon as I figure it out, I'll call you, I promise—'

His words fell off, taken by the wind. Her focus shifted and she became suddenly aware of the traffic thundering overhead. It was as if somebody had lowered the volume while she'd been speaking to him. She thanked her good luck for the lighting from the tidal barrier and the road. At least it gave them some chance in hell of making their way across safely.

Each step was an effort. She'd thought her clothes couldn't get any wetter, but as the cold water crashed and splashed up around her, her trousers seemed to fuse to her skin.

She thought the wooden structure was moving beneath her

feet. Did it really, or was it just the sense of water flowing in her peripheral vision? She couldn't tell, but it was scary.

She felt immediately off balance as she looked ahead at her quarry. He was making better progress than her, faster for sure. Would he reach the other side? And if he did, surely there would be more fencing to deal with, put there to discourage thrill-seeking idiots.

'Please don't make me do this!' she shouted over.

He couldn't hear her. He was intent on getting to the other side now, wherever that was. He was going to take this to its conclusion. Escape, death, or capture. She'd almost ruled out capture. The halfway point was approaching, and she didn't think she could make it any further. Hollie was out of courage; this was too much. It was just too exposed and precarious. She didn't dare to go on. Maybe her team was right. Perhaps she wasn't the right person for this job and was better suited to pen-pushing now. She couldn't risk not seeing the kids again, not with things as they were. She wouldn't take that chance.

Hollie tried one more time.

'Please, come back and talk to me—'

The wind changed direction suddenly and the man stopped and turned. He looked at her as if he hadn't expected her to follow him that far. He seemed surprised to see her so close.

'Please don't follow me, DI Turner. I don't want you hurt—'

She clocked it straight away. His language was different. Usually, there'd be some idiot threatening to harm her or her colleagues. She'd heard every threat under the sun. Often, they moved on to what they'd do to her kids. They loved threatening daughters, too. There was usually something horrific they would suggest about harming her daughter that could still make her flinch. But if she'd heard him right, he was more concerned about her safety than anything. Again, her cop's instinct went off like an incessant alarm.

Hollie felt the pressure of her team and the DCC to get

the case resolved. There was always that relentless force in the background: make an arrest, press charges, get a conviction.

He'd stopped in his tracks now and seemed aware of what he'd done and how far out he'd walked. The sight of him mid-river with a storm of fierce, swirling water around him made her shudder. This was crazy.

'I promise, DI Turner, I'll hand myself over to you as soon as I can. But not yet. I can't leave this to the police. I can't let you lot mess this up—'

She heard those words perfectly, as if the wind wanted to help – like it could see the danger of what they were doing, and it wanted to urge them to safety.

At that moment, Hollie considered letting him go.

Her phone vibrated in her pocket. What a time to call. She glanced ahead at the man. He was looking at her. It seemed to her as if he was trying to see if he could trust her. She was wondering the same thing herself.

She pulled out her phone, glancing down quickly to see if she needed to answer. It was the office. She'd have to take it.

Hollie looked up. Where'd he gone? Shit. Where was he? Had he fallen in? She hadn't heard any cries. She searched the water around where he'd been, but she could see nothing that looked like a body being washed away.

She moved to place the phone back in her pocket, but she paused. She was going to act on her hunch and give him a head start. She'd leave it in the lap of the gods. He had the duration of the phone call to get away. If he couldn't press it home to his advantage, she'd have to collar him.

Hollie answered the call.

'What?' she snapped.

'It's DC Langdon, ma'am—'

Hollie turned her head to find an angle where she could hear properly without the wind crashing in her ears.

'Sorry to call you, but I thought you'd want to know immediately. We've just had a major development in the case—'

'This had better be important. I'm in a bit of a situation right now.'

'It is, ma'am. We'll need to get over there ASAP, I think.'

Hollie looked ahead. She'd as good as lost him now. Why hadn't she called for backup? She'd keep this little cock-up to herself. The last thing she needed was another setback with the team.

'Okay, enough with the dramatics, DC Langdon, what's happened?'

Hollie was annoyed with herself for taking it out on the young officer. She checked herself. It wasn't so many years ago that her ill-tempered superiors were biting her head off whenever things weren't going their way.

'Apologies, ma'am, it's just that it's a big catch and I thought you'd be excited,' DC Langdon continued. Hollie detected the frustration in her voice. She forced herself to calm down and listen.

'I'm sorry, go ahead—'

'Mandy Tyson just walked into Osborne police station. And she confessed to the murder of Sister Brennan.'

A LETTER FROM THE AUTHOR

Thank you very much for reading *The Fallen Girls*. If you enjoyed *The Fallen Girls* and would like to join other readers in keeping in touch, stay in the loop with my new releases by clicking on the link.

www.stormpublishing.co/paul-j-teague

Or sign up to my personal email newsletter on the link here:

www.paulteague.net/storm

I'd be grateful if you would leave a review if you enjoyed the first book in this DI Hollie Turner trilogy, as this helps other readers to discover my books.

It's been wonderful to write a book based in and around Hull. I moved to the city in 1994 and worked there until 2000, with two of my children being born at local hospitals. One of them spent time at Hedon Road maternity hospital. We lived at the side of the River Humber, in North Ferriby, then moved to the city centre along Beverley Road, finishing up in Beverley itself.

I worked at BBC Radio Humberside during those six years, mainly as a radio presenter, but also as a reporter and producer. I was lucky enough to present virtually every programme on the radio during my time there, starting with the *Drivetime* show, moving on to the breakfast programme and taking in mid-morning, the *Soapbox* phone-in, the afternoon show, Saturday & Sunday breakfast and no doubt a couple of others I've now forgotten. I interviewed the local MPs while I was working there, as well as all the movers and shakers in the city.

As a journalist, I visited and reported from all four corners of the Humberside area, including Scunthorpe, Grimsby, Bridlington, Withernsea, Hornsea, Goole, Brigg and many villages and communities in between. It is this experience which inspired me to set this series of novels in the region, with my primary focus on the city of Hull.

The Humberside area was a brilliant place to work as a reporter. I got to cover an amazing array of crime incidents, as well as dealing with political stories, rural and industrial issues, the ferries and the local sports scene, which is very strong in that part of the world. John Prescott was the deputy prime minister at the time, I got told off by both Michael Howard and Ann Widdecombe for pushing too hard about issues relating to Hull Prison, and I enjoyed the daily crack with the locals on the phone-in show.

Yet the inspiration for this particular trilogy came from a remarkable lady who used to pick me up in the mornings to run me in for the BBC Radio Humberside breakfast show. If you're first on the radio in the morning, you start work at an unearthly hour, so a variety of taxi drivers would arrive to pick me up from my house, and we'd call into the newsagent en route to pick up that day's papers, and I'd get dropped off outside Chapel Street, which is where the radio station was located when I worked there.

I got particularly friendly with one of the female drivers who I used to love chatting to on my way in to start my shifts at those godforsaken hours. As we got to know each other better, one day she confided in me with a deeply moving and personal story. It emerged that as a teenager, she had become pregnant out of wedlock. Just like hundreds of young women in the sixties and seventies, her baby was taken away and given up for adoption. This lady's son had got in touch with her, and they were going to meet up. She was emotional and over the moon to be reunited with the son she never thought she'd see again. She was also very angry about what had happened to her when she was younger.

I asked if she would be happy to be interviewed for the radio about her experiences and she agreed. What followed was a week-long series on the mid-morning show, which was an emotional roller coaster. Many topics and news stories had a profound impact on me when I was working in radio, and this story was one of them. I can't imagine what it must have been like to have been condemned by all the adults around you at such a young age and then to have to give up the baby you've carried for nine months. Most of those girls would have gone on to have other children, yet they never forgot the babies they lost. And as the world's moral compass turned around them, what must it have been like to watch as the country became completely at ease with having children out of wedlock when you were ostracised for exactly the same thing when you were still a child yourself?

This story is entirely fictional, but I have tried to capture some of the sadness, anger and lack of agency that I learned about in my radio interview as I explore the story of Mandy and the girls she encounters on her journey. The women whose babies were stolen from them are still waiting for an apology from the government for what happened to them decades before. I've lost touch with the taxi driver who shared this personal story with me, but it would be lovely if she knew what a lasting impact knowing her has made on me.

There's a strong flavour of the seventies in this story. I was born in 1965, so I'm very much a child of that decade. I was buying vinyl singles then – by Mud, Suzi Quatro, Slade and The Sweet – and I even used my comic money to purchase selective issues of *Jackie* and *Diana*, depending on which pop stars were featured as poster pull-outs. We spent our tiny amounts of pocket money on Fruit Salads and Sherbet Dippers, and a bar of Old Jamaica chocolate really did seem like a purchase that was only for the affluent.

I even had a paper round in the eighties, and Mandy's experiences are directly based on mine. The lady who I worked for was called Mrs Mouncey and she had one of those heavy, black delivery bikes with a basket at the front. Sometimes, if I lost concentration, I'd lose track of where the front wheel was pointing underneath the newspaper-packed basket, and I'd have to correct a severe wobble or even brush myself down after a minor prang. I wasn't a very good paperboy. I got fed up with a dog chasing me along the road at the far side of the village, so I just threw the owners' papers in a nearby ditch and cycled off at great speed.

I loved my time working at BBC Radio Humberside. It was such an exciting time in my career. I'd always wanted to be a radio presenter, and in Hull, I got to do so much live broadcasting; it was a wonderful experience. I worked with a great team – many of whom still work at BBC Radio Humberside – and we had a lot of fun putting the programmes out every day. The news agenda was so varied, too. It was never boring, not even after six years of covering the news there.

The Humber Bridge just had to feature in this first part of the trilogy. My dad worked for years on the south side of the Humber, at one of the oil refineries along the estuary. At the age of sixteen, having just finished my O levels, I tagged along with the village primary school and went to see the Queen officially opening the bridge in 1981. I crossed the bridge many times in the course of my BBC work, but also when visiting my parents in Lincolnshire. In those days, I'd keep a booklet of red tickets in the car because you have to pay to cross with a vehicle. These days, it's all electronic.

I even abseiled off the bridge on live radio, which is what gave me the inspiration and detail to come up with the gruesome death which begins this story. It's the most counterintuitive of things to do. You get fitted into a harness and then climb over the side railings, hanging on for dear life, I might add. You then release the rope that controls your movement and speed so you're at right angles to the bridge. At that point, you kick away and hope like hell that the harness holds you securely. Did I mention I did this on live radio?

I'd set up the entire thing so I could give live commentary as I went over the side of the bridge. This might be hard to believe, but as soon as I knew the harness had taken my weight, it was fine. I had complete control of my movement and, at one stage, just sat there in mid-air, describing on the radio what I could see. It was a fabulous experience and one of the many brilliant things I was privileged to encounter during my working life with the BBC. None of this stuff gets wasted.

If you're new to my trilogies, it's worth knowing this: all the loose ends will be tied up throughout the story. I like to leave readers with a cliffhanger, but I do resolve all the mysteries by the end of the third book. I'll talk more about the stories in books two and three, but for now, I'll detain you no longer. An adult Mandy has just walked into the police station to confess she's responsible for the death of Sister Sophia Brennan, the same Mandy whose sad story we've just been following over the past forty chapters. Could she really have done it? All will be revealed in book two, *Her Last Cry*.

Before you go, please connect with me on social media.

Thanks once again for reading *The Fallen Girls* and I hope you'll enjoy the further twists and turns in *Her Last Cry*, the second book in this DI Hollie Turner trilogy.

Paul Teague

facebook.com/paulteagueauthor

x.com/PaulTeagueUK

Printed in Great Britain
by Amazon